# DIVE

A totally gripping, breathlessly twisty crime mystery

# JON BARTON

Joffe Books, London
www.joffebooks.com

First published in Great Britain in 2023

© Jon Barton

Cover art by Nick Castle

ISBN: 978-1-80405-021-7

# CHAPTER ONE

The dead girl's eyes were yellowed at the whites and staring at the sky as if she knew what was coming.

'Pull closer,' said David.

The Ribcraft boat came about to the corpse, already drawing off on the ebb tide and catching the maelstrom made by the outboard engine.

David Cade extended a long pole with a large plastic loop at one end and flopped it onto the water.

Naomi Harding watched the loop catch the corpse around the neck, and grimaced as David wrestled the dead weight over the trim and onto the deck. She could see that a mane of flaxen hair was constricting the lifeless head and obscuring the victim's face.

David rolled the body so the dead girl lay on her back. Naomi wasn't sure she liked the way he was manhandling her. Nevertheless she kept quiet. She had learnt that there was no respect for due process in this unit. The dead, she had discovered, received no special treatment.

Naomi stood back and let David study the cadaver. It wasn't as if he hadn't seen death before, but all the same he seemed distracted. Naomi wished she understood why, but then, how well did she really know him?

'Twenties,' David guessed. 'Possibly Northern European.'

Naomi looked at him before studying the corpse again. The girl was tall and her long hair fell tendrilled on the deck. Her skin was cold to the touch. Mud and exposure to the elements had cast her skin a bronze hue, and the acid copper stench of blood had bound with the ammonia smell of the blowflies drawn to the corpse.

The heatwave meant scavengers were spoiled for choice that summer, as London burned under blistering blue skies. There had been no rainfall in weeks, and this Tuesday morning was no exception. It would take more than a breeze off the river to stir the stifling air.

Naomi pinched at her wetsuit, her own sweat meshing it to the small of her back. By way of distraction, she stared into the dead girl's eyes. They were discoloured in death and devoid of hope, as if her last thought was frozen in her eyes — she knew she was going to die.

The victim was wearing a black dress that left her shoulders and collarbone exposed, but there were no signs of a struggle. Naomi threw a glance at David, their thoughts simpatico. It was impossible to drown an adult without leaving bruises because of their violent struggle for breath.

David looked askance. Naomi pretended not to notice his hand shaking as he paused to light a cigarette, showing nothing of the interest that had gripped him only moments ago.

'Hazard a cause of death?' Naomi said.

David shrugged.

'No bruising. No petechiae, the hyoids look intact,' Naomi continued. 'No sign of ballistics, open or closed . . .'

David was watching the river.

'Sergeant?'

He took a long drag before turning to face her.

'What do you think?' Naomi asked.

'Does it matter?'

She eyed him with the forbearance she'd perfected over the last three months they'd been working together. 'Humour me.'

Another long drag, before David flicked the butt so it vanished over the side. 'It's an overdose.'

He sounded even more inattentive than Naomi was used to. She eyed him carefully and asked, 'How could you possibly make that call?'

'You ever seen a beam swinger in a cocktail dress?'

Naomi found herself holding her breath as she reeled from his answer. Coppers were known for dark humour, but nothing had prepared her for the callousness of the Marine Police. To David, she understood, it was merely a statement of fact. At forty-three years old, he outranked her both in age and experience, and his twelve years as a police diver had shown him the dark heart of the river. The Thames attracted suicide by its nature. She knew how quickly a person could go under, pulled down as if snatched by invisible hands. Drowning was a way to disappear without trace. When divers found people in the river, it followed they never meant to be found.

Naomi followed David's gaze as he bent to examine the corpse. A sunspot had caught for a second, in the small, clear gemstone in the girl's left ear. The other earring was missing. Crouching on one knee, Naomi could just make out the pinprick in the girl's right earlobe. But David paid no attention to that. He was busy examining the blotch that stained the back of the girl's left hand. From a distance, it could have been mistaken for a birthmark. But it was neither of those. It was a club stamp.

A shadow — was it discontent? — flickered across David's face, before something else caught his attention. He pinched a strand of the dead girl's hair between thumb and forefinger, leaning in to study the grit before it came away in his gloved hand. Swarthy, like old iron — it lacked the orange hue of rust.

As Naomi looked between David and the body, she wondered about the parents and how they might react when they discovered their little girl was dead. David stood and Naomi met his eye. She was probably one of the few women

3

he'd worked with in the Metropolitan Police who was tall enough to look him in the eye standing face-to-face. 'You told me bodies land where the river bends,' she said.

'Yeah. Usually they do.'

'We're downriver. This area is a dead straight — why did she land here?' The question had been bothering her since they arrived.

David searched the sky as if the answer might fall into his brain. Above them, the trains clacked through Blackfriars Station, their shadows riding by on the water. The day was young, but that did not prevent London's skyline from heaving in the heat, parched air draping itself around them like a shroud. He felt like the world was trying to tell him something. It was a message easier to ignore in the tall shadows of the streets, where shade was a fleeting commodity.

Naomi read back over her notes as David instructed the crew to zip the dead girl into a body bag before waving the all-clear to the Port Authority Watchdog. The skipper, who had found the corpse first, was blowing out his cheeks, still turning over the catch like a find. 'She's young,' he called out. 'Must have been a wild night, eh?'

David made a face. 'Let's get her back.'

Naomi looked over at that, a knot of concern forming in her stomach. 'Shouldn't we wait?'

'What for?'

Before she could answer, David started the outboard engine. There was nothing more to say.

It was a short ride back to the pontoon. Travelling at speed, the RIB flew up a spray that doused the men in a mist. Naomi found her attention returning to the body bag at her feet. When asked to pronounce judgement upon the drowned, the coroner would often deliver an open verdict. There was seldom any certainty the deceased had intended to die, and suicides were not the only traffic of the Thames. Yet when she first set eyes on the body, bloated and broken on the surface of the water, Naomi had sensed foul play. Women killed themselves in all sorts of ways, but not like this. Dead men meant suicide or an accident, or a murder. When they found dead women, it was usually the latter.

To educate herself, Naomi had spent the last few months scouring the registers of the National Missing Persons bureau, weighing up facts and figures with David's superior knowledge of the waterways. He had told her that women, as a general rule, did not end their lives by drowning themselves in the Thames. Naomi was inclined to agree. Her mind, these days, worked like a criminology review. If years of criminal investigation had taught her anything, it was that she should listen to her intuition.

In the commotion of the return journey, there came a non-descript chime of David's phone sounding off. She watched him out the corner of her eye as he quickly checked the screen, and irritation crossed his face. She didn't know him well, but they shared one thing in common. Home life was off-limits.

David tied off the boat as they arrived back at the dock, and Naomi disembarked, stepping aside so a pop-up stretcher could be wheeled into position. She watched the body get sloughed heavily onto the stretcher before it was taken away, and pictured its onward journey to the forensic van parked on the street. The remains would be handed over, and the Unit would rinse and repeat. Divers recovered evidence but they did not investigate. Her job was to bring up the bodies and pass them along.

The last part of that mantra would take some getting used to.

# CHAPTER TWO

*Thirty hours earlier*

MONDAY 21 JUNE
Low tide: 00.18 (0.82 m) / 12.24 (1.14 m)
High tide: 06.18 (6.42 m) / 18.26 (6.25 m)

The radio hissed into life, then crackled as a voice broke through. *'Don't be stupid, David, pull astern.'*

He began the arithmetic. Fifteen seconds — or ten — before the outer gate raised. He leaned on the throttle, and the rigid inflatable boat listed with a roar of horsepower.

Somewhere over the chaos, he heard the voice on the radio urging him to stop. *'Pull astern right n—'*

The vessel tore through the lock before the outer gate reared up. David cut the engine, which sent a wall of water at the inner gate as if to hail the dockmaster.

On short nights like this one, the water shimmered with moonlight, unhindered in the blue-black sky. At this time of year the searing summer days were long and cloudless. Then the nights cooled slowly and graveyard shifts felt longer for it. But David Cade didn't care. Long shifts were his forte.

Apart from a tank and regulator, he was kitted out in diving gear. Broad and solemn, with a firm face and steel-blue eyes that flashed when the mood took them, David was taking a risk by setting out alone. Officially speaking, it carried heavy penalties. Lynch had warned him at length, wielding words unfit to repeat. But tonight, there was nowhere he'd rather be.

Now that the spectacle was over he cruised into the central basin and slowed by a silver-haired man vaping on the deck of a flat-top barge.

Connor Beckett's face was fixed with exasperation. 'Are you trying to give me a heart attack?'

David said nothing. The team leader knew his efforts were wasted before he opened his mouth. He leaped up to the floodlit barge, ignoring Connor's eyes scaling his height. David took care of himself as ex-Royal Marines were wont to do. Following naval service, he'd joined the Military Police before transitioning to the Met, drifting through various specialisms before winding up as a diver. Despite the mileage, David had done his best to keep fighting fit.

'What have you got?' he asked.

Connor shrugged. 'Come and see for yourself.'

They were standing on a steel platform at least twenty feet long, and the flotsam of construction was everywhere. Hydraulic fumes rose all around St Katharine Docks, and at the centre of things, an excavator choked engine smoke into the restless night. Workmen huddled at the water's edge to catch a cool breeze off the river.

A Marine Police presence was simply a safety measure, and Connor's team were on call tonight. They had spent the shift enjoying the peace and quiet until the excavator backfired. An obstruction had entered the hot zone and so the foreman had punched the panic button. They could not continue until the site had the all-clear. This would only come after a crew of commercial divers had spent several gruelling hours clearing the bed of the central basin to access the waste-water pipe that serviced the Tower Hotel.

David examined the excavator billowing steam by way of complaint. Most likely it was just sediment dregs or the filigree of a shopping trolley causing the obstruction. That was no excuse for complacency. These drills were dangerous, and the divers were loath to investigate the hindrance. With David showing up unannounced, they knew they wouldn't have to. David was married to the job despite the dangers it involved. In fact, he didn't seem to care about those dangers, and it was this obsessive behaviour that sequestered him from his personal life.

David glanced at the Ivory House clocktower. Three in the morning. They had to get on.

Connor was consulting the foreman when he noticed David surveying the water. 'Don't even think about it.'

David didn't listen. He waited for Connor to turn back to the foreman before putting his mask on and kneeling on the edge of the barge.

Connor spun back round. 'Hey, *don't*—'

Too late. It was all Connor could do but gawp at the rippling water.

* * *

It was full dark below the surface. This was David's world — one he knew and saw, as if seeing were possible down here in the darkness. He was deaf to everything but breath down here. The mask tombed his eyes, ears and sinuses. He felt the pressure line grasp his body on the short descent to the basin floor.

*In. Out. Inhale. Exhale.*

He blindly examined the floor with his hands. He found pipework and a trench, then felt the familiar shaft of the excavator. It rose like a flexing bicep.

There was something else too, a white-rabbit object in the hot zone. He grappled with a handle, pulled it close and made for the surface. He felt his ears pop and his body decompress.

He surfaced to workmen hauling him onto the barge. Through his mask, he could see Connor yelling at him, but couldn't hear the sound. Water was draining out of his ears and the neoprene hood held much of it in.

David lowered the hood to catch the end of Connor's tirade. He'd taken worse from power-drunk commandos and senior officers scolding him for whatever would kill him next. What did it matter? The deed was done.

He removed the rest of his apparatus before inspecting his prize: a hard-backed case, scuffed but otherwise unscathed. David dug his gloved fingers into a groove and tried to open it. When that didn't work, he took a knife from his belt and prised open the lid.

There came a floral scent with a stronger chemical undertone, like burning plastic on a fire. Packed into the case were three sodden brown parcels. Prompted by a swell of interest from the workmen, David made an incision in one through an outer layer of kraft paper, cling film and duct tape, and into the rubber that served to waterproof the alkaloid. He then used the knife's blade to extract a trace of the powder.

He stopped short of lifting it to his tongue. The powder was potent, and the river had not distilled it. He expected the cocaine to numb his gums, but a deeper instinct told him not to try it. With that unease playing on his mind, David forbade the all-clear. The site was now a crime scene, and it would have to be shut down until an SIO could clear things up.

In the time it took for the foreman to protest, David had returned to the RIB, revved the outboard engine and peeled onto the water in a tight hairpin.

He was away before Connor could stop him.

# CHAPTER THREE

The temperature had dropped fractionally overnight, and although the sun was still some way from its peak position, the Monday morning rush hour felt stiflingly close.

Naomi Harding relished the short walk from Wapping Overground to the dock, savouring the rare moment of headspace. She was blasted on all fronts, at work and at home — to say nothing of her social life. It was more than the job, although that played a part. Naomi could handle getting browbeaten at every possible opportunity by the toxic culture of the Marine Police Unit. There had always been a legacy of chauvinism in the Met.

It was getting overlooked at home that proved harder to take. She had barely seen her nine-year-old daughter in the three months since she had returned to work. In that time, she'd been through the wringer with the inquest regarding her conduct, and worked tirelessly to hide her deep unease from Amy. There was more to it, besides. Amy was growing up — and Naomi felt left out. There was no doubt in her mind that her husband was inclined to keep it that way. If Miles meant to prove a point, she wished he'd leave their daughter out of it.

Wharf buildings offered plenty of shade on the way. Naomi never minded train travel usually, but with the mercury this high, the Overground made for sticky business. She checked her watch. Still early. Veering off the street, Naomi wandered into Wapping Rose Gardens to steel herself for the day ahead.

Thames River Police was visible through the garden gates. The large Edwardian building ranged up behind a row of police vans and stood flush with the river wall. Beyond it was the river itself and a walkway that officers referred to as 'the brow', which led down to a floating pontoon where several Watchdog police boats were almost always tethered.

If the police station was a showroom, the dock was the factory floor — although a pedestrian walking by wouldn't notice the difference. Set apart from Wapping Police Headquarters, the Marine Police dry dock itself was little more than a husk: a liminal space that cut into the foreshore, admitting a pair of dock lanes to slope down into the water. The Marine Police Unit's segregation suited the divers. 'Real' police work was siphoned off, so the Unit was left alone. No appraisals from the rank and file and, more importantly, no paperwork. A small price to pay for the diciest job in the Met.

She remembered her first day on the job. The sun had been in the sky for almost two hours that April morning. Naomi had thought she was in the wrong place — the dry dock had looked like a fossilized warehouse that ought to be condemned. It was the blue plaque on the wall that had confirmed she was in the right place.

She'd had no idea what to expect, and unease had crept up on her like a particularly anxious insect. She'd shivered, despite the warmth of the spring day, her CID days feeling like another life long since behind her.

She didn't mind slumming it — a decade in the Met had seen to that — but this building was in its own league, barnacled with decay and resurrecting old thoughts she'd no time for just now. Stranger still was how outlandish it looked, wedged between two wharves and the police station itself. She had tried to ignore the shabby man sucking a vape at the entrance, studying her but pretending not to. Vapour clouds had curled past his tired eyes and thinning silver hair. The man's shirt had been open and ripe from overuse. In contrast, Naomi's tunic was crisp and white, her brogues freshly polished. Naomi was a striking woman, with hematite eyes and long black hair that matched the suit she'd chosen for the day ahead. Either this man was wildly underdressed or this was par for the course.

She had left the kerb and crossed the street, closing the gap between herself and the vaping man. An ersatz smell of strawberry had filled the air as she'd buzzed the intercom and stepped through the main door.

The air inside had been almost thin. The reception hall was drab and dirty, strip-lighting a thin atrophied carpet. Scotland Yard was no looker, but at least it was fumigated. This place looked like a slaughterhouse.

*All right, that'll do. Play the hand you're dealt, Harding.* The rebuke had rattled sharply round her brain like a coin in an antique kettle. Before she had approached the reception desk and encountered yet more perennial indifference, a bald square man had rounded a corner to meet her. He was heavy set and haggard with a face like melting wax.

'You're late.'

Naomi had blinked. How could she have been? Hadn't she been standing on the street for ten minutes, heart in her mouth, allowing the time to crawl by before braving a punctual entrance?

The bald man had clearly had no time for pleasantries and had turned away by way of instruction. Naomi had followed him down a long angular corridor the colour of old gravy to an office cramped with filing cabinets and a lacquered desk. She had noticed idly that there was a glass partition where the wall should be.

'Sit,' the man had said, jabbing a finger before rounding the desk.

Naomi had appraised a tired chair of the sort you might find in a dentist's waiting room and reluctantly lowered herself onto it. The bald man had sat heavily and leaned back in his own chair.

Not for the first time, Naomi had felt the scrutiny of strange eyes, and realized she hadn't studied the man properly. That was unusual for her — she still identified as a detective, and observation was an occupational hazard. The bald man had returned her stare. His skin was so pale as to have almost no pigment, and there were nests of burst capillaries beneath his eyes. When he spoke again, his voice had poured like syrup over the desk. 'I asked for more men. And they sent you.'

Naomi hadn't flinched. She was used to this. Even so, she hadn't been certain if she should speak her mind yet. Better to get the measure of him first.

'Harding, was it?'

'That's right, sir.'

'Do I need to introduce myself?'

Naomi had chewed a wasp. Then she'd said, 'I was told to ask for Stephen Lynch.'

The man called Lynch had cocked his head. 'Six years in the Criminal Investigation Department,' he had growled, giving no indication he was impressed. 'Until three weeks ago.'

She had felt his silence then. She'd braced herself for questions — if only there were answers to give.

Lynch had taken a file from a drawer, opened it and flipped to the last page. 'Officers down — three of them, was it? Killed in action? On your watch, I understand.' He had spoken tonelessly but the threat was there. His was a voice that inspired vertigo, unpicking the scab of recent events.

Naomi had led a joint operation with the National Crime Agency to seize a shipment of cocaine that had come to the UK from Columbia. During the raid, three officers from the SCO19 Firearms Unit were shot dead. She should have known better. The ability of the police to perform their duties was dependent upon the public approval of police actions, and Naomi was seen to be responsible for a serious public humiliation. An investigation had been launched, but since evidence was still being gathered, Naomi had been permitted back to work. Not with Major Crimes as a serving officer, not with her titles. She could still be a police officer, but not as she knew it. Corporate spin might have framed it as 'light duties', but they were demoting her as far as it was possible to go. Down the drain. To this shithole.

How she had longed for it then: the thrill of the chase, the adrenaline of a job well done. Being a DI at the Met Police had given her life a sense of purpose. The impulse to come through in the hour of need was what propelled Naomi to fight the good fight, and like most young women forging a career in a male-dominated profession, it had become about discovering who she really was.

'I don't have time for damaged goods,' Lynch had told her. 'Not in this economy. They've cut my budget in half and treat my team like waste disposal experts.'

Naomi had been surprised to feel relief. Waste disposal — so she wasn't the only one that had been relegated to the dregs of the Met.

Lynch had leaned back in his chair again. 'How's your maritime knowledge?'

'There's room for improvement.'

'Had any training?'

'I'm a licensed search officer. And I'm a qualified BSAC diver so—'

'That's not what I asked.'

Naomi had hesitated a second too long. She would not easily forget her time at the diving school in Jarrow. She'd made sacrifices to be there of course, but kept that part of her life strictly to herself. It had proved more than a disruption. It had caused the fault line in her marriage to splinter and split open.

And it went further. Naomi's mistakes had meant her reputation had taken a dive all of its own. She was bad news wherever she went. No matter how hard she tried, Naomi could not fabricate confidence when her self-worth was shot to pieces.

That was not what had rankled her that day, though. She had excelled in every module and mastered underwater search patterns. She'd made it her business to know her way around the specialist equipment, and that was *before* she had even entered the diving tank. Admittedly, she hadn't managed to avoid decompression sickness over the course of that fortnight. This was an expected side effect of diving that her instructors had warned her about, but even so, Naomi had not anticipated spending most of her downtime bent double over a toilet in Tyne and Wear's cheapest budget hotel — she had kept that to herself, too.

What had rankled was being interrupted by Lynch. Naomi had spent ten years working hard enough to bite back when it happened. She hated this disregard: the lack of control over the conversation. She thought she knew why Lynch thought so little of her. Her mistakes had cost lives. She was a cop killer. That was about as far as the captain's imagination was prepared to stretch.

'I suspect you have all the notes there.' Naomi had nodded once at the file. 'I was put through a refresher course.'

'In a tank.'

'Yes, sir.'

'So nothing inshore?'

'No, sir.'

That had evidently been the wrong answer. Lynch had given her a look that could curdle milk. 'We'll have to fix that. You're banned from the water until we put you through your paces here, understand?'

The dismissive tone had been all too familiar. Yet if Naomi had strained to listen, she could have picked up the additional note of apprehension.

'With respect, sir, I understand the dangers of—'

'No. You don't.'

Naomi had flinched at this second interruption, but Lynch had taken no notice. 'You can't see shit in the Thames,' he had continued. 'You're blind. Nil vis. That scare you?'

'No.'

'It should.'

'With respect, sir, I've been cross-examined to death.'

'One more exam won't hurt then.'

'*Look*. With all due respect, sir, I'm tired of being told what I can and can't do.' Naomi had felt herself scream on the inside.

Lynch had watched her. For a moment, she'd had the sensation he was staring right through her. His mouth was fixed in a stiff downward crimp, and his eyes were softening. Then he had laced his fingers. 'For what it's worth, I sympathize. We've all been shit-canned. One way or another.'

He had stood up and moved to the sideboard and a waiting pot of coffee — fresh, she had hoped. He had poured two mugs (alas, no steam), offered one to Naomi and kept one aside for himself.

'I don't like being a baggage handler, but I need you onside, so listen up. Any notion you may have had about this unit is wrong.' Lynch had paused to seal her interest. 'We're not regular police. We are not special. We work in the dark. Total Policing means nothing here. We don't serve the public, we bring out their dead. Dredge their bodies and pass them along. Is that understood?'

Naomi had considered the coffee. Perhaps to make a point, Lynch had left it black.

'Perfectly.'

'Good,' Lynch had said. 'You're in the pit now, where all the shit gathers . . .' He had walked to the door and bidden her to follow. 'Would you like to meet the shovels?'

* * *

Naomi wished she was heading inside the river police station to enjoy an air-conditioned office bustling with activity. Instead, she begrudgingly quit the garden and trudged to the dock via the sliding gate to the side of the building.

As she wove through the warren of corridors to the dry dock, she recalled the first time she had entered the cavernous space. Arriving now, a familiar chill swept through her bones. It was a depot of stone walls and rusting girders, and the river's alkaline odour mingled with men's sweat. It was a tired, weatherworn place.

Her eyeline settled on the dock lanes and the hydraulic slips backing into the Thames through a pair of hangar doors. Both were open, the water lapping hungrily at the threshold. Masks, demisters, davits, nose bars, regulators and steel-capped boots were piled on iron shelves on the walls. Cages of gas bottles formed rank beneath a motley row of crudely customized helmets. Behind her, bifolding doors opened to the street — the better for the police vans to receive the grim garlands divers dredged from the Thames.

Naomi had long been desensitized to the sight of a corpse, but that hadn't stopped her eyes from magnifying like wheels of shock the first time a body was reclaimed, watching divers roughly slough a body bag on a pop-up stretcher and wheel it off to a waiting Forensics van.

*Dredge their bodies and pass them along.*

The words were stamped on her mind. Yet the divers had seemed inured, numbed. She had gathered later that finding dead people was commonplace and she became anaesthetized to it soon enough.

Male eyes now followed Naomi as she approached the dock lane. She had never quite got used to that. That they were all men was no surprise. Women in the police had to work twice as hard to go half as far, and it was even worse for people of colour. Of those that made it to the Marine Unit, it seemed impossible anyone with visible barriers would succeed.

The morning he'd showed her around, Lynch had dismissed the team with a hand, as if demotivating a fly he held a secret fondness for. Naomi had since learnt the hard way that the divers were difficult to ignore. This lot were as unsavoury as they came: old-school arseholes receding from middle age, counting the days until their index-linked pension kicked in. With pale skin and eyes sunken into their sockets, they looked as though they might be used as test subjects for insomnia surveys.

Both dock lanes were currently empty. Peering out to the river, Naomi could see a RIB coming in. As she stepped forward, she paused instinctively. Then she took a step back.

Lynch had done the same the first time a boat had hydroplaned up and into the dock lane. She recalled the horsepower — how it had crashed against her eardrums as water thrust forward. Naomi smiled at the memory. She'd had trouble with a fellow diver that morning. Bow-backed with tree-trunk arms, the primordial grunt might have emerged from the soup mere hours before he'd met her. When he was certain Lynch wasn't looking, the man had pushed his tongue between his index and middle finger and wagged it in her direction.

Her jaw muscles had pulsed, and the fingers of her right hand closed to make a fist. She was a city girl. Her veins were sewers and subway maps. *If I have to get into it with this prick*, she had thought, *then so be it*. But before she could react, a boat had surged into the no-wake zone and soaked the man head to foot at the slip.

Naomi's smile broadened remembering that. She stood well back as the same boat now swept into the bay and a voice barked over her shoulder.

'David. How many bollockings do you need? I'm starting to think you collect them.'

Lynch was striding over, aiming the venom at the man vaulting the trim of the boat. The fugitive gleam flickered in David Cade's eyes as the captain continued. 'What have I told you about going it alone — and never on graveyard shift.'

'Rules, huh?'

'*Yes*, rules. Don't give me that.'

'You need more men,' David replied in a sombre London accent.

David's brinkmanship was derisive. No one denied he got the job done, but each time he bent the rules it was another step towards chaos. Naomi often wondered why the captain allowed it. There was something in the way Lynch spoke in a low growl, but with a certain care bubbling beneath it. Care, or mutual respect — she couldn't tell which. He muttered something about slinging David's overtime sheet through the window before turning away.

Naomi's gaze fastened onto Cade's cargo. The colour drained from her face, and quite suddenly, she felt her blood run cold. There was a hard case on the deck — and she had seen one like it before. It was identical to those used to courier drugs around the city. Her heart beat a series of staccato notes as David placed it on the dock by her feet. He ignored her, nodding to Lynch as he opened the case, treating it like an antiquity.

Three brown parcels, each the size of a brick, were packed into the case. One of them oozed white sludge where the rubber packaging had been cut and water had seeped inside.

But this didn't make any sense. The last time she'd seen a case like this one, there had been dozens lined up on the floor. This was customary practice following a bust. Evidence would be placed on the ground, and fixed with property stored dockets before being whisked off to evidence storage. She'd spent hours staring at photographs of the contents in the CID bullpen. But that was before three officers were killed in the line of duty, when the worst had yet to happen.

Now here it was — the contraband she'd seized that fateful night. What was it doing here?

'Where did you find that?' she asked him softly.

'Who cares,' snapped Lynch. 'Get rid of it.'

The captain walked away, disinterested and disgruntled as he often was on an empty stomach. Naomi watched helplessly as the case was carried off down a mangy hall to the evidence holding on-site. But she did not relax. The Met had done their best to swat it, but the detective inside of her was buzzing still, infesting her mind with questions. And she had to admit: it felt good.

One question in particular came thundering to the front of her mind. What did it mean if the consignment had been jettisoned into the river?

When she turned back, David had already gone.

# CHAPTER FOUR

David Cade looked out over the river and felt his muscles relax. For a moment, the moving water had taken the city away.

He waited until he was alone before stepping onto the foreshore. It was just him and the river now. In the middle of this grimy polluted city, the foreshore was where he came to watch the seasons change and gulls swoop low over the water.

When David was by the river, he was a world away from his problems. It was where he went to forget about his failed marriage, his difficult daughter — and the accident, which was never very far from his mind.

*You lied. You left. She'll always hate you for it.*

Leaving was the only way he could keep Lex safe. He didn't feel like he knew how to be a father, without putting her in harm's way. She was better off without him. It had always been a painful thought, and the river, he had decided, was somewhere he could come to make sense of the world. When life became too much, he would steal half an hour in its company.

Audrey had once told him that if you tell the sea your troubles and stand with your feet in the water, the tide will pull your troubles away with it. He wasn't sure if that was true of the Thames. He would often catch himself testing the theory, letting his troubles recede from his body, exorcizing feelings he could not name as he walked beside it for miles. David often haunted the foreshore, trying to fathom what he thought he should be feeling. It was the perfect place to hide.

The morning shift had passed without incident as the new rotation began. David had done his best to ignore the banter in the locker room, full of men yawning and bothering their eyes. The whole place had rung with shower steam and shit impressions, and while bodies were dragged into their clothes, David had kept his distance in a quiet corner. He had a habit of keeping people at arm's length, collecting acquaintances rather than friends. But all the better should someone he loved ever again nearly drown on his watch.

For their part, the divers knew it was simply David's way. Putting his behaviour into categories could be as fruitless as catching the wind with your hands. Besides, David worked double rotations for no reason other than wanting to. No one could relate to that.

But work was diverting. That was a soft version of the harder line his ex-wife had taken — and his daughter too in the fullness of time.

Talk of a round at the Captain Kidd drew David's attention. He realized he was being invited to the pub, and that he ought to say something like 'Maybe next time' or 'Thanks for asking'. But nothing came. Somehow optional phrases left a spindrift taste in the mouth, the way lies do if spoken aloud. He was so accustomed to estranging himself, the team just shrugged as they left.

Sidling back up the river steps from the foreshore, he tried to refocus on the spoils of the shift to come.

'David. Cute outfit.'

Alexis Cade was leaning against the wall by the fire exit. The doors were wide open, catching her in a shaft of strong sunlight. Hearing her voice, David felt his heart slam into the earth and his shoulders constrict. What was she playing at? To come *here* of all places . . . Shouldn't she be in a library somewhere studying? He looked through to the dock to check he wouldn't be heard.

'Whatever happened to "Dad"?'

'You tell me.'

He winced. Talking to Lex was like trying to stand your ground in an earth tremor. When you thought you'd found your footing . . .

David beckoned her away from the door and she trailed him down the lean walkway. They were now sandwiched between the station and the tumbledown wall of the dock. One fenced end linked the brow to the foreshore. The other bled out to the street. A southerly wind was crying through the cleft between buildings, carrying the torrid midsummer heat.

Trying not to inhale the aroma of baking rubbish, David took the measure of his daughter. Lex was fifteen, with mussed hair she'd recently bleached. She was lanky, not quite David's height, with a frayed backpack slung over one shoulder. Her bronze eyes were fringed with eyeliner that had run and stained her face.

David realized he was sweating, and suspected it was not from the heat. He appraised her clothes the way he supposed a good parent should, and she waited, unsmiling, willing him to speak first. What was it this time — money? A sofa to crash on?

'You can't show up like this.'

Lex blinked. It was the smallest of gestures, but small things were seismic: an eyelid flicker, a brow twitch, an imperceptible bow of the head. Lex used muscles in her face most people didn't know were there. Or perhaps she was simply imitating him. She took after Audrey, but had inherited her father's introverted thoughtfulness. Lex could be unknowable too.

'You're ignoring me, David. You haven't returned my calls.' As she spoke, her words sashayed between irony and self-deprecation.

'I'm working.'

'Try parenting, it lasts longer.'

Allowing that to sink in, Lex reached in the folds of her jacket and produced something small and thin. David felt a twinge of helplessness as she drew a matchbook from her pocket.

'You're smoking now?'

'I learned from the best,' she answered with the cigarette pinched between her teeth. She struck a match but the wind killed it. She tried another, but the wind did for that too.

David unzipped the pouch on his breast and handed her the lighter he kept there. She looked at him as if she'd stepped in something unsanitary.

'What is it?' he said.

'Matches are better. You don't burn the tobacco.'

David heard himself laugh. He couldn't help it. She spoke in terms that would brook no argument, but he had to wonder where she'd picked that up.

Lex took the lighter, handing him the matchbook by way of a trade. She lit the cigarette before wheeling around, and the lit end crackled as she took a long drag.

'You know you can't just come here—'

'Yeah, yeah. You told me the first time.'

There came a sharp high-pitched sound David recognized as the rotation bell. The tide was beginning to retreat. Time to work.

'You should go home, Lex.'

'I had a fight with Mum.' She took another drag.

'Wouldn't be the first time. Going to tell me what happened?'

'Nothing happened. She overreacted. You know what she's like. She worries about everything.'

David sensed she was downplaying it. For her part Lex averted her eyes, and worried a dark mark on her hand.

'All right, fine. If you really want to know — I went to a club.'

'When?'

'Relax. It was last night. No harm done.'

23

David bristled at that. 'No harm? You're underage for a start.'

'What's the big deal?'

David paused. It occurred to him that she had a point. Teenagers pushed boundaries, he had done it himself. Did he expect her to live under a rock?

'You came down here to tell me this?'

'Something like that.'

'Why?'

Lex didn't answer. Possibilities whirled through David's head like clutter caught up in a cyclone.

'What kind of club?' he asked dimly.

'Come on, David, what do you think?'

She gave him a cutting look, ignoring her phone as it blipped in her pocket.

'What did your mother say?'

'Nothing.'

'Lex.'

'She said I couldn't go, OK?'

'Why?'

'Because clubs are *wild*,' she trilled, in sarcastic sing-song. 'You drink and meet boys and do drugs.'

'Why won't you listen to your mother?'

'Here we go.'

'You're fifteen.'

'I'm not a kid!'

He heard her phone blip a second time. Strange — he'd never known his teenage daughter to ignore a text so willingly. David took the measure of her again. Then he realized she was shaking, minutely at first, but now it seemed like a tick she chose to ignore. He'd seen recruits shake like that. A nil vis dive could cry havoc with your head. It was a kind of post-traumatic stress. Surely she wasn't suffering that?

Her phone went off yet again. For a moment, it looked like she might burst into tears.

'Lex,' he pressed, 'do you want to get that?'

'Battery's about to die, I don't wanna waste it.'

'So turn it off.'

She thrust a hand in her pocket, retrieved the phone and stabbed the screen with her finger, holding it for him to see. 'Happy now?'

The rotation bell rang a second time. David felt himself tense. 'Look — I have to go.'

'What? Why?'

'Some of us work for a living. I can give you some money for the train if you need . . .' David trailed off. He had already faced away from her, but now he could feel pressure on his upper arm. When he looked back at her, he found her fingers latched to it, and her thumb was squeezing the elbow crease. This time, her voice was soft and bruised.

'Dad, I need help.'

He inhaled. Let the moment pass. Then he grasped the nettle. 'How much do you need?'

'It's not about money.'

'Then it can wait.'

Lex gave him a stilled look. 'Can I crash at your place?'

'What?'

'Please. Just for a few days.'

'Get it out of your head,' he snapped. 'It's not happening.'

'What's the big deal? I won't get in the way.'

'You *are* in the way. You think you can show up like this and expect me to drop everything? I have to work. You think child maintenance is cheap?'

'I think it's convenient.'

He felt that: hornet words that stung his thoughts, bursting venom into his bloodstream. Before either of them could speak again, the fire door swung open. Naomi Harding came into view.

'Uh, sorry, but I think you're needed.'

'One minute.'

David exhaled — it was not how he wanted to end this. The bell chimed again, and Naomi lingered in the doorway as he peeled away from Lex.

'I have to go back to work.'

'Can I wait for you?'

'No.' His voice was flat and final.

'But what am I supposed to do?'

'Go home to your mother.' With that, David left her in the alley, moving to the fire door and closing it behind him.

It would be the last time he saw her.

# CHAPTER FIVE

Hammersmith foreshore was ten miles downriver, reachable in as many minutes if travelling by RIB. The winding route added a mile or so to the journey, but on sweltering days with the wind in your hair, the city was something to behold. It was early afternoon, and lingering skirts of cloud held no purchase in the sky. They broke up and left a canvas clear and hard, roasting the skyscrapers that rose into it.

The Ribcraft boats were swift agile machines that listed with the horsepower of twin engines. Naomi sat back, enjoying the turbulence as it whipped against her face. David stood at the helm with a hand on the throttle, arcing the boat to avoid chop from Thames Clippers and a barge sliding past on their left side.

Soon they reached the stretch of river flanked by City Hall and the Tower of London. As if in reverence they slowed past HMS *Belfast* before accelerating again, hurtling under bridges criss-crossing the river. They passed Southbank and the Palace of Westminster, Lambeth, Vauxhall and Pimlico. The river's winding route began to straighten out near Battersea, cresting south, then north, like the upright curvature of a serpent. Eventually, Hammersmith Bridge emerged through the glittering haze of the day.

David pulled back on the throttle and the RIB began to slow, as close to the foreshore as he could get. Tunde, another member of the team, leaped off the boat and bound a line to a groyne. There were no pontoons here. They all had to wade in to reach the shore.

Soon Naomi found herself standing on the frontier between river and land. It was a sorry sight drained of life and colour. The foreshore was packed down hard with mud-grey rock and set apart by Victorian revetment timbers as far as she could see. A wrought-iron levee lined the North Bank, and the retreating tide lapped the rim of the bank with dull relish, jettisoning a huddle of human waste. Anything that could be flushed down the toilet shoaled nearby: sanitary towels and condom wrappers, wet wipes, cotton bud sticks, and lipstick-stained fag ends. Replacing the usual caustic odour of the river was a repellent human essence that thickened at the back of her throat.

Pollution in the river hinged on many variables, including tidal and seasonal changes, but there was no doubt it was teeming with dangerous microbes. There were several sewage outfalls along this central London stretch, so the Environment Agency had classified the Thames as unsuitable for swimming. Months before her first dive, Naomi had been inoculated against countless pathogens, including tetanus and hepatitis. To Naomi's mind, it was like throwing snowballs at Everest. There was little protection from waterborne parasites. She knew that microbes entered the body through cuts or abrasions on the skin, or through the eyes, nose, ears or mouth. Diving apparatus was the first defence, next to personal protective equipment. Serving the Marine Policing Unit required personal management of these risks: she had signed a waiver to that effect.

Naomi examined the water again. It was black, nacreous where it licked the foreshore. Rank feelings trammelled up her throat. It wasn't the thrill of the chase that moved her. The good fight was losing its edge. In its place was a deep-seated insecurity that had made her lose sight of things. She was not accepting of how her mental health was suffering through this ordeal. Naomi saw it as frailty, and she'd receive no support from the miscreants in the Unit.

Shuddering in the shadow of the luxury apartment block rising hard against the sky, she heard David issue instructions, and the Dive Team began to unload equipment. They knew the drill, even if Naomi didn't. Despite her relative confidence she still had to wrestle information out of Cade.

And that was how it had been for months. Her days were spent adrift, asking questions with no answers. There was an unspoken assumption that her interim training would fill in the gaps.

Naomi made to help Tunde unload a weight off the boat. 'What's this? Routine sweep?' She was trying her best to make herself sound casual.

Tunde nodded. He didn't look at her, but he sympathized. 'Don't worry. I knew jack-all when I started, too.'

Naomi said nothing. She felt quietly grateful for his pity.

'We have four hours of low tide,' Tunde explained, strewing equipment about as if it were flat-pack furniture. 'When the Feds are quiet, we come fishing out here.'

'Feds?'

'Your lot,' he said. 'At the Met.'

He meant criminal investigators. The Marine Police took a call if there was any indication that evidence, or a person, would show up on the river's slack tide. They'd received no such call that day. Nonetheless, she thought she heard a note of sourness catch the vowels in Tunde's voice.

The diver just shrugged. 'You guys are the real police. You leave the wet work to us. If you haven't called us out, we're free agents.'

Feeling far from free, Naomi caught herself scanning the shoreline again. 'Why here?' she asked. She'd never been on a rotation with Tunde, and was loath to admit that she'd not come out this way before.

'Ah. Good question.' Tunde nodded once at the current. 'Notice anything?'

Naomi did. As the river changed course the current had made one subtle adaptation. Two slipstreams were now colliding in a riptide, and she could just make out the line in the water.

Tunde was bobbing his head, the air of a schoolteacher about him. 'The current slacks on the river bend. This spit of shore is one of our hotspots.'

Naomi had more questions but Tunde had moved on.

'You know what a jackstay is?' He was fastening a wire to a pair of weights, thirty pounds apiece by her estimate.

Naomi shrugged. 'You drop the weights over a search area and the diver follows the wire.'

'That's it. You'll be working in nil vis down there. If we think there's something to find, we scatter the weights in the search area. Makes for a nice even search.'

He negotiated a petrol compressor, a cylindrical canister tethered to a gas pump, the source of oxygen for a sweep, quite unlike a bailout tank suited to scuba. But Tunde did not need to explain. She had gleaned all of this from her training. Divers would never perform a routine sweep on a bailout tank. Those were for emergencies only. In any case, she knew you only had about ten minutes of oxygen in a tank. A petrol compressor gave them hours of it.

Tunde tapped the compressor proudly, as if it were a racehorse he had high hopes for. 'She's a beauty. You'll be glad of her on a Gucci dive.'

'Gucci?' Naomi met his eyes, and Tunde offered a toothy grin before turning back to his work. 'What's a—' She paused. Naomi didn't get it, but she didn't want to admit that either.

'It's a corpse.' David supplied the answer. His words had the ghostly ring of repetition.

*Dredge their bodies. Pass them along.*

Naomi swivelled to him but David was already busying himself with equipment. 'Dare I ask why we're calling them that?'

30

Tunde shrugged wickedly. 'We take bets on whether we find one. Keeps it interesting.' He noticed David's side-eye before adding, 'Might be my luck's about to change.'

Naomi didn't know what to make of that. She felt stupid. Naivety taunted her like a flicker of madness. She thought about her friends in the CID, and the forensic experts she knew. If you were surrounded by death and decay, then black humour was bound to wall you in. It was no wonder that the same brand of wit had tailed her here. It was as if coping mechanisms were somehow being bandied about on a Mobius strip around the police — shared, but never spoken of.

'Bodies sink in water until the cavities fill with gas,' Tunde continued. 'Makes them hard to find. They're swept downriver until the tide slacks.' He swept a ceremonious hand across the landscape. 'This is where the current slacks hardest. A lot of bodies wash up here if they've been ditched upriver.'

Naomi studied her surroundings with fresh eyes. 'So it's a point of no return.'

'Exactly.' Tunde offered a tight smile to make light of things before he returned to his work, leaving Naomi to weigh this information. The science was spurious at best, but the same forensic experts had taught her that science was to be taken at the service of justice. Taking facts hard won in the laboratory and using them in the uncompromisingly real world of the crime scene was all she had ever known. To her mind, finding a body was the beginning of the forensic building of a case against a defendant. But divers didn't build cases. They did the wet work. Patterns emerged and events recurred and divers dredged bodies in all the familiar places. It was bleak but strangely logical.

A voice came to mind that sounded like a glitch in her thinking — *You're starting to think like them*. The old temptations she'd left behind were stirring again, and her head was filled with questions.

Naomi cleared her throat. 'How often do they land here?' She found herself refusing to call them Guccis.

'Most days,' Tunde said, disinterested. 'You not done one of these before?'

'Not yet.'

'Well, it's about time. Most land in Hammersmith. Among other things.'

'What other things?'

'How long were you in the CID again?' Tunde was trying to read the expression on her face.

'Long enough,' Naomi allowed.

Tunde gave her a half-smile. 'Fine. Point is, you're about to see all the worst shit about humanity down here. If it's not a body, it's something else. Hearts and lungs and bits of people. You get me?'

'Why?' Naomi spoke fast, not wanting Tunde to think he'd affected her with his words.

'Thames mud preserves all sorts. It's anaerobic. Means the mud—'

'Lacks oxygen, yes I know.'

'So things survive in the mud so long that they get preserved. Once they're exposed, it's a race against time to save them.'

Naomi rolled her tongue over her gums to blanch the bitter taste this information had left. She understood now what it was about Tunde she couldn't put her finger on: it was the shadow of things he still couldn't speak of lurking in his eyes.

David had clearly been listening and decided that the conversation was over. Reaching down to raise an Arvest harness out of a crate he'd dragged to the foreshore, he lobbed it to Naomi. She caught it neatly and made to put it on, but David took her aside, using the pretence of checking the gear to speak. 'This will be your first real dive for us,' he said. 'But I think you're capable.'

Naomi pulled a face. There were many things she wanted to say, but better to hold her tongue.

'It's dirty work,' David told her, matter-of-factly. 'You don't have to do this if you don't want to.'

*You'd like that, wouldn't you? Patronizing prick.* 'I didn't come here to keep my hands clean.'

David looked unconvinced. 'If you want out, say now.'

She zipped herself into the vest.

# CHAPTER SIX

Ten minutes later, Naomi was standing on the RIB deck. The boat had been taken further out into the centre of the river, and a jackstay sweep was now set between the foreshore and the boat itself. Her eyes were drilling into the murky water. The Thames had formed a thunderhead of silt and algae, and the wind had dropped, so that the putrefied smell she had failed to get used to was beginning to swell.

Naomi cast her eyes back to the foreshore. There were two teams working off two compressors, the first of which had been set up on the foreshore for one team to conduct a wade search. The second had been set up on the deck, and was now ticking at her feet like a bomb that was about to go off.

Tunde was threading the umbilical cord that channelled through her vest to the oxygen bottle strapped to her back. The same cord was coupled with their compressor. Though she could see where her oxygen was coming from, the operation offered only a fleeting reassurance. But there was no way she would back out. Not now. The apparatus had been checked and triple-checked. There was no more time to procrastinate.

David moved to the trim and raised his voice so both teams could hear him. 'It's a routine sweep. Waders, you know what to do. Keep it tight and watch for snags. Arm's length on the wire. Understood?'

Satisfied by the chorus of agreement, David turned away. Tunde seemed to sense Naomi's disquiet and offered a cautious nod. 'Relax. You've done all this before.'

'I've never been down there looking for dead people.'

'First time for everything. It won't be the last time, Naomi. We do this every day.'

He was right. She'd become intimately acquainted with violence and death in her time in the police. If she found a body today, it ought to be no different to being summoned to a crime scene in the middle of the night. But the rationale felt empty, just left a hole that was growing deeper. Beneath the canvas of a forensic tent, with industrial lamps lighting the ground, it was impossible to lose your footing. But here it was different. Months of training had not, in the end, prepared her for rooting around for corpses in the cold, wet darkness.

'Sure.' She could hear the hollow ring in her voice, and was hoping Tunde hadn't noticed.

'Don't think about it,' he said. 'You'll be down there for a few minutes, then we'll tap you out. Just remember to breathe . . .' His words fell short when he noticed David rounding on him.

'Tunde, you'll work the umbilicals. You're my eyes on river traffic.' David raised his voice to address the others. 'We'll regulate at ten bar. Check your weight belts and suit inflation. I want this all done with signals.'

On the shore, one of the men yawned with affectation. 'It's only a hundred yards weight to weight. You want to do *signals*? That'll take twice as long.'

'It's Harding's first time in Hammersmith,' David yelled back.

Tunde turned to Naomi and used his back to shield her from the death stares the divers were aiming at her. He ran through what she needed to do if she found something under the water. But Naomi wasn't listening. The notion that the other divers were bored of protocol did not put her mind at ease. A pang of angst crept up as the river lapped hungrily at the boat. She had a sudden feeling that she was about to be swallowed whole.

David joined them where they stood at the trim. 'All set?'

Naomi nodded.

'Listen,' he said, 'this is important. If you get in trouble, tug on the cord twice. You've been trained for this. You've done it countless times.' He left the words to sink in before handing her something small and black, which Naomi recognized as a charting watch.

'It's got a doppler velocity log built in and—' David paused, boring himself — 'it's so we can find you if you don't tug the cord . . .' He made the universal gesture for *the rest is history*. Then he stepped aside, nodding at the starboard ladder.

Naomi steeled herself to step down into the water. She watched as Scud, one of the other divers, went first, breathing in to fight the cold-water shock response. Then he disappeared. It was like watching someone step through a tear in space. The umbilical cord in Tunde's hand slackened at first, then gave enough leeway to pull taught, indicating that Scud had reached the second weight.

Naomi approached the ladder with a confidence she didn't feel. After weeks of gruelling sweeps and tests, and all manner of search patterns under intense scrutiny, she should have felt ready. She had the occupational diving experience, and the College of Policing had fast-tracked her through the HSE qualifications, to say nothing of the training Lynch had thrust upon her. He'd made her perform wade sweeps and drain searches, and various confined space tests, several of which she felt sure he'd made up on the spot just to terrorize her.

She felt a sickening lift-drop in her stomach. The reality was that no amount of training could prepare her for the dangers of inshore diving in the Thames, let alone a Gucci dive. She'd covered the bare minimum to satisfy competencies and Diving at Work Regulations. It was barely a crack in the dam. Diving was dangerous. Deadly. She had heard stories — the men had made sure of it.

Naomi rallied. If this was going to be her future, so be it. She put on her mask and tasted frigid, alien air through the regulator. With a glance at David and Tunde, she took a step down. How could the river be so cold in this heatwave? It made her blood feel like it was actually thinning in real time.

Another step, then another, until the cold surrounded her in its terrible grip. She pushed her weight into her boots and made to take another step — there was nothing but empty space.

A disposable razor bobbed by her face: a repulsive reminder of the shit she was getting into. The water chill stabbed at her neck, and she forced herself to slow her breathing. Her heart thudded in her ears.

Her mask dimmed with condensation, and a voice deep in her subconscious screamed *No* like a drumbeat. *No . . . No . . .*

*Now.*

\* \* \*

David watched in silence as Tunde fed Naomi's umbilical cord with his hands. Both men honoured the *omertà* that came with the job, trying to ignore the dangers they'd decided not to tell her about. How a sudden rush of water into the nose and throat could inhibit a vital cranial nerve and cause sudden loss of consciousness — and death.

David recalled his first dive at the National Police Diving School in Sunderland. He'd been training to lift heavy objects underwater, in this case, enclosed airbags. He had been given a lifting strop, and securing it to the bag, the strop had caught somewhere on his suit. He had almost drowned trying to swim free. Looking back, David was glad to have learnt this lesson early. To dive in the Thames was to roll the dice, and while training could protect you up to a point, the risks were never far away. Diving in freshwater lakes and rivers was a far cry from nil visibility. He'd seen the Thames best countless divers in his time — even people that had been to war zones were no match for it. For when you found a body down there in the kind of dark that spoke back, you wanted for all the world to fill your lungs with air. Against your instincts you had to learn to relax.

When he was by the river, he was somewhere else, a world away from his problems. It was how he had been able to disassociate from the screams of terrified parents as he'd dragged his little girl from the water all those years ago.

*You lied. You left.*

Naomi surfaced suddenly. She was rasping, coughing hard.

David bent down. 'You're in shock.' He spoke in a murmur so the others couldn't hear. 'You're all right. Steady your breathing. Stay calm. Breathe in.'

She did, her eyes meeting with his own.

'Do you want to stop?'

She shook her head. David nodded. 'You've got this. Go again.'

Naomi ducked under, and silence fell once more. Tunde watched the water anxiously.

'David—'

'Give her a minute.'

Tunde felt two tugs on the line. 'David, my cord—'

David hauled his mask over his face, took a deep breath, and folded into the water. He was instantly met with the ferocious cold. The shock was a familiar pain that tentacled through his veins. His ears rang with the grinding harmonics of shifting water.

He came to the jackstay wire and fed himself along its length, his right hand sweeping ahead. His fingers grazed a hard surface. Then Naomi's hand. It gripped him fiercely, as his free hand travelled along her lower arm. She was snagged

38

on something. He fumbled in the dark for the knife on his belt and used it to cleave her vest buckle.

Naomi was free. David followed her as she rose.

Residue dribbled down his mask and through the refractions he witnessed Tunde helping Naomi onto the boat. She ditched her mask, and retched over the side several feet away from where he was treading water.

Before he could reach the boat, David heard the alarm. Tunde was waving to turn about. It was then that David noticed the blood. A red mist was clouding around Scud as he surfaced, panting hard. Something had impaled his right arm.

David swam over and dragged him back to the RIB. Tunde and three others hauled their colleague onto the boat, laying him cruciform on the deck.

\* \* \*

Scud lay inches from where Naomi was hunched catching her breath. She saw his teeth clenched in pain. She saw the blood, the tear in his suit. The shaft lodged in his arm was six inches long and perhaps a millimetre wide.

'Fucking shopping trolley,' Scud rasped.

Naomi watched Tunde douse his hands in chlorine from the first aid kit. David was looming over them now, and he was positioning his weight on the wounded diver. She knew what was about to happen.

Scud howled, then swore again as Tunde doused the wound with a vial of sodium chloride. As he lay there clutching his arm, Naomi was struck by a merciless thought: *It could have been me.* The dangers meshed together and ran like dark seams that closed around her heart.

Naomi set to reclaiming the weights as Tunde radioed in and David fired up the engine. With all the gear stowed on deck, David opened the throttle and the boat leaped away from the foreshore.

# CHAPTER SEVEN

Naomi watched as the stretcher was wheeled away, with Scud still smarting from the shaft that speared his arm. Tunde assured her (with an apparent lack of irony) that medical attention was not only common but necessary — the Thames was no place for open wounds.

A sudden thought blazed across her mind. *It could have been a needle.*

She walked quickly to the locker room, the better to be alone. Once inside, she sat looking down past the creases in her hands, at a dread so acute it seemed to manifest before her eyes.

*There's no point dwelling on it,* a more reasonable voice cut in. *Time to go home.*

She craned over at the shower cubicles, pining for a hot shower despite the heat of the lagging afternoon. Afterwards, she dressed in linen trousers and a top as non-descript as they came. But before she could gather her things, her phone rang.

'Are you done yet?'

Miles Harding kept his voice flat and even, like someone not prepared to brook an argument.

'There's a few bits and pieces I need to square away. Why? Everything OK?'

'Amy. You're supposed to pick her up from school.'

Naomi felt her heart vault. How could she have forgotten? 'I'm sorry, I . . . I really can't.'

'Figures. I knew this would happen. I already called your mother.'

'Right.' Naomi cringed. This felt like a trap. She knew she hadn't been reliable lately, but she'd not expected Miles to enjoy taking major in Amy's life so much. She was stuck in minor. Amy had grown used to her absence at the school gate and the dinner table. Naomi hated this situation. She was failing her daughter.

'You know at some point you're going to have to get over yourself,' Miles added. 'Your life is here with us.'

Naomi ended the call. Not for the first time she wondered what it was about her that meant she was happier dealing with drug dealers and psychopaths than her own husband. The anger she had been ranging at herself until that point was now fixed firmly on Miles. It was exhausting being blamed for everything. She was tired of it.

As she left the room, she spotted Lynch at the end of the corridor and her attention immediately pivoted away from her marriage. The captain was speaking to another man, barely contained in an overbearing suit. She could just make out the commander's insignia on the man's shoulders — a crown over a single pip.

Naomi didn't know what to do. The sight of Roy Bishop was a welcome one — he alone had defended her against the allegations of gross misconduct. It was Bishop who had shielded her when the coroner had completed the inquest. But commanding officers didn't come to Wapping, and Lynch's body language suggested that he was just as uncertain about the visit as she was. Stephen Lynch was clearly a man who distrusted the fat cats. Yet here he was, playing host to the top brass, the breed of which Lynch despised most.

Someone else stepped into view. Detective Chief Inspector Shannon Baines had the unnatural appearance of an action figure, built like an ex-Soviet missile train, bulletproof the way people are when they take no shit and speak their mind. Unlike Bishop — who had the air of a Roman statesman — Baines was streamlined and formidable.

Naomi knew she would not be a welcome sight. Baines had known the men in the Firearms Unit well, having spent a lot of time together in the officers' bar and drinking into the small hours. As far as Baines was concerned, their deaths should be accounted for, and Naomi should be the one to do it.

Naomi went unnoticed as she watched them from the end of the hallway. She found herself wondering how tall the woman was, and what she benched. Maybe a family car.

Bishop made to introduce the woman and Lynch shook her hand. When they laughed, the sound carried, and Naomi sensed it was being absorbed by a second set of ears. She looked over her shoulder. There was David, several feet away, apparently as vexed as she was. She turned back, unwilling to draw her eyes away from Lynch, Bishop and Baines. Paranoia swirled inside her brain.

The company parted ways. As Lynch loped off, Commander Bishop began to forge a path in Naomi's direction. His eyes looked past her, connecting with David's for a moment. Upon reaching Naomi, he beckoned her into the women's changing room.

But Naomi stayed put. Her eyeline was fixed pointedly upon Baines, who was walking after Lynch down the hallway. Then, noticing David had also gone, Naomi trudged into the changing room, and waited until the door snapped closed before she spoke.

'Roy.'

'Naomi.'

Commander Bishop was standing by the lockers, and easily filling the room. He was a man of imposing size. His smile faded to a pained expression that made Naomi wince.

'So this is where you ended up.' He spoke in his customary drawl as his eyes roamed about the barren room. 'I didn't think they'd send you down *here*.'

42

'It is what it is.'

'Is it?'

Naomi folded her arms. Her head quested to the wall.

'I defended you,' he said.

'I know, I was there.'

'You shouldn't be working with the frogmen. A woman of your experience, you're wasted in this unit.' He let out a sigh. 'I suppose you're better off out of it right now.'

'Oh, sure. Tell that to the IOPC. Tell that to Baines. Tell that to anybody else who wants my head on a spike.'

'You know it's not that simple.'

Bishop scratched his double chin before returning her gaze. 'The drugs squad arrested a few gangbangers last night. We're attempting to prove they shot the men in the Firearms Unit.'

Naomi flinched, but said nothing.

'Criminal charges take precedence,' Bishop continued. 'The case against you is being put on hold.'

'Why?'

'Sub judice.'

'No. I mean, why have you come down here? To suspend me again? Because I'm done with all that. I'd rather give you my resignation.'

Bishop's face formed a mask of surprise. 'That's not what anyone wants.' He slumped on a bench, the wood creaking awkwardly under his weight. 'Look,' he said, 'if we can charge those men, you're in the clear. No misconduct, or malfeasance—'

'Save it, Roy. There's no evidence to put to a discipline board. You know that. Three men were killed and people want me to carry the can. That's all there is to it.' Naomi turned away to hide the emotion that warped her face. By the time she had grasped the nettle, Bishop's head was bowed, his hands pressed together. 'If you're not here to suspend me again, then why are you here?'

'Because I believe you — for what it's worth. That, and CID is a mess.'

Naomi wanted that 'mess' to have been caused by her absence, but when Bishop pinched his nose, that glimmer of hope began to fade.

'You didn't hear this from me,' Bishop said conspiratorially. 'The drug squad are trying to keep a lid on several dozen overdose victims. In fact, they're filing them round the clock. DCI Shannon Baines is the skipper these days, but she asked me to help out with her investigation.'

Naomi frowned. She took a seat on the opposite bench, and Bishop leaned closer to her. 'She thinks some dodgy gear found its way to the street. Some twaddle about purity, or something like that. The last thing the Met need is a public health scare with this thing.'

He was talking about narcotics — but if he was saying it for her benefit, Naomi couldn't be sure. Bishop had been her commanding officer, and had proven an ally when she needed his support, as far as that went. If Bishop had come down here to seek help from Lynch, he wouldn't get it. What did the Marine Police have to do with it? That's what Lynch would say.

'I hear a diver found a kilo of the stuff this morning.' There was a leisurely note in Bishop's voice, a childish enquiry.

'They don't tell me anything. Divers pass the work on.'

'Come now, Naomi, we're not talking about a couple of nine bars. This is serious weight.'

Naomi's eyes widened. A nine-ounce block was one of the standard units in wholesale drug supply. Bishop was being very clever in choosing his words. Despite herself, Naomi could feel the good fight warm her blood, the thrill of the chase returning. It was exhilarating. She knew he was playing her, but it didn't matter. She was being drawn in. There was a flicker of a thought that reared up like a flame: if Bishop needed the divers onside, perhaps her rotation had been no accident. Perhaps Bishop had been pulling the strings.

'We need you back at CID — it was an obvious mistake to rotate you down here. But maybe we can make a good fist of it.' Bishop rose to his feet. 'If you see anything strange, or hear anything unusual, call me. I'll make it worth your while.'

'Funny. I've been told to set my mind to wool-gathering mode.'

Bishop narrowed his eyes. 'How long can you keep that up?'

'How long do you need?'

'Six.'

'Six *months*? Jesus, Roy.'

'That's the best I can do,' Bishop insisted as he ushered himself to the door. 'You've got my number. You know where I am.'

'That's it?'

Bishop nodded.

Naomi rose too, and for a moment, she wondered if she should share her suspicion that the case David had found was connected to the raid somehow. On the other hand, she didn't want to waste the commander's time with mere supposition. Hard cases were a dime a dozen in drugs investigations. Yet, after all that had happened, Bishop had stood by her — and she felt she owed him something.

'I'll call you if anything comes up,' she promised.

'Good. And obviously—'

'I'll keep it to myself.'

\* \* \*

David wedged a loose brick in the fire door to sneak a cigarette in the alley. The wind had dropped since his argument with Lex earlier that day, but the heat remained unbending.

His phone rang. It took a moment to decide whether to answer.

'Is Lex there?' Audrey's voice was laced with acid.

'Afternoon to you too.'

'Is she there or not?' More acid. Urgent now.

David doused his cigarette and began to pace. 'She was.'

'When?'

'This morning.'

'Where is she now?'

He recounted a range of options, settling for the one he presumed the most likely. 'My place, I think.'

'What do you mean *think*? Don't you know?'

'I'm at work. I've not been home.'

Audrey said nothing. He could hear her breathing.

'I don't know what you want me to say,' he added.

'Did she go to that club?'

David stopped pacing. A moment passed.

'Well? Did she mention anything?'

'No,' he said. 'She didn't.' He ran a hand through his hair, nursing the lie.

'Tell her I'm looking for her.' Audrey was clipping her consonants. She only did that when she was seriously worried. 'Get her to call me. Don't let her leave if she ends up at yours.'

He frowned. What was she talking about?

'I'm serious, David. Don't let her go to that place.'

'Audrey, wait—' No good. She'd ended the call. He quickly dialled another number. There was just one ring before an automated voicemail message kicked in.

*Hi, it's me. If that's you then talk to the beep.*

David scowled. He never liked these things. The phone beeped, and he spoke. 'Lex? If you get this, go to my place. Key's in the usual place. I'll see you later.'

He hung up, texted her the same message, and started to pace again. The exchange with his ex-wife had left his thoughts in a dull, thick state. Anxiety began to climb his spine, its cold fingers touching each vertebra. He'd have hoped the daily dose of citalopram would take the edge off. Another cigarette would have to do for the time being. He padded himself down, looking for . . .

'Need a light?' Roy Bishop was inching sideways through the gap in the door, as if waiting for permission to commit himself to the cause. 'It's David, isn't it? David Cade?'

David nodded, recognizing the commander's insignia. 'That's right, sir.'

'Oh please, do away with the "sir". Rank gets lost in these woods. Roy Bishop. I'm very pleased to meet you.' He held out a hand to shake and raised a lighter with the other. It was an expensive lighter, the kind that stayed lit until it was closed manually. David watched the flame shiver and dance before he bowed his head, holding the cigarette between his teeth until it was lit. He kept his eyes raised.

'Trouble at home? Couldn't help but hear . . .'

David took a long drag. 'My daughter.'

'Wild one, is she?'

'Something like that.'

Bishop offered a saccharine smile. 'Your captain says you're the best he's got. Did you know I run things at CID?'

David shrugged. 'I didn't know. Sorry to disappoint.'

'That's OK — why would you? To get to the point, there's a recent recruit in your team. Naomi Harding used to be one of mine.'

'That I did know.'

Bishop looked around furtively, as if he thought they were sharing covert information. 'Nasty business, all round. I want her back in active service as soon as possible.'

'Wasn't she suspended?' David chose to ignore the slight — apparently the diving unit didn't feature in Bishop's definition of service.

'She was,' Bishop agreed. 'But the matter is on hold for the foreseeable.' He marshalled his words gingerly. 'Since you are the best Lynch has, I'd like to think I can trust you. Can I trust you, Sergeant?'

'Depends what you want from me, sir.'

'Oh, nothing taxing — I'd appreciate you keeping an eye. Looking out for her, perhaps. She's not cut from the same cloth as the frogs in this unit.'

'What's your interest in her?' David took a drag.

'Between you and me, the mandarins want to keep an eye on things down here.'

'They've never bothered before.'

'Times change,' Bishop said brightly. 'All to the good. You lot have long been the black sheep of the Met Police. The boys at the top think you're going the way of the horse and cart.'

'No doubt that's why she was sent here.'

'Quite. In any case, it's high time we turn that around.' Bishop shuffled a business card out of his breast pocket and handed it over. 'If those eyes of yours see anything strange, or you could do with a voice from the top of the food chain, that's my number. I think we can help each other.'

David eyed the home number scribbled on the back of the card.

'Trust me,' Bishop added. 'Favours go a long way.'

David supposed it cost him nothing to play along, so he pledged to do what was asked.

Before he lumbered back inside, Bishop reprised that saccharine, media-trained smile.

# CHAPTER EIGHT

It was getting on for evening when David left the dock. It was still warm, but the sun was beginning to soften its stranglehold on the day, and the dappled sky hewed yellow and gold. A breeze threw clouds of dust and leaves into the air and across the road as he stepped out into the still bright sunlight. Now in jeans and a faded shirt, he set off in the direction of home.

Of all the places he knew well on the tidal Thames, Wapping was the most evocative. The streets were often eerily quiet and, though private developers had done their best to block access to the river, myriad narrow passageways endured as cobbled time capsules. In places they led to equally ancient stairs, rotten wood and stone steps worn by millions of feet into a series of sagging crescents. Even the birds were different on the river. Unlike the greasy, maimed London pigeons, knots flocked in their thousands in secret places on the water. Sunlight would hit the flock on one side until, turning as one, they'd vanish. Every day the river promised portal moments that seemed miraculous to him. On these breathless summer nights Wapping was a tranquil place, all tumbledown streets and quiet gardens shoring the river as it writhed a course through the city.

He took a passageway to the foreshore, passing the Town of Ramsgate pub and Wapping Old Stairs. The tide was rising, so now the stairs belched straight down to the water. When Lex was little, sleuthing ginnels and snickets were a constant source of delight. He'd shown her the routes of the tributaries, from the Walbrook to the Westbourne. Her favourites had been the underground rivers that passed unseen, visible for moments before they vanished. She'd liked the Westbourne because it crossed Sloane Square Tube platform. She'd also loved the Fleet, the route of which could be traced through the centre of town and found trickling out beneath Fleet Street, before emerging from a storm drain at Blackfriars Bridge. He'd even showed her the unmarked place on Hampstead Heath where the Fleet embarked on its dark and sinister journey. It was often missed — very few people knew of it. David had told her it was a secret place, and only they knew where it was. Lex had clucked and flapped with glee, wrapping her arms tighter as she'd nestled her head in his shoulders.

But those times had grown scarce. David hoped the shoulder-nestling wouldn't disappear completely, but if it did, he only had himself to blame. Joining the Marine Police after the accident had put him well out of reach by design.

*You lied. You left.*

By the time he'd reached his apartment building the afternoon sun was gilding the streets. A group of feral school-children chased one another in the park across the street, and a gang of older teenage boys were pushing one another around by the gates. David paused, checking Lex was not with them. It occurred to him that he really didn't know where she'd go, or who her friends were. It was ridiculous he did not know the answer.

Tower View was a handsome zinc-clad apartment building that looked across the river to Tower Bridge itself. David had not intended to live so centrally, but around the time his marriage capsized, a police captain was retiring to the Emirates and was subletting his crash pad. Thanks to mates-rates rent he'd somehow managed to land on his feet. It was a functional and otherwise unaffordable one-bed flat, but it was fit for purpose. He spent little time there. He only wanted to work. There was no time for anything else.

Audrey for her part had moved back to St Albans. Lex had been caught in the middle. She'd been a born-and-raised Londoner until only a year before, and had yearned to remain part of the city's fabric. It had caused no end of friction.

David tapped his fob and walked inside, ignoring the lift as he took the stairs. On the fifth floor he trudged to number six, where he knelt and flipped the doormat.

The spare key was untouched. It seemed unchanged since Lex had last used it — she'd made a habit of treating it like a free hotel more weekends than David would like. He unlocked the door and stepped over the threshold.

Inside, the flat was ascetic, the stockpiling detritus of a life barely lived, a real life avoided. A small hallway led to an open space with a sofa and meagre dining set he seldom used. He was about to go hunting for the takeaway menus he kept in an empty drawer, when he heard his phone buzz in his pocket.

'Are you back home?'

He hesitated. Audrey again. She could strike a tone which was both accusatory and curious at the best of times, but now her voice was high and muffled.

'Well? Are you?'

'I just got in.'

'She's not there, is she?' He could hear the disappointment ripple through her voice. 'I told you, *don't* let her go to that place.'

'Audrey. Slow down—'

'Where the hell is she, David?'

He held the phone away from his ear. 'You don't need to yell.'

'You lied to me — didn't you?'

A spasm of guilt travelled through his thoughts, as a painful reminder that Audrey knew him better than he knew himself. Deciding all he wanted was for this conversation to end, he made his way to the front door, opened it, and struck what he supposed was a disciplinary tone.

'Lex. You're late.'

There was silence on the other end of the phone line. He sensed Audrey was waiting to hear her daughter's voice. He swung the bathroom door and let it slam with a thud. Then, gagging the phone with one hand, he continued. 'I told you not to go out. Your mother and I were worried sick.'

He removed his palm from the receiver to address Audrey. 'Sorry — she blanked me.'

'Let me speak to her.'

'You can't. She, um, she's only gone and locked herself in the bathroom.'

'Why?'

'How should I know?'

'Is she all right?' Audrey was raising her voice again.

'She seems normal to me.'

That part was true. Storming in without an explanation was exactly what Lex might have done. Feeling the need for an epilogue, David rapped his knuckles on the bathroom door.

'Typical Lex. So mature . . . She's fine, Audrey.' And he believed it. Lex could take care of herself — couldn't she?

Audrey made a sound like losing her patience. 'You get her to call me when she comes out of there.'

'Magic word.'

'Fuck off.'

'Mind telling me what this is about?'

For the second time today Audrey ended the call, leaving David to stew in irritated silence. He glanced out of the window. Then he redialled. There came one ring, followed by a click.

'Lex?'

*Hi, it's me. If that's you then talk to the beep.*

'It's Dad. Call me when you get this, OK?' He texted her the same as before, then discarded the phone on the dining table. Through the picture window, Tower Bridge stood like a beacon against the golden sky.

He decided not to worry about it. He knew Audrey — but he knew Lex better. She was a streetwise teenager. She could get by easily enough, but she had no money of her own. London was a more exciting place with his cash burning a hole in her pocket. She'd show up eventually.

As the day slowly burned itself out, a takeaway and the evening paper sent David to bed. He had to be up early for the morning rotation. But it took a long time to fall asleep. Somewhere in a deep pit of his mind, his subconscious recalled the accident that lingered like the spectre at the feast . . .

\* \* \*

*'Dad — are you thinking about leaving again?'*

*David sat up quickly from his resting position on the lawn chair and stared at her.*

*'Just wondering.'*

*Alexis Cade, eight years old with raccoon eyes from wearing her goggles for too long, was perched on a chair across from him. She was tall even then, but she was self-consciously folding her limbs inward to make herself look smaller than she was. The lido was brand new and pristine, and it was still very much a novelty. David had spent the last two weeks teaching Lex to swim. It had cost him an arm to convince Audrey — promise her even — that Lex would be perfectly safe. That last fortnight had been a golden time. But it was coming to an end. Now he was reminded that he never knew what to say.*

*'Where'd you hear that?'*

*Her mouth thinned to a straight line. She didn't have to say it — he knew where she'd heard it.*

*'Don't listen to your mother.'*

*'Really?'*

*David paused. Was it fair to lie to her like this? Having left the armed forces he was unsure of his footing himself, and he didn't know what the future held yet. He gathered the Military Police might be a good fit for him, but that would take him away from her again.*

53

'Everything's fine. Really, you don't have to worry.'

'But if you do work away again—'

'I'm not doing it again.' He wasn't sure if he believed it himself, but as he looked into her eyes, he noticed they were glistening.

'Mum says you don't have a job.'

'Right now, I don't. But I will.' He wasn't going to make her feel bad for asking, and he was damned if he was going to make her feel as small as she looked. He took her hands and pressed them between his own. 'You're doing it again.'

'Huh?'

'Worrying about me.'

'Because I don't want you to go.'

'Honey, you don't have to worry about that. You're not worried, right?'

Lex shrugged her shoulders. David smiled. 'Your mother's right about one thing: I don't have a job at the moment. But that isn't something you have to think about.'

'Why not?'

'Because you're eight years old. Think about kid stuff. Like Lego and ice cream.'

'Lego? Come on, Dad.'

He returned her glare with a wicked grin. Then he turned serious. 'Look at me, Lex. Do I look worried?'

'No.'

'Then you don't need to, either. Pinky swear you won't worry.' He didn't believe her when she hooked her little finger around his own. He didn't believe it himself. 'Please stop worrying about your dad.'

'OK . . .' She hesitated, and he felt that pinch a little. She never called him Dad. She never called him anything. The shock subsided, but only in the way he imagined there might be a few beats of silence after an earthquake hit before the screaming started.

'How's the water?'

'It's good. Ten more minutes?'

'Don't tell your mother.'

Looking back, he remembered almost everything about that day. The smell of chlorine. Wet tiles with puddles of water and rapidly drying footprints. The sounds of splashing, of shrieking. The gurgle *of pool filters and stuttering voices of swimmers catching their breath. He recalled Lex testing the deep end with her big toe. He remembered the lifeguard greet his girlfriend before turning his back on the water.*

*But he couldn't remember what he was thinking about as his eyes began to close.*

*Waking in fright, he realized he couldn't see her. When he spotted her floating listless in the water he threw himself at the deep end. The chlorine stung his eyes, and through waterlogged ears he heard the echoing screams of children and parents as they hurried down from the stalls. Some were coming down to help, but most were dragging their own children away as if they'd be scarred by the scene. He dragged her to the edge of the pool, heaved her onto the tiles. Her hair tendrilled around her head as David began the compressions. It took him two agonizing minutes to resuscitate her. They were the longest of his life.*

*Later, the sound of his then-wife's vitriol mingled with the hum of the hospital ward. In his dreams, her voice deepened until it belonged to the bogeyman. It no longer mattered whether it was Audrey or his father that spoke the words first. The memories converged as one, but the words were always the same.*

*'It's your fault.'*

*And with it, David's lizard mind formed a conclusion that he had convinced himself was true, every moment of every day since the second he'd first dredged the words from the nightmares.*

*You lied. You left. She'll always hate you for it.*

\* \* \*

He jerked awake again, but this time it was to the inky darkness that fell just before the sun set. He checked his phone and sank back in his chair, panting uneasily. A car door shut somewhere down on the street. Upstairs his neighbour dropped something on the floor.

Another dream. He seemed to collect them these days. His feelings were no longer separate entities. The fault line between guilt and shame had splintered, leaving him with nothing but the sick and angry thud of his heartbeat.

It wasn't that Lex herself blamed him for the accident. It was that when he did blame himself, no one had seen fit to correct him.

*You lied. You left . . .*

She did not call back that night.

# CHAPTER NINE

TUESDAY 22 JUNE
Low tide: 00.51 (0.90 m) / 13.01 (1.30 m)
High tide: 06.55 (6.20 m) / 19.36 (6.07 m)

The sun was climbing through a mist that was quick to disperse and take the wraps off a perfect summer day. David woke, and checked his phone.

*She's fine. She's a teenager.*

The thought followed him around as he showered and dressed, and opened the bathroom cabinet for the box of small white tablets. He took 20 mg of citalopram every day to take the edge off a deep-seated and difficult anxiety, which was often brought about by fitful dreams. The meds were kept well-hidden, concealed in the pouch of an old washbag. He worried about how admitting things like poor mental health could affect him professionally, and the antidepressants remained the only clue to bouts of low moments. His brain had a knack of tormenting him with thoughts of despair and terror, and his mood swings were symptomatic of what was always simmering just beneath the surface. He popped one of the tablets before setting off, checking that the spare key had not been tampered with.

Outside, his fingers gripped the mobile phone in his pocket. Radio silence was not uncommon for Alexis Cade, but if she thought he was worried about her, he felt certain she'd call him back.

*Maybe that's just it. She* doesn't *think you're worried.*

His skin prickled. The dissenting thought had left its mark on his mood. As he marched along the road, the matter continued to coalesce. Alexis — he was full-naming her now out of spite — was in Year Ten at secondary school. It was about the time when exam pressure kicked in, when life became one gruelling setback after another. It was little wonder that she hadn't called. She needed to let off some steam.

The temperature was still rising when David reached the dock. Stephen Lynch was holding a vigil over the overnight team setting up for their last rotation.

David went over. 'All quiet on the Western Front?'

'Not exactly.'

'What do you mean?'

'Found a Gucci at Blackfriars.'

David paused. 'Blackfriars? Why there?'

'Who knows. We need to get it out of the water. The area's a prime spot for tourists.'

'Did you get a description of the girl?'

Lynch swivelled his head.

'The girl. I assume it's a girl. Do we know what she looks like?' David couldn't quite believe he was asking the question — as if there was the slimmest chance his daughter had shown up dead.

*But Lex didn't want to be found last night . . .*

Lynch shrugged his shoulders dismissively. 'It's a Gucci. Does it matter?'

David stepped over to where the RIBs were waiting to launch and boarded one in silence. He sat nearest Naomi, who was loading gear onto the boat. 'Shouldn't you put something on?' she asked him. 'A vest or whatever?'

He just shrugged. Lynch shook his head as he met Naomi's eye. It was easier to let Cade do his thing for all concerned.

Soon the RIB was racing upriver and Blackfriars Bridge was rising into view. David barely registered the Watchdog circling near the south foreshore as if by way of a cordon. Watchdogs were small functional vessels — workhorses for the Port of London Authority, which administered the riverbed and the foreshore up to the mean highwater mark. It was usually when a crime was detected or a body discovered that their worlds crossed paths.

Sure enough, he saw the shape. He found himself standing right on the trim of the boat, staring intently, trying to quell the fear rising in his belly.

'Pull closer.' He pulled on a pair of gloves.

Presently David looked askance, nursing a cigarette, not willing to admit his heart had been thumping in his chest until only moments ago. He flicked the butt over the side, thoughts fixed on his little girl, out there, not answering his phone calls.

'She's young,' the skipper called out, referring to the dead girl. 'Must have been a wild night, eh?'

Most people joined the Met Police because they wanted to make a difference: days would be spent cleaning up the streets, fuelled by a hopeful fanaticism for justice. But the illusion was too often dragged down by casual corruption and piles of paperwork, and the endless stream of Londoners with trivial disputes. By the time he'd bounced between the Royal Marines and the Military Police, and a handful of specialisms that had refused to chime, David had chosen the Marine Police. He enjoyed work that taxed his body rather than his brain, and that his days were purposeful. Somewhere along the line his own fanaticism had mutated into something caught between abstinence and ambivalence, until he'd abandoned the notion of due process altogether. His experience conflated that of every diver on the team, resigned to be seen as non-speaking characters like the frogmen in crime shows on television. David's world may be quiet and empty when he came home each day, but he wasn't hustled by journeymen devoted to data-driven policing. His colleagues didn't harass him or gossip about his personal life. They left him alone.

But now an image of Lex flashed through David's mind. His daughter's face, blank-eyed, wet and pale, hair coiled around her head like a macabre halo.

He wondered if he should mention something to Lynch. He had a duty to report any turmoil to his supervising officer. But he quickly decided against it. Whether it was his duty or not, the captain was cut from the same cloth — what would telling him about Lex achieve, besides suspending him from work, and thus removing him from the one thing that kept his life in check?

David tied off as soon as they returned to the dock and made for the fire exit. In the alley, he took out his phone and dialled a number.

He heard a ring, then her voice. *Hi, it's me—*

This was followed by the beep. David's throat worked, but no sound came out. The wind played a long trombone note through the empty space over his head. He hung up, struggling to climb over the wall of anxiety that was building up around him.

*She's a teenager. This is what they do.*

That thought did not take a wrecking ball to that wall as he hoped. Instead, he stepped back inside and marched himself to a door at the end of a long corridor. He checked the coast was clear before walking into the storeroom and closing the door behind him.

The space was a relic of the past, when it was still respected that the Marine Police had been around longer than the Met. Everything was so different now. Consequently, the air was fusty and the blinds were drawn. Dust filmed every surface, leaden with a soulless assortment of office trappings.

Recently, David had begun using this room to shut out the pressures of the world. It was somewhere to go to keep his mind busy when anxiety hovered in his brain. It was also a place to keep his hands busy too, by idly rewiring switchboards. He requisitioned one now, pulling a chair up to an ageing computer.

He supposed he could have used one of the working boards in the station next door, but he didn't want to attract attention, and he was wary following the visit from the commander.

The machine was past its best, but he only needed the landline phone and the grubby headset hooked up to it. There was a buzz and then a bland neutral voice spoke directly into his ear. 'Name and ID?'

'David Cade. ID 82517, Department 12.'

He heard fingers peck computer keys. 'MPU?'

'That's it.'

'What can I do for you, Sergeant?'

'I need to track and trace someone. Do you still do that?'

'One moment.'

One moment became two. David ran his tongue over his teeth.

'Do you have the form to hand?'

'I need you to bypass the bumf,' he said. 'Try ASAC341.' He remembered the code well. He had used it many times going through the motions, before he'd joined the Dive Team. Somehow the code had stayed lodged in his brain like a radio jingle.

'I'm sorry. I'm afraid that code is no longer valid.'

David was counting on that. 'Maybe you can help me then. I need to trace a GPS on a phone. You can still do that from there, right?'

'Oh. Well, look, new rules—'

'You'll have all the paperwork you need.'

'Yes, but the internal process—'

'I had the wrong code, let's put it to human error. The system was updated not six months ago. Your team should have sent us the literature, but they never did.'

'I'm sorry, Sergeant, I'm just an assistant. If you like I can put you through to—'

'Let's not put you in hot water over this,' David cut in. 'It's a matter of urgency down here. We've got a body on our hands, and I think there's a connection to a person I'm looking for.'

'Everyone has to go through the internal process—'

'What's your name?'

'Pardon?'

'What's your name, son?'

The assistant cleared his throat. 'Pat Driscoll.'

'OK, Pat Driscoll, listen up. I found a dead woman in the River Thames this morning. I hate to bother the super at home, and you have all the updates in front of you. Our PNC hasn't been patched, so it hasn't been updated.' David felt the lies lap his gut. He prayed the assistant's computer literacy was as sub-par as his own. 'Please. Help me find her — you might save a life today. Can you help me do that, Pat?'

In this game of chance, David pictured Pat as a bushy-tailed graduate. He'd adopted a fatherly tone to coax the boy's gaze away from the pencil pot on his desk. He'd repeated Pat's name. He'd cited the superintendent. He'd used the acronym for the Police National Computer. Old tricks still worked on the evergreen.

'Look, I'd do it myself,' David added. 'But we're behind on service updates down here. You should see the code on your screen . . .'

The tapping of keys. 'I have it here.'

'Try my code, would you, Pat? I won't take up any more of your time.'

More tapping. 'What is it you need?'

'GPS on a phone.' David gave his daughter's details. Phone number, birthday, Audrey's home address. By some miracle Pat missed the association by name. Evergreen, indeed.

David held his breath, but it was Pat that exhaled first. 'I'm sorry, sir, I can't process it. Your request has been denied.'

'Denied?'

'Yes. A window came up.'

'Describe it, Pat.'

'It locked me out. Says that someone has been assigned to the case. It says there's a conflict on file. I'm afraid you don't have access for that particular case.'

David felt the muscles in his face tighten.

'Also, somebody must be editing the file at the moment,' Pat continued. 'Even I can't access it from here.'

David hung up the phone and pressed his hands to his head. There *shouldn't* be a case, but there was. An active one at that. He had lied about Lex's association with the woman in the water — he had known his code wouldn't work. Could someone be tracing Lex using the internal server? Who would have been assigned to an open investigation?

He had only meant to test the water. Call the switchboard, get a fix on her location. He suddenly understood that someone at the operations centre *had* been tracking her phone number, debit transactions, even her IP address could be traced to a wireless hotspot.

David stared unseeingly into the room. His mind trawled through the past unbidden, back to the day of the accident. When Lex had nearly drowned, Audrey had been justifiably upset. But she'd taken it too far when she reported him to the police on grounds of neglect. That was the first ripple in the flood. David had spent a painful three weeks under investigation, and though the case was eventually dropped, the damage could not be undone. It was easy to believe he was bad for his daughter, that he should have stayed away from her and the Military Police would help him to do that. So he'd left her.

The thought of leaning into his responsibilities had given way to an act of distancing, of othering himself from Lex. And all the better. He had promised to watch her and failed.

*You lied. You left.*

David closed his eyes. That word — neglect — what did it mean? It meant coming home from the funeral a broken-hearted little boy, with a stomach churning so wildly he'd stolen the grief sandwiches untouched on the trestle table. Worth the risk, if it avoided another lunchbox of crusts so stale they could snap. It meant a slow walk home, part because his feet throbbed in too-small shoes, part because there was nothing for him when he got there. It meant keeping his head down, avoiding both praise and detection, nursing gum for hours to mine its non-existent nutrients. Coming home to blistering scorn with a petrol smell that rose thick. It meant longing for his child muscles, low and tight on his arms, to bulge fast so he could at least fight back. It meant spending too much time out of doors rooting around the tip near the house, clambering over the rubble and seized-up bicycle chains, unaware of the lurking dangers of mercury from broken thermometers.

His father had blamed him for the complications that began with his birth and ended with his mother in the grave. David had picked over the carcass of events long enough to know that if there was one thing he'd never do, it was to teach Lex what blame felt like. If he had it his way, she'd never understand what blame even *looked* like.

But he had to blame someone. It was why he'd cultured a dependency on antidepressants and serial lies, so far gone from his father's pathological honesty.

His eyes opened. He was swiftly disabused of a better past. If he'd stuck it out, if he'd stayed. If everything was different. The notion was a fantasy. There had been too many lost chances for that vision to have played out.

Now there was a case. Another case. Not one of neglect this time, but not so far removed from it either.

A membrane of sweat formed on David's brow. His throat closed as if the room were shrinking. There shouldn't be a case. It was meant to be a lie. *His* lie. There was only one reason for the existence of an open police file . . .

Alexis Cade was in trouble.

## CHAPTER TEN

Naomi found David in the men's changing room. It was smaller than her own, and musky as a monkey house.

The morning had seeped into the afternoon. Ever since David had returned from sneaking off to the storeroom, Naomi had sensed his irascibility. She had been waiting for an opportune moment to talk to him alone, and she discovered him hosing down dive gear with a chlorine wand. Naomi was unfazed. She knew he went to great lengths to busy those idle hands.

'Should you be in here?' he growled.

Naomi was momentarily drawn to David's open locker. There was an old Polaroid photograph wedged in its hinge. A girl — was it his daughter? — maybe eight or nine, grinning on a tyre swing.

David noticed her wandering gaze and snapped the locker shut. 'Do you want something, Harding?'

'We need to talk.'

'So talk.'

'That girl we found,' she said hastily. 'The Gucci?'

David had made to turn away from her but stopped mid-action. 'What of it?'

'The Port Authority said the girl was an illegal. No papers. Nothing.'

'What's your point?'

Naomi heard herself speak with an exasperated forcefulness. 'It looks like an overdose to me. Before I was brought here, I worked in Major Crimes. I was a DI. I've seen overdose victims before — I know what to look for.'

'Why do you care what happened to that girl?'

It occurred to Naomi that she didn't know what to say. Surely it was obvious. 'Do you know what the Met do with Jane Does?'

'Enlighten me.'

'They're chalked up as medical waste and fast-tracked to a crematorium in Hainault.'

David rolled his eyes.

'Doesn't that bother you?'

'Why would it?' David answered. 'We dredge them. That's all we do. The sooner you get used to that the better.'

Naomi felt frustration bubbling up. The Marine Police was perfectly capable of police work — she simply could not understand the apathy. Why wouldn't you want to investigate? Why else would you join the police? The idea you could make a difference, and the hope you *would* was a motivating force . . . yet none of that seemed to mean anything down here.

'Fine,' she snapped. 'Have it your way.'

As she swept from the room, she didn't notice David's attention had piqued. She marched down the corridor, feeling impotent. Moreover she felt she had only herself to blame. The need to find out more was an itch she couldn't scratch. How did she expect to survive here?

Unless she didn't. Naomi turned the thought over. What if she did leave? What if resigning from the force was the sort of action that got results? If what Bishop had said was true about the gangbangers and the criminal charges, it would take *years* for the IOPC to turn their attention back to her. And if she was long out of the game by then, and justice had been served in the courts, there was every possibility the IOPC would close the file and her failures could be forgotten. They would incinerate the paperwork as easily as the girl in the river.

Her thoughts returned to the corpse she'd found. That the young woman may have been forced to enter the country illegally had not occurred to David or the other divers, or if it had, it had meant nothing to them. It was an unwritten law of nature that Jane Does were erased from history. Nobody missed them or mourned their loss. It was Naomi's own worst fear realized.

She soon realized she'd been walking in the direction of the captain's office, because she was standing outside the door. Instinct seemed to have possessed her muscles. She lingered at the glass, peering through. Lynch was sitting in his chair, while DCI Baines was hunched over his desk. What was she doing here? Naomi couldn't help noticing how displaced Baines was, as if she had never seen a desk in her life.

Naomi let her hand hover over the door handle, long enough to ignite a fire in her belly. Then she entered the room.

Lynch rose furiously to his feet. 'Don't you knock?'

'I'm sorry, sir, but this is important.'

Lynch ignored that. 'I suppose you know each other,' he remarked, nodding at the bulletproof woman.

DCI Baines scanned Naomi like a judicious customs official. A shiver ran to the base of Naomi's spine and clung to her dry suit bunching there. She wished she had changed. The dry suit was not just unflattering. Standing before a ranking officer, it was a painful reminder of her failure.

'Ah, David.' Lynch looked past Naomi. 'This is DCI Baines. She'll be working closely with us in the coming weeks.'

Naomi swivelled to David, who was now standing in the doorway, and she thought of one of those wildlife shows, when hyena shuffle at the fringe of a herd. Baines was watching David as if he were prey.

David spoke at last. 'Working with us? Here?'

'That's right.' Lynch offered Naomi a smile, and she sensed this was bad news.

'What for?' David's usual indifference was tinged with ill-disguised suspicion.

Baines's voice was sharp, authoritative, her words carefully curated. 'You found a corpse this morning. The victim is linked to a wider investigation.'

Naomi nodded inwardly to herself. It came as no surprise. She knew that the first forty-eight hours were crucial to solve a murder inquiry.

'There a reason you're here, Harding?' Lynch cocked his eyebrows in Naomi's direction.

'Yes.'

'Make it quick.'

Naomi faltered, realizing Lynch had no intention of ushering Baines out the room. But when she looked at him, there was a glint in the captain's eye. He, like them, hated that Baines was here. She was now a fly on the wall, and there was nothing Lynch could do about it. The captain despised red tape at the best of times. Naomi theorized he'd been relegated himself, once. If that were true, it made the Met the enemy.

'Apologies for the intrusion, sir, but the corpse in the water — I think there's more to it.'

'Oh?' Lynch began, but Baines had already turned her attention to Naomi.

'Thank you for stating the obvious, Harding.' Baines shot Lynch a tight suppressive smile. 'I believe I just said that.'

'But we're talking about a potential lead in a major investigation.'

'In which you are not involved,' Baines said.

'All due respect—' Naomi matched the woman's tone — 'I'm speaking to my captain.'

'None of it is your concern.'

'You think so?'

'I know so. You're a diver now.' Baines smiled.

Naomi stood her ground. 'This girl—'

'She was an illegal, Harding,' Lynch addressed her patiently. 'You're an intelligent woman. Do you have any idea how many illegals we find in the drink, or how many were coked up to begin with? Those girls are off the grid—'

'Listen—' Naomi pressed.

'Abducted from mainland Europe, more often than not. London's a big place, Harding. The Home Office love deporting people who shouldn't be here. You think they care if a few strays turn up dead?'

'Please, just listen to me—'

'Immigrants always get dumped,' Lynch said with finality. 'They're casualties of war. Don't waste my time with this.'

'She was an overdose victim, and if I'm right, she was plied with a potentially lethal narcotic that was supposed to have been taken off the street.'

Something in the room changed. Baines seemed to be studying Naomi with new interest. Lynch spotted that too. Naomi could sense David behind her, watching the war of wills unfold. She felt her blood run hot. 'Don't you care who she is? How she died?'

'It's not in our job description. This isn't your case.'

The captain's words leached at Naomi, but there was nothing more she could say. She would be consumed here. The only solace came from knowing that digestion would take six months.

When she turned to leave, she noticed David had already hurried away.

* * *

Thunderheads gathered in the distance, heralding a high note of the heatwave at last.

The cherry of David's cigarette glowered as a breeze kicked up a frenzy through the alley down to the foreshore. The remainder of the day shift had passed as uneasily as that

69

of the afternoon. He'd tried to call Lex, but each time it had rung through to the answerphone. When he'd returned to the dock, his mind had felt full. Thoughts vied for space in his brain and crept like weeds up a vast wall of anxiety.

As he made his way to the locker room his eyes caught a glimpse of a police van parked out on the street, visible through the open bifolding doors. This was not unusual, but something didn't sit right. The van had plates of bulletproof glass, and the windscreen was blacked out. The rear doors were open and DCI Baines was loading something into the vehicle. It was solid and scuffed and he recognized it almost immediately: the same hard case he had salvaged from St Katharine Dock the night before. It was now wrapped up in a sealed plastic evidence bag and tagged with a property stored docket. He knew the case would have been secured in the evidence holding on-site, or even at the police station next door. That was where it ought to have stayed — unless the case proved relevant to an ongoing investigation.

Baines positioned the case inside the van. Before she closed the doors, David caught sight of the body bag on the stretcher inside. As she moved to the driver's side, Baines noticed David watching her. For a moment, neither moved, the wind whistling through the empty space between them. Then, as David took one step forward, Baines climbed into the cab and started the engine, apparently aware there was nothing he could do to stop her.

It was all David could do to watch the van pull away, reach the end of the street, and turn off out of sight. He stood in the street, not quite sure what he had witnessed. Baines was a ranking officer. By all accounts, she had every right to reclaim evidence herself. Still, it didn't sit right. There was something about the way she had looked at him in the captain's office, almost like she had wanted to get under his skin.

His phone buzzed in his pocket and he grabbed at it, all thoughts of Baines forgotten. But it was just an alert from his calendar reminding him to take his meds. He thought of the last time he saw Lex, of how she had seemed so vulnerable, with her bleached hair and eyeliner-stained eyes. He caught himself wishing that she had gone to his place in spite of what he'd told her, and ignoring frustration that she hadn't.

He edged carefully down to the Alderman Stairs and found that the rising tide was ravenous. But the thrash of the water failed to clear his mind as it usually did. The only constant was the coming storm, which continued to menace the horizon.

Reaching his apartment, David noted the spare key remained untouched under the mat.

David sloughed off his shirt as he walked into the muggy living room and opened the windows to air the space. He hunched on the sofa, checked his watch. It was almost six. He hadn't eaten since the morning, but even so, his stomach felt heavy. It didn't help that thoughts of Lex played in a constant loop in his head, her face branded on his mind.

David had told her to go home. She hadn't gone back to St Albans. And that was all he knew. She couldn't be missing. Tragedies like that only happened to other people.

* * *

In dreams the smell of chlorine merged with petrol fumes and the taste of lies as they formed in his mouth. Eventually they drove him awake. The room was darker now, though a spray of sun lingered to bleach the horizon. He must have passed out on the sofa, and bringing himself groggily to his feet, David glanced at his watch. Hours had passed, it was almost ten.

He checked his phone, but there were no calls. He dialled Lex's number and jabbed the loudspeaker. Then he made his way to the bedroom. He had no business there, but it was the longest walk he could take.

The phone rang once.

*Hi, it's me. If that's you then talk to the beep.*

He threw the handset down on the bed in frustration. It slipped off the side of the bed and landed with an invisible *thunk*.

A memory rode upon the sound: Lex creeping into his old bedroom in the dead of night. Audrey asleep next to him. He remembered gathering Lex up in his arms.

'It's OK — it's not real.'

'But I heard him.'

'You couldn't have, sweetheart. There's nothing under the bed.'

And there wasn't. Look, he would show her. Take her back to her room and drop on all fours and crawl underneath . . .

David did it now. As his hand quested for the phone amid the clutter of shoes and dust bunnies, his fingers came upon something.

The cardboard box slid out easily. It was full of ornaments from reconnaissance past: schematics, blueprints, maps of the waterways — and a folded sheet of paper. David opened it. He stared down at a blown-up aerial photograph of central London, the city reduced to abstractions. The corners of the map were mussed and the paper felt aged between his fingers. The blue line of the river roved across the page as a familiar meandering line.

David could not explain why he pinned it to the wall. He only knew he wouldn't sleep again tonight, and that his strings were being pulled by something other than himself.

He took a marker pen from a desk drawer and drew a line on the map, a crow's flight from the Marine Police back to his apartment. She had wanted to come back here. And he had said no.

If she had not come back here, she would have headed back to the river and followed it. She would have done that because it would comfort her, and because it would take her to Blackfriars Station if she'd meant to go home. Since she had not done that, where did she go next?

# CHAPTER ELEVEN

WEDNESDAY 23 JUNE
Low tide: 01.27 (1.01 m) / 13.41 (1.48 m)
High tide: 07.38 (6.01 m) / 19.36 (6.07 m)

The city awakened to an ant-march of commuter traffic. Vapour trails scored the sky and though black clouds speckled the horizon the coming storm was no closer to its execution.

David had abandoned sleep altogether and consigned himself to the sofa. As the morning came, he took a shower. His body bore marks of exposure to the sun. The skin of his forearms, his neck and the V of his collar were now scorched an angry red.

He dressed and took his pills. He'd been glued to his phone all night, but he checked it again as he opened the front door and flicked the doormat with his foot.

The key was untouched, dormant like an unused puzzle piece.

He closed the door and went to the window to gaze at the river glimmering in the sun. Panic felt so close, it was like standing at the edge of a wildfire. Frenzied thoughts danced and blazed. He'd not seen hide nor hair of Lex for two days now. Were she a few years older, old enough for student bars, he wouldn't mind.

*But she's not. She's fifteen.*

Maybe he wouldn't go to work today. He could call the police — the real ones — and report her disappearance. Dickering with his phone, he summoned these words to the screen:

> *You can make a report to the police immediately — you do NOT have to wait until twenty-four hours after a disappearance. Once you have made a report, action will depend on the given circumstances and how much they consider the missing person to be at risk.*

A litany of questions ran round his head like a wind-up toy. Was she at risk? If so, from whom? What would he say when the police pressed him on it? He read on:

> *If you have serious concerns for the welfare and safety of a person, and their whereabouts are unknown . . .*

David poked through recent events, as a doctor might hunt precancerous cells, struggling to determine whether Lex had given him cause to believe she was actually in danger. She had asked for help — she wanted to stay with him — and she was shaking while she did it. He'd insisted she was in the way. If he called the police, what would he say — that it was his fault?

David spent the better part of an hour calling hospitals across London, but there were no admissions to chase up. He considered her term dates. Lex was supposed to be on a study break to focus on exam revision but he phoned the school office all the same. Nothing. It was only then that he reluctantly returned to the open tab with the Met Police website and scrolled to the options on-screen:

> *What would you like to report?*
> • *A missing person*

- *A sighting of a missing person*
- *A person I haven't seen or heard from in days, weeks or months*

He tapped the third option, and the screen changed again: did he think she might be in immediate danger? David pressed *No*. To his annoyance the site offered links to the Salvation Army. He went back, hating himself as he instead tapped *Yes*.

*Call 999. Please have the following information ready.*

- *Date and time the person was last seen and who by.*
- *What they were wearing when they were last seen.*
- *Their description, such as height, colouring, marks or scars.*
- *Their address.*
- *Any family, friends, or places they often go.*
- *Do they have access to a car? If yes, please have the registration number, if possible.*
- *Other means of transport (do they have a bus or rail card?)*
- *Any enquiries that have been made to find out the person's whereabouts.*
- *Any vulnerabilities they have, such as medical needs or a disability.*
- *Why you consider them to be in immediate danger.*

David felt an emptiness in the hollow part of his chest. There were so many variables at play. The first four points were straightforward but the fifth rankled. *Family, friends, places they often go.* If only he knew the answer. There was always the chance, not a pleasant possibility but one that endured all the same, that Alexis Cade was not missing at all, and that she had simply run away . . .

David flushed hot with anger at himself for not knowing his daughter well enough. Why didn't he know who her friends were? How could he have let this happen?

He stared at his phone, remembered her own phone battery often died from overuse. It infuriated him that she didn't charge it properly. But maybe that was a good thing. Lex had sequestered his phone on family holidays. Why hadn't he thought of this before?

Hedging his bets, he opened the Facebook app on his phone, and at the bottom of the screen a window slid up with her details. David's heart bounced. She had stored her password on his iCloud keychain. He quickly logged into her Facebook page. He could even link to her Instagram from here.

David scrambled to read the comments feed. Lex had not used social media since Sunday, nor read private messages from friends. He spent time messaging some of the people that commented regularly, hoping they were more than casual contacts. He was dismayed to learn her best friend from school had recently been blocked, but private messages did not disclose why. He wondered about that. He clicked through photos of her, scanning the heart emoticons and comments until he realized he kept seeing the same name. He opened the person's profile. Staring back at him was a young man in his twenties, with a dicky bow and a haircut styled into a quiff. His name was Piers Larwood. His profile's privacy settings were set to friends only, so David returned to Lex's Facebook page to read the comments he'd left her.

*Thanks for last night.*

*Beautiful.*

*See you later ;)*

There was a video uploaded from her phone a week before. The footage was shaky — it looked like Lex and Piers were lying on a beach. They were staring at the camera and pulling faces. Piers, he noticed, was wearing an expensive pair of Ray-Bans.

'How much do you love me?' Lex asked.

Piers cackled, raised his hands to the camera to make the universal symbol for *this much*. The dirty joke Piers cracked was enough to make David's skin crawl. Piers was clearly older than Lex. But maybe that was why she liked him . . .

The footage on the phone suddenly whipped around to a new angle, and it was then that David recognized the place. It wasn't a beach at all. It was a stretch of foreshore near Wapping Wall.

'What a lovely day,' Lex sighed.

The video reached its end.

David had been pacing the room as he watched, but now hunched on the sofa to make sense of his thoughts. Who was Piers to Lex? Was it possible he'd know where she was? On closer inspection of her Instagram feed, he realized she'd shared more videos. In one of them, Piers was on a dance floor. In another, they were lying in bed.

David trembled. He pictured himself storming into the room, dragging Piers half-naked to the floor. He imagined wrapping his fingers around the boy's throat, reminding him Lex was underage, and didn't he know that, and *what the hell was he thinking dragging a kid into all this*?

It was a terrible moment it took a long time to recover from.

Eventually he selected a third video. In it, Lex was scurrying through a blur of undergrowth. Piers had to be clutching the phone because he could be heard off-screen. 'Where are we going?'

'You'll see.'

It was difficult to tolerate Larwood's cut-glass vowels, the public-school accent present and correct.

Lex hopped onto a fallen oak tree and turned to laugh at the camera before she leaped out of sight. The camera shook frantically in its pursuit. On the other side of the tree, the camera craned down into a deep ditch which led to a hole in the ground. David recognized the sound of headwater and knew at once where they were.

It was the secret place. The entrance to the Fleet.

David felt the heat of betrayal. That was their place — only *they* knew where it was. He felt utterly lost, uncertain how to process this onslaught of new information. He shook himself. Hidden among the other messages on Facebook he found a note Piers had posted several weeks before. Lex had commented on it with a heart emoji, and Larwood had replied to it, with a mobile phone number.

David's finger loitered over the screen. He glanced at his watch. Half seven in the morning. He didn't know if it was too early to make the call — he was so used to graveyard shifts and early morning rotations, it occurred to him that Larwood didn't share the same sleep patterns. But having barely slept and grown anxious with it, now was not the time to fret over Larwood's reaction. Wasting no more time, he jabbed at the number and the call rang through. On the sixth ring the call connected.

'Hello?' The voice on the other end was hesitant, somewhat higher than David expected.

'It's David Cade. I think you know my daughter.'

He was subjected to silence before Piers Larwood spoke again. 'Oh. Hi. I don't know where she is if you want to know . . .'

David clicked his teeth. 'She's not been in touch with me or her mum. We're worried sick. Can you tell me when you last saw her?'

'Oh. I, um . . . When did you last see her?'

'Sunday,' David lied. If Larwood was innocent, then there was no point him asking the question.

'Sunday, huh? Well, it was Saturday. Yeah. Saturday, I reckon it was.' It sounded as casual as choosing an answer to a pub quiz question.

'Whereabouts?'

'At a party.'

David sensed Larwood was playing it safe. 'Was she acting strange?' he asked. 'Was anything going on?'

'I don't know. I don't know where she is either, OK?'

'Has she contacted you?'

'Why would she?'

'You seem pretty pally online.' David didn't feel the urge to lie this time. 'Are you her boyfriend?'

'What? No, no. We're . . . we were casual.'

'*Were?*'

A panicked breath rattled the cut-glass vowels like a wind chime. 'Look, if she's missing, I don't know anything about it.'

'Who said she was missing?'

The panic in Larwood's voice intensified. 'Would you mind calling back later? It's, uh, not a good time.'

The line went dead before David could answer. He flopped back on the sofa to stare at the living room ceiling, as if he'd find the answers haloing around his head. He replayed the conversation in his mind. Nothing felt right about the exchange. Nothing felt right about any of this. The more he imagined the danger Lex might be in, the less he felt able to act. He felt poleaxed. That was the thing about anxiety: it felt like he was the only one who could smell burning.

The criteria tab from the police website remained open on his phone, and David gazed at the outstanding points on the screen. Some were dead ends by default. Lex couldn't drive, didn't need a railcard — she was eligible for a child's fare until her sixteenth birthday. The last point had been framed as a question: why did he think Lex was in immediate danger?

Truthfully he didn't know. He could sense it brimming at the back of his eyes like a headache in the wings. Something deep down told him she *was* in danger, but the reason eluded him. There had to be one.

'There has to be,' he whispered aloud, baring his teeth at the endless and incomprehensible nothingness that should have been populated by personal information. He didn't know any more of her friends, nor any of the places she would go. All he knew for sure was where he'd last seen her.

And yet, it was not Lex he saw weightless in the empty space in his mind. It was the dead girl, floating in the river, the domes of her eyes sunk into her skull, gaze fixed at the empty sky.

\* \* \*

David hurried to the dock. He had decided it best to tell Lynch the truth, and hope that compassion would give him time to set out and find Lex. Stopping by to explain his absence couldn't hurt, and he could drop into the station next door to file the missing persons report.

Upon arrival, he spotted the blacked-out van parked in front of the station. Did that mean DCI Baines was close by? The dock was oddly quiet, given the day shift had only just started.

David made his way to the changing room, but as he approached, he heard voices bickering from the corridor.

'Step aside, Harding. Don't embarrass yourself.' The bulletproof woman's voice.

'I want answers,' he heard Naomi retort. 'What are you hiding?'

David carefully crept closer to where Baines and Harding stood out of view. He could see their shadows in a streak of sunlight on the far wall.

'You're not a DI anymore,' Baines snarled. 'This has nothing to do with you.'

Naomi stood her ground. 'I only want to know what Major Crimes want with these women.'

'I don't answer to you — *your* mistakes cost lives. Last chance, Harding. Get out of my way.' Baines bullied her way past Naomi, straight into David's path. A contemptuous look shrouded her face.

'Help you with something?' he asked quietly, blocking her route.

'I'm waiting on your captain,' Baines said.

'Rare we get skippers down here. Time was they sent bobbies to do their dirty work. What's changed?'

'I suggest you step aside for your own sake, Sergeant. I'm investigating a case.'

'Why are you here?' he repeated.

'Lynch found another girl. I need a debrief.'

'What are you talking about?' David's mouth dried. Baines seemed to enjoy his reaction.

'You haven't heard? They found another one. At Blackfriars.'

'How do you know?'

'It's my job to know — it's part of a case.' Shannon almost smiled. Almost. 'Whatever went down, it must have been a wild night.'

\* \* \*

David leaped up the stairs and tore onto the street. Mercifully, he spotted a black cab and splayed his hand. It was all the driver could do to finish pulling up as David tumbled into the back.

'Blackfriars — *quickly*.'

The bridge was two miles upriver, easily reached by boat, but there was no way he'd make it on foot. He soon learned the hard way that a car in rush-hour traffic was insufferable.

'Morning rush,' the cabbie said dismissively. 'Nothing I can do about that.'

David stewed, unable to part the sea. As they grovelled along the next street they were met with another jam passing Southwark Bridge. He leaned forward and spied Millennium Bridge striking out over the river.

He threw open the door and charged off at a dead run, dimly aware of the cabbie hurling abuse over his shoulder. There were people filing on either side of the bridge, and suitcase wheels zinged along the ridged metal path. David ran with the assurance of an athlete — for a moment, he was a Royal Marine again.

Trains clacked through Blackfriars Station as music drifted from buskers on the river path. At the end of the bridge he scrambled down to the foreshore. It was less protected in this part of town. Without a large river wall to hide from the modern world, the dredging would be exposed.

David spied the boats and the Port Authority Watchdog bobbing near the shore. Lynch, Connor, Tunde and several others were gathered outside a forensic tent. Boots on the ground were doing their best to move people along but it had not stopped tourists from rubbernecking. Flashing his ID at the cordon, David hurtled into their midst.

Lynch looked up with a start. 'David? What are you doing here?'

David's eyes fixed on the girl. She was tall with long hair and she was wearing a black dress . . . but she wasn't Lex.

A hand yanked him up by the scruff. Lynch got right in his face and lowered his voice to a lethal whisper. 'For Christ's sake, wind it in.'

David pulled free of the man's grip. 'Did you find her like this?'

'Not us,' Connor replied. 'One of the lightermen. Tunde fished it out of the water.'

David examined the body. The girl's arms lay pale and splayed on the foreshore. Grit glistened in her hair. There was a club stamp on her hand, identical to what they had found on the first body the morning before. This stamp had left a much stronger impression — it was clearer than the last. It formed the shape of a stallion.

David stood up and took Lynch aside. 'There's a pattern here. There were similar markings on the girl I found yesterday.'

'So?'

'There's . . . I don't know. I think there's a connection.'

'Good for you. Tell that to the detectives when they show up.' Lynch glanced at his watch. Because the body had been found close to the foreshore, they couldn't move it. It was not a diver's job now. This was a crime scene.

David lost his patience. 'Stephen, listen to me—'

'Save your breath. I don't care about an illegal.'

'I care.' And as the words formed, David heard his own voice as if he was outside himself.

'Enough,' Lynch growled. 'Go on, piss off. You're making a scene.'

He was right. There was nothing to be done. As police officers began to step down onto the foreshore David made his way back up to the river path, an ominous compression heavy on his chest.

# CHAPTER TWELVE

David was torn between trying to get the image of the girl out of his head, and trying to keep it there. He had no idea what to make of the victim's resemblance to Lex, nor where that notion would lead him. The business with Larwood had shaken him, and his failure to file a missing persons report had only deepened his concern, to say nothing of the twin encounters with Baines and Lynch.

At a loss over what to do, he headed home. When Lex tired of her adolescent haunts she always showed up there — he wasn't about to raid every student bar and gig venue in the city. He could go home and wait. She might even have already gone there. The idea spread a warm feeling of anticipation from his heart to his legs, and he quickened his pace along the cobbled terraces.

The sun was well-established by now, unleashing yet another blazing summer day. The newly christened heat sent what remained of the early morning pall shrinking to thickets of shade.

David reached the building and moments later approached his front door. The doormat was skewed at an angle. The spare key was gone. His heart snared in his chest as he charged into the flat.

'Lex! Lex—?' The breeze of cheap perfume, the crisp packets and fizzy drink cans were nowhere to be found. The flat lacked the carbon footprint he'd expect of his daughter. Before he could bang on the bathroom door he was cut off by a familiar accusatory voice.

'You lied.'

Audrey Cade was standing in the blind spot around the corner of the open-plan kitchen. A bar of sunlight was falling through the room and had drawn up a line of battle. At the sight of her, a flurry of feelings cascaded through David with the force of an avalanche.

'She never came back here, did she.' Audrey didn't bother to frame her words as a question.

'I can explain.'

'Can you?' Audrey moved towards him.

'Yes, I—'

Her hand flashed up, and he registered the pain swelling across his temple. Her fist must have closed at the last moment because Audrey was now racking the knuckles of her right hand painfully. Her rage seemed barrel-aged.

'Please don't do that again.'

'Give me a reason not to.' Audrey's eyes — the same bronze eyes she shared with their daughter — flashed angrily.

'I told you not to let her go. You had one job.'

'I was at work, Audrey. What was I supposed to do? Or should I have marched her back here and locked the front door behind me?'

Audrey glowered at him, and David wondered how much more could be left unsaid between them.

'Anyway,' he continued, 'I think you owe me an explanation first.'

'What?'

'You two had a fight. You hung up the phone before I could ask you about that. So, let's rewind.' David raised his hands by way of a truce. 'Yes, you told me not to let her go, but you didn't say why.'

'We didn't fight.'

'That's not what she said.'

Audrey placed her hands on her hips. Though she was shifting her weight impatiently from one foot to the other, her voice was measured and clear, like a teacher trying to enlighten a toddler. 'Fine. We had words. What do you want to know?'

'Lex told me you were overreacting about her going out to some club. She said she wanted to stay with me because of it.'

'She told you about the club, did she?'

David entertained the eerie sensation of standing on a chessboard as the pieces were starting to move. 'She mentioned it, but that's it,' he admitted. 'Why is that important?' Then he hesitated. The dead girl from the foreshore had fallen to the forefront of his mind, but it was not her face he pictured this time. It was the club stamp on the lifeless hand. 'Tell me about the club,' he said. 'Why is it such a big deal?'

Audrey faced the window. 'She's too young for all that. I shouldn't have to say it.'

'She's pushing her limits.'

It was Audrey's turn to hesitate. David watched as her hand found its way to her pocket. She pulled out a small and square object. 'I found this under her mattress.'

The wrap was no bigger than a penny sweet, but David knew at once that a gram of cocaine was enclosed inside its folds. 'She didn't tell me.'

'Why would she — you're her father.' Audrey folded her arms. 'I bet she didn't tell you about the boyfriend either.'

David held his tongue. He wasn't sure how much Audrey knew about Piers Larwood, and he didn't want to admit he'd been snooping around. From the very beginning, Audrey had been able to read Lex's every mercurial mood. Whereas he had felt awkward, scared of the fragile weight in his arms, unable to tell what she wanted when she cried.

'Are you telling me you didn't sneak around when you were a kid?'

'Oh, wake up,' Audrey snarled. 'She's out there doing Class A drugs with strangers — and you're doing nothing about it.'

'That's not fair, Audrey, I had no idea she was doing anything.'

'You hide yourself away, pretending she's a little girl.'

'Stop it, Audrey.'

'She's a child. Our child is out there—'

'I said *stop*.'

Audrey glowered as she stood her ground as if charged by a bolt of lightning. They were nose to nose now. It was the closest they'd been for a long time.

'You don't give a shit, do you?' Audrey's anger sounded porous. 'You only care about yourself.'

'That's not true.'

Audrey managed a pitying look before removing herself from his orbit. 'I need to find her. I'm going to the police.'

'I'll come with you.'

'No. I want you to go and look for her.'

'Where do you think I've been?' he demanded, smarting under the truth Audrey had so easily gleaned. He didn't like being told what to do.

'Work probably. It wouldn't surprise me.' Audrey stepped even closer to him and looked in his eyes. 'Whatever's happened between us, she's our little girl. We need to find her. Can we agree on that?'

He nodded once.

'Good. I'm going to the police.'

'I'll find her.'

'You'd better.'

She brushed past and dumped the spare key on the coffee table. 'You'd better fucking find her, David.'

* * *

Audrey lowered herself into the car parked across the street and began her breathing exercises. In a few short moments, her heart rate began to drop. Clearing her mind proved trickier. She'd had years to put what had happened between them into words, the anger and the bitterness at a marriage that was made to last but doomed to fail. It was still too challenging to contemplate. Life with David had been far from simple: here was someone who loved her and wanted to be with her. All the things that went towards building a life together made sense. But they were not for ever.

She had known that in her gut. It was a familiar guilt she felt now, a punch working the same bruise. She'd known it would get messier as time went on but she hadn't bargained on the third party in their relationship. David's commitment to diving was unbending, and his gift at unmooring emotions she kept at bay. That in itself was not the issue. Her own career in corporate law was no picnic, but she had never let it define her. Audrey knew what a workaholic looked like, but David took it too far. He was obsessed. What made it worse was that Audrey had seen it happening, but couldn't explain why she didn't stop it.

She ought to have told him to say no. Many times. Even as things had got messy and his wandering eye returned to the water. On nights he had not come home, Audrey had fought her jealousy. Knowing he was wrapped in the embrace of the Thames did nothing to console her. The pressure of the week would be behind her, and they would stare down the barrel of a weekend — all that time together. She had grown so used to being apart, so used to playing second fiddle to his work, that time felt like false victory.

She should have said no when he went down on one knee. Audrey couldn't explain why she didn't. *There's no such thing as perfect*, she had insisted. *Besides, he'll be a great father.*

She had tried and failed to logic her way through the marriage for years. She had managed to find brief spells of happiness. The baby's arrival was one thing, but that period came and went. When David came to bed after a night on the job, she had never completely relaxed, wise to the river's stench filling the bedroom in the darkness.

Doubt about balancing motherhood and a career had become another muscle to her. But her body rarely lied. Audrey reminded herself of this as her muscles relaxed and her shoulders fell away from her ears. How was she so tense? The question lingered, as Audrey felt the muscle around her atlas bone contract as if an invisible hand were pushing on the back of her neck.

Butting heads with David was the closest she'd felt to him in years. It was nothing physical. It was more like their needs had finally aligned. She was sure that David didn't know how she felt. That true intimacy, the ability to read each other, had come and gone.

When the plan had been explained to her, Audrey had agreed without question that David could be leveraged. Old wounds were useful, and she had come here to open them again.

She took out her mobile phone. David had no idea how deep the trouble Lex was in, but she had known what would make him want to find out. She had set out to summon a version of David: the obsessive, foolhardy workaholic who had sequestered himself from their marriage.

The cocaine wrap was a trigger. She had come here hoping that he had learnt nothing from their estrangement. He had not disappointed her.

Exhaling, Audrey sank into the driver's seat. Her own wounds were unstitching, as she had known they would. The phone was ringing on her lap, and someone answered on loudspeaker.

'It's me,' said Audrey. 'It's done.'

\* \* \*

*Hi, it's me. If that's you then talk to the beep.*

'You need to pick up the phone and talk to me. I'm not joking. Call me back — the minute you get this.'

David ended the call and immediately sent a text with the same message, ignoring that previous messages remained unread. Now he was circling the room as if a new direction would yield fresh insight. He returned the spare keys from where Audrey had abandoned them to their hiding place under the mat.

His stomach began to groan. Anxiety had diminished his appetite, but he knew he had to eat something if he was to have any hope of finding Lex. He also had a strong craving for a cigarette. Nicotine would help him think. He opened the windows and set about in search of a lighter. Checking his jacket pocket, he discovered something small and lean, and drew it out to see what it was. The platoon of ten black-head matches were neatly ranged in a row, visible through a letterbox seam at the front of the eggshell matchbook.

*Matches are better. You don't burn the tobacco.*

David turned the matchbook over in his hand. He was expecting to find a strike surface. Instead there was an address embossed on the inlay.

*THE PALE HORSE, 666 SHOREDITCH HIGH STREET, LONDON E1.*

David trembled. Was this the club Audrey had warned him about? If not, how had Lex get hold of it? The twin questions goaded him. He could go there and investigate, see what all the fuss was about.

*But what if Lex comes here?*

David took a drag. He couldn't stand by and rely on what-ifs. This could be a lead. He may even find her there. He could speak to the owner — someone could give him answers. Though it was possible they would not let him in. David hadn't set foot in a nightclub in decades. Despite the misgivings, Audrey's warning hung spectrally in the air. *You'd better fucking find her, David.*

He would go. Tonight. He had to. Because his daughter had vanished, and it was probably his fault that she wasn't calling him back. Because he missed her voice, her smile and her arrogance, and those moments in her company when he came alive, when he finally felt like he was living, not dying by inches.

He took a long drag and set his mind to it. After dredging the familiar places — TikTok, Instagram, any other apps she might use — he would follow her trail like a network of wires.

He thought about what he would say when he saw her again. He pictured her running in for an embrace, and he longed to fill the space in his arms with her being. He imagined the first thing she would say. Something dry, belittling. She wouldn't call him 'Dad'.

The fact was, there was no order in chaos. The police refused to help and clues led to dead ends. Having come to doubt the religion of technique, where could David turn? He had never been a detective, nor trained as one. But twelve years in the Marine Police had nurtured instincts that had always turned out to be right. He was a diver. He saw things no one else could. The perfect dark beneath the Thames was his to master — but technique was no substitute for instinct. The men on the Dive Team trusted his intuition. Lynch too. He had never been wrong about anything he thought to be true.

If the next move was to report her as a missing person, Audrey would see to that. He pined for a trace of physical data like debit card transactions, or Oyster card activity . . . She had eluded both her parents so far. It made him believe that either she did not want to be found, or worse: that someone else didn't want him to find her.

## CHAPTER THIRTEEN

Down in a disused office of Wapping Police Headquarters, Naomi Harding considered her options. The malodorous room was a storage area for disused office equipment she had found while exploring the corridors. The air in here was cool and still. Decorators had once tried to brighten the space, but the result looked no more cheerful than a funeral home. Naomi had adopted the room for the purpose of being left to herself. Hidden among the empty shelves and broken fixtures, she came here to segregate her feelings. To show emotion was to admit weakness in the police, and that wouldn't do at all.

As she paced the threadbare carpet, Naomi compiled her thoughts. She hadn't been a diver for long, but old muscles were working again, and so were the old temptations tethered to her time in the Met. For as long as she could remember, Naomi had fixated on joining the police. She had been bullied at school, and kept to herself shielded by a wall of books. The classic adventure stories she tore through as a child by Bernard Cornwell and Patrick O'Brian were stories of men (and they were usually men) doing good in impossible circumstances. They had led her to loathe the frailty she perceived in her friends. Her mother had weaponized her vulnerability so well that she refused to drive at night, and she had made herself so reliant on the men around her that she had become a victim of fraud and lost a chunk of her pension. There had been other formative moments too, which was why Naomi fell hard for a calling in which protecting others was more than a job — it was a deployment.

Since the discovery of the two dead girls in the Thames, she had decided, with a Baptist's zeal, she was going to go after whoever had killed them. Naomi still considered herself a detective. She had worked too hard for too long to ignore that obsession. It didn't matter that the CID was trying to throw her away like she were a rag. It couldn't be coincidence that David Cade had found that cocaine in the water — indistinguishable from the contraband she'd spent months chasing back at the drugs squad. Naomi was too experienced to multiply assumptions unnecessarily. Occam's Razor stated the simplest solution fit the facts, and now that dead girls were being dredged from the river, she had to prove, beyond reasonable doubt, that those were the drugs that killed them, and pin it to the person who had given it to them. She needed to weight the scale of justice in her favour. And since Lynch would insist that investigating was 'not in their job description', Naomi had elected to take matters into her own hands.

There were good reasons to investigate. Naomi had spent months on the drugs squad. She'd witnessed first-hand what drugs did to people. If her suspicions were correct, the girls had died painfully, perhaps horribly. She refused to let that stand. The other reason was personal: Shannon Baines had spurred her on. There was nothing Naomi hated more than to be told she couldn't do something. It was what made her too hot-tempered to work with sexists and bigots, and what excited the jealousy of her superiors. Only Roy Bishop seemed sympathetic. The commander had perceived something in her that she did not see herself.

She vowed she would have her day — if only to prove Baines wrong. So now she would focus her efforts on the girls themselves. When she was at Major Crimes, Naomi had singled out coppers with a shared drive to fight the good fight with purposeful resolve, and had fostered a few close friendships. With help from those contacts, she was convinced she could identify at least one of the girls.

She called her old muckers at CID, to see if any information had come their way. She sidestepped the drugs squad as best she could — she did not want Shannon Baines to catch wind of her plans. She was in her second hour making calls, blowing stray strands of hair from her face, when she struck a dead end. No one in CID or subsidiaries at Major Crimes had heard about the girls. In fact, according to the internal database, there was no record of them at all. Not even a record of an open investigation.

It seemed impossible. The first body was found yesterday, the second only hours ago. How could the Jane Does have already been wiped from view, as easily as condensation off a window? Why weren't they in the system? Their very existence should have been a trigger for someone to find out who they were.

Naomi leaned back in the rusting chair she'd commandeered for herself and pressed her mobile phone to her chin. A large spider drew her eye, slinking to the topmost corner of the room. Naomi watched it awhile, wrestling with a question. *If there's no investigation, where are the girls now?*

The phone in her hand rang so loudly that she almost dropped the handset in alarm. Nerves jangling, Naomi composed herself and checked the screen. *Withheld.* In normal circumstances, she'd have declined the call.

'Hello?'

Instantly Naomi cocked her ear away from the phone. There came a loud hissing down the line, and when a voice arrived, it was deep and throaty.

*'Harding. You need to look for the drugs.'*

'Who is this?'

*'Don't ask questions — just listen. Look for the bodies. Find out how they died.'*

The line went dead, leaving empty silence in its wake.

Naomi sat back and stared at her phone. The caller had clearly obscured their voice somehow. Who was it? And how had they known to contact her?

*Find out how they died.* What did that mean?

She took a deep breath, the better to manage her thoughts. Whoever called had known exactly how to spark her interest. The words, the urgency: they had delivered just enough of a clue to appeal to her uncompromising, pig-headed preoccupation with the good fight. To her steadfast nature, the smallest clues were as sparks to dry straw. Her mysterious co-conspirator clearly knew her well — but did that make them a friend or an enemy?

*Look for the bodies. Find out how they died.*

Almost without realizing what she was doing, Naomi dialled a number. It was a contact she'd been sitting on for some time, and as the line began to ring at one end, she caught herself holding her breath.

'You're through to Forensics.'

'Hi, yes. This is Naomi Harding at MPU, I need to speak to Sofia Pérez, please?'

Naomi held the line, tapping her thumb and fingers, a vague sense of her pulse quickening. When the phone rang through, she heard a voice savour her name. 'Naomi Harding. Can it be she?'

Naomi leaned forward. 'Sofia . . . um, how are you?'

'I see you kept my number. That's sweet.'

Forensic pathologist Dr Sofia Pérez spoke with exaggerated precision that fused fondness with righteous anger. Not so long ago, she had been Naomi's drinking buddy and sparring partner, coaxing her to rage against the institutional life of the Met's utilitarian settings. In times of high stress and mounting paperwork, Naomi had enjoyed listening to Sofia's lightly sarcastic barbs. They'd talked brightly, picking out the positives in unlikely prospects, joking about the men they'd hurt. In the bluster of mutual reassurance, Naomi and Sofia had unwound in the officers' bar. The domestic it had once caused with Miles had led to a night on Sofia's sofa.

This was followed by a second night. Then a third. By the end of the week, Naomi had felt like she could return home and her bond with Sofia had strengthened. Sofia became someone Naomi could rely on when things with Miles got too heavy.

But then came the investigation. Naomi had hidden from the world, and her friendship with Sofia, like so many others, had fizzled. If only she had answered Sofia's worried texts, or reset their friendship on respectful terms, but she had been too much of a coward.

But then, what if it had been more than friendship? She was scared to admit it to herself: the existence of a co-dependence, and more than that besides. She wished she could make things count again, but more than that, she wanted to feel like she was worth something.

'Sofia, look, I, um . . . don't know if you heard. I'm down at Wapping these days?'

'Yes, I hadn't seen you at the officers' bar. Still drinking for England?'

'Actually, I'm trying to cut back. Never just one, is it?'

Naomi tried to keep her voice steady through Sofia's patient silence. 'Look, Sofia. I'm sorry to trouble you with this . . .'

'No, no. It's no trouble, whatever it is. I'm sure there's a good reason for ghosting me completely. Did your husband ask you to do that, or was that one of your own bright ideas?'

'I'm genuinely sorry.'

'Are you, Nay? Because it seems like you want something. I'm not a toy in the attic. You don't get to pick me up and toss me aside when you're done.'

*Look for the bodies. Find out how they died.*

'You're right,' Naomi conceded. 'I shouldn't have cut you off and I'm sorry for that. You want me to jump hoops, I get it . . . but we're still colleagues, and I need your help.'

Sofia's voice turned waspish. 'Make it quick, I'm very busy.'

*Find out how they died.*

'I'm trying to identify the remains of two women that may have ended up in your lab.' Naomi found herself possessed by the same urgency as her mystery informant. The words she'd used would send Sofia back to those terrible lectures at King's College, with endless slides of brutalized women (and they were usually women) opening every module. Naomi had a way of heightening attention when she was coming to the point, as she did now. 'They were fished out of the Thames. If my hunch is right, you had the drug squad on the phone. They want full pathology on them. Say nothing if I'm right about that.'

Sofia breathed down the phone.

Naomi pressed on. 'I would think the girls I'm looking for were, say, late teens? Everything tells me the drugs squad won't ID them. They'll be for the crematoria. If I'm right, say nothing.'

Naomi listened intently. She could tell she held Sofia's attention. 'I want to do what I can for them, but I need a look at a pathology report—'

'If you want to discuss a case, you'll have to take it up with a case officer.'

'But that's just it,' Naomi urged. 'There is no case, at least not one I can find listed on the database. There isn't even an open file. I've been digging around and I can't find anything.'

'Why do you care who they are?'

Naomi faltered, hadn't expected that. 'Because it's the right thing to do.'

'Cut the crap, Harding. What do you want with them?'

'If I find out what killed them, I'll catch whoever's responsible.'

'And you can assure me of that, can you?'

It was Naomi's turn to say nothing, but Sofia cut in. 'I thought you were a diver, now?'

'I am.'

'So what's your stake in this?'

'There's no mystery to it, Sofia. I'm just trying to tie up a case. That's all.'

'But you're not a DI now.'

'I know. But I'm doing it anyway.'

'Still fighting the good fight, huh?'

Lurking beneath Sofia's intended slight, Naomi detected the same vulnerability, something that needed protection. Or perhaps it was simply the Met's latent chauvinism rubbing off on her.

Sofia cleared her throat, and Naomi could picture her pinching her nose affectedly. 'Look, I'll meet you somewhere, after hours.'

'Sofia, I can't thank you enough.'

'Text me.'

Dr Pérez rung off, leaving Naomi to smile to herself.

In the corner of the room, the spider was weaving a web.

# CHAPTER FOURTEEN

*Two days ago*
*1.04 a.m.*

Piers Larwood was slumped in a chair, attempting to draw air out of the room, which had seemed to have plenty just a few minutes ago. It was only when he had caught sight of his reflection in the wall-length mirror at the other end of the bar that the situation had begun to coalesce. The surface of the glass was speckled with blood now, and his features were frozen in a mute communication of horror.

At some point he discovered he had remembered to breathe again. He had been paralyzed with fear but not because of the girls. He was no murderer. Even if he was, they were nothing to him. Less than nothing. They had made their choices in life and there was nothing more to say about that. More frightening was the sense of the real weight of the axe dangling over him.

He could not go to prison. Not over this. But the system would not be sympathetic this time. His reach and his father's legacy would not save him. It was a tall order to ask any court to overlook his police record — to which he had been adding to ever since his first arrest. Larwood was a new face in the laundering racket, and had worked tirelessly to legitimate himself in an illegitimate trade. Peddling drugs was a lowlife's game and he was clearly not cut from that cloth. Nevertheless he promised security, high margins, and a reasonable rate of return. He promised no risk in the portfolio. He'd pledged that and more to Mark Cronin, the bagman who came to the club. He'd presented the pitch from the same chair he was sitting in now, from behind the same large desk, flanked by thick-necked steroid junkies not unlike the muscle the bagman had brought with him.

As Larwood eyed the hard case lying open on the floor, he recalled the conversation he'd had several nights ago with his point of contact. Cronin was ex-police as Larwood understood it. He had a need to sell a lot of his product fast, to a direct competitor. The police had rumbled his supplier's operation and left a huge dent in the profit margin. This was seven months back, and although not all the gear had been seized, they'd had had to wait for things to settle before trying to shift it. And now it was deemed prudent to get the gear moving again.

Larwood found himself smiling: the wild, crazed grin of a man with the winning hand. He was valuable. The criminal element needed his client base. The art of the deal relied on what people tried to hide from you, not what they wanted to show you. He'd searched for it, the same way you might sift through a landfill, for evidence of what they wanted to bury. And when he was presented with a ready supply of narcotics in exchange for a quick sell, he'd seen his chance to negotiate.

Larwood had studied Mark Cronin suspiciously, not wanting to demonstrate his eagerness to buy. Cronin was a young man, late twenties by Larwood's estimation. He wore dark clothes and a leather jacket, and a permanently amused expression that impugned his piggish face.

Larwood had sneered at the hard case on the table. 'More where this came from?'

'Much more. Nine hundred keys.'

'Pounds?'

Cronin rolled his eyes. 'Kilos.'

'So what's that?' Larwood settled the maths in his head. 'Street value, seventy-five?'

'Six,' Cronin had corrected.

Larwood had whistled. Not bad. If he could shift it. It was enough. 'All right,' he'd said. 'So where does it land?'

'Ninety-six on the pound.'

'Ninety-one.'

'Fuck you and your haircut. You obviously don't know who you're dealing with.'

But the muscle guarding the room had made Larwood cocky. 'Look at this place,' he'd purred. 'I've built it from the ground up.' (A blatant lie, his father had fronted the cash.) 'And if you don't know it, the security here won't allow for blind spots. I have cameras that saw you come in and they'll be watching you on the way out. Besides—' Larwood had added a menacing edge to his voice — 'if ever the police were to track you and your people down, all the incriminating evidence is right here on tape. It would be easy for me to cut a deal.'

Cronin had sneered. 'So that's why you're still in the game. I wondered what we needed you for.'

'It's no secret. Now you know.'

'If you didn't have your guard here—'

'Well, I do,' Larwood had broken in. 'And there's nothing you can do about it.'

Cronin had shifted in his chair.

'Relax. Let's all just calm down.' Larwood had raised his hands and waved them at everyone in the room. 'The nick know nothing about the set-up and it's better for everyone if it stays that way.' (That was another outright lie.) 'My point is, there's nothing in your hand. You don't have a buyer — if you did you wouldn't be here.' He'd heard a scary laugh, and realized it was his own.

With a fleeting half-smile, Cronin had cast his eyes over Larwood's entourage. He was assessing the risk, trying to decide how it would go. 'There's no way at ninety-one.'

'You've gone to the mattresses. Don't try to negotiate the price.'

'There's no way,' Cronin had repeated.

Larwood smirked. 'Fine. We're fill or kill at ninety-three.'

'Kill or what?'

'Means we have a deal.' Larwood had shaped the words with a patronizing overture, making sure to roll his eyes as Cronin had done a moment before. 'So are we done?'

Cronin hadn't flinched but Larwood could tell he was desperate.

'You can promise you'll sell it to the right people?'

'Competitors, you mean?' Larwood's eyes had narrowed. 'What are you up to — a hostile takeover or something?'

'Between you and me, this gear is two-bit. We're having a little spring clean.' Cronin had tapped the case and leaned back in his chair.

Larwood had reappraised his position. Selling dodgy gear would bring the police to their door, to say nothing of the casualties it could produce. On the other hand, it was the only way to clean up. If the club closed down in the end, so be it. He'd had assurances. There was no chance that this trail of criminality would find its way back to him. This was the only way to clear the black spot against his name.

They shook hands. The deal was done.

\* \* \*

Tonight was only meant to be a small affair. A taste. He hadn't thought that a skim off the top would amount to much. There had been every reason to celebrate.

But now he didn't know what to do. He had pledged to shift the product and return the profit quickly. He had promised. But now he couldn't pay off the debt — *any* of it — and the people he represented were not the kind to care why.

Terror returned to Larwood's mind, and cliches of what would happen to him if he didn't come up with the cash.

Thoughts of nail guns and refuse compactors raced through his head. He pictured his skull in a vice.

It had not yet occurred to Larwood that Cronin had weighed his options carefully that night and concluded that Larwood liked to sample the goods. Larwood reckoned that it could have been him lying dead on the floor tonight. Perhaps it *should* have been, and Cronin was setting him up.

He knew he had to get away from here. He would have to convince Lex to go with him, or if he couldn't convince her, he would have to do it by force. He needed that girl. One more chance to get clean. That's all. One more chance. He would promise her. This time he would make her believe it.

It had taken a long while to form the skeleton of a plan, which he ran over and over in his head until there was some flesh on the bones. It was OK. Not perfect. Not a sure thing. But it would do. He would have to be careful. He would have to keep his eyes and ears open. The state of the club didn't matter much. He'd bleach everything in sight. The carpets were scheduled to be changed soon — no one would care if the floor was wrecked through the back rooms.

Pushing that aside, his thoughts turned to the riskier part of the plan. He would make regular visits to the secret place, from its source down to its mouth. Larwood almost smiled, a mad loopy grin as his hand gripped the phone in his pocket.

He dialled. It rang through.

'Christ alive, it's half one in the morning—'

'Are you alone?' Larwood's own voice crackled as he heaved with breath.

'Yes.'

'I need you to come to the club.'

'The club? Why?'

The man's voice was sharp and shocked him into fitful attention. Sweat greased his palms. His flannel shirt clung to the folds of puppy fat on his stomach, and he felt his temples pulsate as blood flooded his face and brain.

'Just *get down here.*' His throat felt tight, and he shrieked his words into the receiver. 'We've got a problem.'

In that moment something changed between the two people on the call. It was as if the person at the other end had already registered that the worst-case scenario had come to fruition. Tears formed hot and thick and streamed down Larwood's face. He couldn't stand still for a second. As he moved around the room, he was careful not to step in the blood soaking into the carpet or catch his Chelsea boot on the tangle of limbs forming a ghoulish web on the floor.

'Please,' he begged. 'I need you here. Now.'

The man spoke again, this time in a low tone. 'Listen to me very carefully. Don't touch anything. Here's what I need you to do . . .'

Larwood listened, hell-bent on carrying out the instructions to the letter. His eyes tumbled down to where four dead people lay sprawled across the floor. He could still salvage this. It was now or never. He looked at his watch.

It was now.

\* \* \*

An hour later, Piers Larwood was driving through the city, careful not to let the speedometer needle climb over the limit. He had wanted to get away sooner, but it had been difficult to empty the packed club and convince the bar staff not to clean down for the night, to say nothing of the time he had taken to wash the blood off his hands.

He slowed at the intersection at East Smithfield, and felt glad that the area was quiet. Only the night buses roamed the streets. It was too early for newspaper drops and the bakers were just beginning their work. He turned down St Katharine's Way, mindful of the case stowed in the footwell on the passenger's side, trying to ignore the smell of vomit carrying from the boot of the car.

As he sped beneath the underpass the lifting bridge came into view. It straddled the lock via a steel grid carriageway flanked on both sides by a red steel frame. If Larwood had not been wrecked by panic and the blind desire to rid himself of the evidence, he'd have noticed the central basin had been cleared of yachts and other vessels, forced to crowd moorings at the West and East basin. He'd have noticed the flat-top barge and the workmen manning the excavator. He'd have noticed the restless water, which lapped and writhed as the machinery went to task. He may not have drowned out the sound of the generator filling the restless night.

But he did not notice. He only had eyes for any surveillance cameras as he left the car idling beneath the underpass. Once he had recced the area and the loading bay servicing the hotel, he took the case from the footwell and crept to the net cordon at the edge of the water. There was one more frantic look around before he dropped the case over the side. It fell like a dead weight.

But the work wasn't over. It wouldn't be — until he got rid of the girls.

He returned to the car and sped off into the night. Had Larwood waited a moment longer, he'd have seen the hard case emerge, float for a moment, bob towards the excavator, and tip beneath the water once more.

## CHAPTER FIFTEEN

There were people in Naomi's life who laboured under the misconception that policing was regular like clockwork, but she'd accepted long ago there was no clocking off from the Met. Her working life had formed habits so ingrained she barely noticed them at all. These habits cordoned her from close friends and detained their curiosity, as Sofia Pérez had learnt when she became another casualty of Naomi Harding's good intentions.

Naomi's habit was to arrive early for meetings, to observe the specific meeting point from a distance. She lingered in a side street off Broadway, near St James's Park. The breeze had picked up, and the early evening sky was overcast for the first time in weeks.

Sofia Pérez was punctual to the minute. Thirty-four years old with dark curls that reached her waist, she was dressed in charcoal-coloured slacks and a sleeveless number to complement her complexion. She wore no jewellery, but she was wearing make-up. She could not have come from the lab.

Naomi checked herself in a compact mirror. She removed her wedding ring, along with the gold stud in her ear, and stowed them both in her bag before crossing the street.

'Sofia.' She felt a pang in her chest as Sofia met her eyes. 'Thanks for this.'

'Uh-huh.' Sofia kept her hands in her pockets. Her voice, usually wry, was brusque and quiet. 'Buy me a drink, it's been a day.'

They chose The Feathers pub so they could avoid the subsidized bar at New Scotland Yard. With its red-leather-backed booths and floral wallpaper, it was a place to guard from prying eyes and open ears. Naomi fetched a round of drinks from the wood-panelled saloon bar and brought them to Sofia, who was settling herself in a corner.

'Heard you were sacked.'

'Who told you?' Naomi slid into the booth.

Sofia just shrugged.

Naomi raised her glass. 'It's, um, good to see you . . .'

'How's Miles?'

'Oh, you know.'

'Do I?' Sofia had noticed her ring finger. 'And Amy, she must be, what, eight now?'

'Nine. Think we can do this without the small talk?'

Sofia looked unimpressed. 'No we can't. You want to pick up where we left off — remind me where that was again?'

'I'm sorry.'

'You ghosted me.'

'OK, that's not what I'd call it.'

'What else would you call it?' Sofia had her arms folded. She spoke with that exaggerated precision again.

'Didn't we already have this discussion on the phone?' Naomi kept her voice to a hush. 'I can only say sorry so many times.'

'Six months, Naomi. Nothing. Zip. Now you show your face.'

'Like I said on the phone, I'm trying to find out what caused two women to overdose.'

Sofia raised the highball glass halfway to her lips. 'How do you know it's an overdose?'

'I don't,' Naomi admitted.

'OK — say they were drug addicts. How do you know you can catch their dealer?'

'I don't know that, either.'

'So why do you need to know who they are? What are you trying to prove here?'

Naomi hesitated. 'Even if I had an answer, I couldn't tell you.'

'Exactly,' Sofia said, the air of an argument won. 'And that's where this conversation ends. You want me to share a pathology report under the table? Do you understand what you're asking of me? If it's an open investigation, I could lose my job. I have my career to think about. Unlike you.'

Naomi's temper flared a little. She wasn't angry at Sofia. It was just the situation. Irritation that things were not going as she hoped. 'There can't be an ongoing investigation because there is no open file. Believe me, I've asked around, I've checked all the familiar places—'

'That doesn't mean there isn't one.' Sofia lost her patience. 'And for that matter, maybe people don't *want* to help you, now your career's on the rocks?'

Sofia's words burned. Naomi felt them curl around her head like smoke. But somehow, beyond that, the notion of the good fight held firm. It was a beacon stronger than any other source of light. Stronger than reason, and doubt. 'Humour me. Please. If there's no open investigation, nine times out of ten that means there's no one working the case.'

'What's your stake in it? Why are you doing this?'

'Because no one cares who the girls are. They're immigrants. Illegals.'

Sofia looked away at that. Naomi saw her opening. 'Surely you understand?'

Sofia, a Sephardic Jewish immigrant, understood 'otherness'. She'd moved around often as a child before finally settling in the UK, and when she took her citizenship test, she was required to know that the Queen was head of church *and* state. When she had first joined the police, there was no Hispanic/Latinx tick box on the HR form. Coupled with the

107

standard-issue racism and systematic bigotry UK law enforcement doggedly refused to acknowledge, Sofia was tired of batting against the glass ceiling like a bee in a jar. Given luck and circumstance, she could be forgotten as easily as the dead women destined to burn.

'Even if I could show you a pathology report,' Sofia began, with a stony look, 'from one professional to another, there's a reason it's not being recorded on the database.' She pinched her nose. 'The officer investigating told me it's need to know.'

'Meaning?'

'You don't need to know.'

'Sofia, listen to me—'

'No, *you* listen. I was given explicit instructions not to share a peep with anyone. I don't know what's going on. All I know is I shouldn't even be talking to you about this.'

Naomi struggled with the impulse to tell Sofia about the informer on the phone — the one with the deep throat voice. Then she talked herself down. There was no knowing whether that call had been meant to aid her investigation or hinder it. *Look for the bodies. Find out how they died.*

'Sofia, if you really can't help, why did you meet me?'

'Because you're my friend,' Sofia hissed through gritted teeth. 'And despite everything, if you say you're fighting the good fight, I actually believe you. Do you think I enjoy seeing young women on my table? The sheer *number* killed this year alone — it never gets easier. Even if I could help you, how do I know you're not on the creep? You could be one of the moles I was warned about.' Sofia caught herself with a sharp intake of breath, but it was too late.

'So there is a case,' Naomi said.

Sofia pinched her nose again, then downed her gin and tonic.

'Tell me,' Naomi urged. 'You ever heard of a DCI Baines?'

'I know what you're doing.' Sofia's words came tumbling out too quickly.

'I know I don't deserve your trust,' Naomi said, 'but at least let me earn it. Just tell me this. Was it Baines who approached you?'

Sofia said nothing.

'The cadavers are in your lab. Baines wants you to fast-track bloods. The work's being carried out as we speak.' Naomi sat back. Despite herself, she couldn't help feeling a giddy surge of triumphant adrenaline surge through her veins.

'Nice detective work. I hope you're happy,' Sofia said miserably.

'So what happens next?'

'What do you mean?' Sofia spluttered. 'What happens next is I'll do what I'm told. I'll get back to ticking off my to-do list of fatalities, victims, suicides, and the countless other ways to die in this city. I'm doing my job. So should you.' She had clearly decided enough was enough. As she rose to leave, Naomi stepped around the table.

'I didn't want to upset you. I just want to help.'

'You can help by keeping a lid on it. We never had this conversation.'

She was about to step away, but Naomi placed a hand on her arm. Her grip was light and reassuring. 'Sofia . . . if you really can't tell me anything, and you didn't intend to, then tell me honestly: why did you agree to meet me?'

Sofia raised her hand so that it met Naomi's, who felt the piece of paper being pressed into her palm.

'I'm good at what I do,' Sofia said matter-of-factly. 'It doesn't mean I have to like the red tape all the time. This should get you started.'

Naomi slipped the paper into her pocket. When she looked up, she realized Sofia wasn't finished.

'There's something else . . .' She leaned in. Her voice almost broke. 'I came here to warn you off the case.'

'Warn me? About what?'

'I've just got a bad feeling about this one. I think it's dangerous. I can't say why, I just feel like something else is going on.' The expression on Sofia's face was solemn enough to take seriously.

'You think I'm in over my head?'

'It's not that.'

'Then what is it?'

'I've never been asked to withhold information from ranking officers. Have you?'

## CHAPTER SIXTEEN

The storm was closer now. The air fizzed with static and rainclouds were filling the darkening sky.

As the bus trundled towards Shoreditch, David watched the rain begin to smatter the top-deck windows. He had been keen to investigate after hours when The Pale Horse opened its doors, but his patience thinned as the weather turned. It was close to ten in the evening, and the black clouds were chiselled hard against the heavens. A celestial hole had opened in them, rimmed with embers as the evening's fire-glow finally burned out.

Though Shoreditch had gentrified at alarming speed, London's dark underbelly had not disappeared completely. He could still hear the symphony of police sirens over the rain. Though he rarely came to this part of town, he had spent time dredging the Regent's Canal for pollutants, and fondly remembered trips to Brick Lane to feast on salt beef bagels smothered in no-nonsense mustard.

Lex had loved Brick Lane too. Memories of showing her the sights rattled around within the confines of the top deck. There was comfort in street food and world music, in Lex learning to widen her horizons, before adulthood had wiped the enchantments clean. He forced himself to think about the present and looked around instead at the passengers, encumbered by the code of silence that was unique to London transport.

The rain was falling in earnest as he disembarked at Old Street Station. His bomber jacket was insufficient to weather the storm, and his clothes pressed to his skin. He jogged along the busy main road. Hedonism aside, it was a modest part of town. Buildings were a random mix of converted Georgian warehouses and graffiti-canvased shops. But when he reached Shoreditch High Street the place morphed into a mecca of neon bars and Vietnamese street food. David ploughed forward, buffeted by the rain. Through narrowed eyes he saw a queue forming beneath the facade of a large listed building that was painted midnight black.

A brass sign swung over the crowd. The logo appeared as a blotch in his vision at first, but as he approached, he could make out the stallion. It was the same logo stamped onto the hands of the girls dredged from the river. They must have come here within the last few days. They had been dressed up for a night out when they were found. If they had died the same night, this could be where it had happened.

He had to get inside, but he wasn't sure what he hoped to find. Lex herself — or evidence of her disappearance? Perhaps there was something worse waiting for him in there.

He slipped into an alcove on the other side of the street to get a measure of the place. Once out of the rain he spotted the six cameras facing the road. The wall that ran the length of the club had high windows with blacked-out glass. Along that wall, the queue snaked the building through a black gate, where he could see heat lamps glowing in a smoking area beyond.

David wafted to the back of the queue. Overhead, lightning forked and thunder cracked through the sky. A second streak of light tattooed the clouds, and he counted — one, two, three — before the thunder came again: this time as a single coughing bark.

It took a half hour to reach the club's bouncers. He was nearly twice the age of this crowd, but the doormen stamping hands didn't bat an eye. The rain eased as he stepped into the dark of the club. The stamp had been pressed down forcefully onto the top of his hand, and he ran his fingers over the stallion as though it were a scar, smudging the ink in the process. He made his way to the dance floor and paused.

Lex had made a video of Larwood, her boyfriend, on a dance floor. She had definitely been here. This was the club Audrey had warned him about.

Instinct bade him break away and head towards the smoking area. Outside, he discovered a small floodlit courtyard leading out to an alley. Apart from a white Range Rover parked by the furthest wall, there was nothing in the alley but potholes and burnout tracks and a stage door being used as a drop-off point. And more cameras. There were eyes on every angle of the place. Not completely unusual for a Greater London nightclub, but this bore the hallmarks of a compound.

David was about to go back inside to commence the investigation when he stopped. The whiff of chlorine coiled into his nostrils. He hated that smell. It reminded him of Lex, in that pool . . .

The odour drew his eye to the ground. It looked as if the area had been burnished with bleach. In spite of that and the rain, dark spots remained that were easily recognizable to a diver's eyes. 'Blood is thicker than water' — it was one of the first things David had learnt diving in shallow pools. Blood did not long survive the ravages of the tidal Thames.

The trail, such as it was, led across the courtyard to the Range Rover parked in the alley. David followed the trail the way he had come — with his nose more than his eyes — through the doors and back into the club.

Soon he found himself standing in a thin corridor with paint peeling off the walls. It was dark as a dungeon, and thumping bass filled his ears. There didn't seem to be anyone around — the crowd were drawn to a band about to take to the stage. He scanned about for more cameras, then tapped the torch light on his phone and dimmed the beam with his hand.

The trail had become blotchy and yellowed where bleach had soaked into the carpet. The chlorine smell had not dissipated fully. If anything, it was stronger inside. If there had been blood on the floor, someone had tried to treat it with industrial disinfectant. A cleaner would have known better than that.

As he skulked deeper into the labyrinth, the bassline grew louder, and the reek of booze overwhelmed the chlorine smell. David found himself thinking long and hard about why Lex might have come to this place. She had bothered a dark mark on her hand when he saw her last. His first idea had been to interrogate the manager, but the cameras outside had put him off. No sensible business operator would admit foul play based on presumption alone, to an off-duty frogman no less. In any case, it was a busy night, and it seemed unlikely any manager would be able to speak to him anyway.

He looked down and realized he'd lost the trail. The carpet here was dusty and moth-eaten. He doubled back and found the telltale signs once again. The stains were easy to miss in the gloom. Staff probably assumed it was legacy damage if they assumed anything at all — it was unlikely they were paid enough to care.

David followed the trail down the corridor from which he had come, verging right before he reached the stage door. He moved silently as he slipped by doormen and came to a backstage area. Now he was staring down the barrel of a long, claustrophobic corridor. A door to one side labelled *Green Room* was ajar, and David peeked inside. The band paid him no mind as they argued about sound levels.

So it was band night. If this lot were gigging, they might have a small entourage, maybe a driver and a sound guy, although it was equally likely that the band had rocked up with their guitars on their backs and were dealing with an in-house technician. Either way, he would need to tread carefully.

Almost immediately the bleach trail grew in saucers on the floor. The carpet here was particoloured and crusted where the abrasive had dried on. David retraced his steps to where the widening trail vanished under a door.

He gingerly tried the handle. It was locked. He took a minute to steel himself, and another to check the coast was clear. Then, with a breath, he slammed a boot against the door. There was a sound like that of a loose bolt rolling away as the door broke open, and David marched inside.

# CHAPTER SEVENTEEN

The room was a private bar of sorts, enclosed by wall-length mirrors and plush velvet sofas, and the carpet inside was bejewelled by tiny fragments of glass. A glass table, oval-shaped and discoloured, dominated the lounge area. It had been wiped clean in a hurry. There was a minibar taking up one corner of the room. The backlit map of subterranean London framed on the wall between a pair of ornamental brackets drew his eye for a split-second. The space was otherwise small and dormant.

David's eyes scanned every inch of the room. It did not seem to support life just now, and there were no signs of a residual presence or a booking for later that evening. The walls looked immaculate, suspiciously spotless. More than that, the usual odours of alcohol and sweat were overpowered by fresh paint and cleaning fluids. It smelled too clean.

David studied the walls and quietly wondered if there had been cause to hastily cover something over. It wasn't impossible. This was where the trail began, or where blood had been spilled — he wasn't sure which. The door had been locked, which meant there was something here that someone didn't want anyone to see.

A bead of sweat settled on the nape of his neck. He had the sense he was being watched. David winched his head with that thought, and looked straight up into the eye of a CCTV camera.

It gaped blankly. The lens had shattered, leaving a hole starred at the edges. And he could see that the wiring had been ripped out from the back of the device and was hanging down at strange angles.

Fresh anxiety braided his thoughts. A stained carpet. Painted walls. A sullied table. A broken camera. What did it add up to?

He would have to keep searching. To do that he needed to press deeper into the club.

He stepped out of the room and pulled the door closed before he returned to the backstage wings. He followed the electrics, which trunked from steel tracks above his head. They merged with a distribution board that hummed with a constant drone, and it was then that David noticed the wires feeding another security camera. This one was in rude health. There were three more, all of which were fed by the wiring along the baseboard that rose to the second floor.

David reached a set of steel stairs and found himself on a gangway with high ceilings and matt black walls. His eyes retraced the electrics along the baseboard to a door at the end of the gangway. It was the door to the surveillance room. He wiped a hand across his forehead, where a solid sweat had broken. He twisted the handle.

There was a stocky-looking technician perched on a stool reading a book, with his back to the door. He had head-phones on and hadn't heard the intrusion.

David quickly cased the room. It contained an impres-sively high-tech digital security system that could rival the control centre in any of the London Underground stations. The back wall was dwarfed by a master screen, where the view from every camera was displayed in a checkerboard of images, each with a timestamp and caption in the bottom right of each square. Every inch of the frontstage area was monitored, along with every entrance and exit. One square stood out among the rows as a solid black screen. Was this the feed to the private bar where the lens had been smashed?

David spied the router gathering dust on a high shelf. If this was a digital system, footage could be deleted with a button-click. Where was he supposed to look? Sweat pooled in the hollows of his temples.

The technician started at David's reflection in the empty square. 'Hey! What are you doing in here?' The man swivelled round.

David straightened up to full height. 'What's wrong with you?' he demanded with a grimace. 'What do we pay you for?'

The man's mouth fell open. He was large and square, a match in a fair fight.

'Just *look*.' David jabbed a finger at the empty part of the screen. 'What do you call that?'

'Umm—'

'Our contract said full coverage,' David snarled. 'The lads want to go twelve rounds with you.'

The colour drained from the technician's face. 'Are you — are you with the band?'

'What do you fucking think?' David had become one of those people who bandied their lofty status about wherever they went. The effect seemed to be paying off, because he could see bright spots of colour flourishing on the technician's cheeks.

'Don't blame me. The feed's out in the VIP Bar. We're not using it, are we?'

David's heart thumped but he worked hard not to break character. 'Look, mate. Don't make me an arsehole. When the lads get nervous, so do I. They're saying they won't play — *look*.' David leaned in to tap the screen. 'You've got blind spots right there in the lobby.'

'I — I do?'

There was no blind spot of course. Now that he was asked to find one, David couldn't do it any more than he could have stilled his own heartbeat by thought alone.

'Listen.' He dropped his voice to ooze menace. 'I've worked in gaffs like this my whole life. I've seen it all. It only takes one bad seed on his rattle. A blind spot can be the difference between a quiet night and a loud one.' He ushered the technician off the stool as he spoke. 'Now, I want at least three more cameras downstairs, and I don't want to see you again until it's sorted.'

There was a glazed expression on the technician's face now, as if he'd been asked to perform brain surgery with no medical training. 'What will you do?'

'Your job, apparently. Now do me a favour and jog on.'

David slammed the door in the technician's face before spinning around to the screens. He knew the bluster wouldn't last — the technician would realize what had happened. He needed to be long gone by then. He spun the stool away to access the control panel, turning to a smaller monitor displaying the system's interface. He was familiar with the set-up. Cameras recorded for a set time, uploaded to a server, got wiped after a week if no one actively saved it. A week's worth of footage seemed likely: a night club had security demands and a duty of care to its patrons.

He noticed that there were folders marked with each room in the club, and found one marked *VIP Bar*.

Before David opened the folder, panic quickened his heart. He realized he had absolutely no idea what he was looking for. David clicked a folder clocking the date it was last opened — Sunday gone. He scanned the contents. A file was missing. The same person who had broken the camera in the bar must have come up here to conceal evidence.

David found a new line of enquiry: *iCloud Drive > Desktop*.

His frantic tapping of keys brought about a mad frenzy he recognized from his days in the Military Police — the satisfaction of a job well done, and the knowledge that his insight had paid off. The username and password auto-filled, and bestowed dozens of files. There was a smoking gun somewhere. Trying to cover his tracks, the culprit had deleted the file off the main server but had failed to attend to the cloud storage. These were the actions of someone working too fast, not thinking straight, caught in a panic. In other words, the conduct of a criminal.

David took the USB stick from his pocket and jammed it in the nearest port. A new window flashed up — it would take almost five minutes to copy the files he needed. He didn't know if he had those minutes to spare. Since he had no choice, only one other option presented itself.

His cursor hovered over the first file, and a window bounced onto the screen. A low-resolution colour image appeared. Everything was so still, it took David a minute to realize it was a video, rather than a screenshot.

The footage showed a corner angle of a front-facing hallway with clubbers passing through. David dragged the slider back, creating a time-lapse, blurring the image so that the people moved backwards.

He saw something.

David froze the image. A flash of blonde — but not her.

He moved on. Backwards. *Not her*. Forwards. Pause. *Not her*. Forwards again — *stop*.

This time, he did see something. Before he pressed play, David took note of the on-screen display.

*C000346_Pale_Horse*
*QFD_Corridor4.mov*
*DATE_21/06/21*
*CAM06_01:19:00AM*

Alexis Cade was running. He recognized her bleached hair, her stained eyes. She was trying to get away when a figure caught up to her, apparently more quiff than man.

Lex spun round. She struck the man hard across the jaw. The quiff man staggered back, tottering like a decapitated bird. Lex turned and fled, beyond the range of the camera.

David pressed pause. He leaned close to the monitor, trying desperately to identify the figure. The camera's limited range meant the footage only went so far — the culprit's features were ill-defined. Was it the boyfriend? Was this who he'd spoken to on the phone?

David ran a hand through his hair. He longed to put the jigsaw together but he only had half the pieces. His instincts had been right to bring him here, however. He had evidence Lex had come to this place. And when she had, she'd fled. Something had spooked her.

There was a ping as the files finished transferring. Five minutes had passed quickly. He glanced at the screens — no sign of the technician. Was he on his way back? David didn't want to take any more chances.

He pulled out the USB stick and made to leave, but something caught his eye on the master screen. The camera had picked up a familiar face, with a familiar quiff, walking into the gents. This time, his identity was unmistakeable.

It was Piers Larwood. The man who attacked his daughter.

# CHAPTER EIGHTEEN

Naomi had been itching to investigate all night. It was getting late now, and she had spent the evening with Amy. Teatime and a bath, and a longer bedtime story to make up for lost time. Now her daughter was in bed and Miles was binging a box set in his man cave, she could finally return to her work.

For the last half hour she'd sat hunched over her laptop in the home office, scrolling results from searching the names Sofia had provided. So far social media had not borne fruit. Naomi switched to Google, hoping she'd uncover something soon — the girls' names were all she had. She clicked through to an article from a Greek newspaper dating back several years and stopped. The image of a blonde-haired girl she recognized stared back at her. Naomi clicked on the small icon of the English flag at the top of the page and read hungrily. Her elation evaporated. The article gave few useful details. The girl, Eleni Balaskas, had won a beauty pageant several years ago, and the main image showed her smiling on a balcony overlooking the coast of the Athens Riviera. Her name matched one that Sofia had given up in the pub, but beyond that and her relevant physical characteristics, there was nothing more to find. How had she gone from pageant winner to a nameless victim bloated on the surface of the Thames?

Naomi considered the second name, Varya Kastrati, but the Google search yielded even less than the first. Varya had been quoted (on a Reddit forum no less) complaining about the cost of dance classes in the Albanian town of Saranda. Apart from living in coastal regions, where she supposed it was possible to snatch young women and traffic them illegally, there didn't seem to be any further connection between them.

In the normal course of things Naomi could create a reconstruction, building victim profiles and tracing movements to create a timeline of the crime. But every time she attempted it, a smokescreen came down.

Rufus, her daughter's tomcat, padded into the room and sat gingerly on the carpet beside her. Naomi looked down and sighed. 'It's lousy, Rufus. Lousy to the core.'

Some cases felt like staring at the sun and calling it night. Something about this case wasn't right. Everything looked fine from here, but down in the place where instinct lived, none of it made sense. Distance would make her understand. Battles often made more sense when viewed from the sky.

Supposing drugs were the killer and not domestic violence, rape, or an unintended slight, the result was the same: two bodies in the morgue with tags on their toes. Naomi had questions, a few vague disquiets, but even if she had full forensic access, the river would have washed away any trace evidence. She wished it was simpler. Naomi was thinking of the crime dramas on television that annoyed her — cosy teatime mysteries in which the time of death was set between five o'clock and ten past the hour. After all her years in policing, Naomi knew better than that.

'It's lousy,' she said again, eyeing the window that faced the street. A welcome shower of sheet rain was cudgelling the quiet neighbourhood, and the shadows of rustling trees flickered on the walls of the room.

*Find out how they died.*

The discreet voice recited the phrase in her head like a psalm. Naomi knew there was something here — there always was, if you looked hard enough. *Come on, Harding, think.*

Naomi laid out what she knew to be true: if both girls had died by suicide, Baines would not have placed an embargo on the outstanding toxicology report. She'd had a concrete reason for doing that, and it made sense that it was something to do with the drugs David had found, in a hard case identical to the ones she'd seized months before. There was her link between the drugs and the girls. Furthermore, the river was a vector for male suicide, not female. That was backed by her own research. There was a computerized register of missing persons the Marine Police cross-referenced when a body was found in the water. When the dead were positively identified, the database was updated by the UK Missing Persons Unit. These were not impulse crimes committed by women whose sanity had broken. There was more to it than that.

Naomi glanced at the newspaper article again. The photo of Eleni Balaskas — the first corpse they had found — smiled through the laptop screen. Her eyes were not yet doomed to die. They were not yet yellowed at the whites. Hadn't David confirmed she was an overdose at first sighting?

'OK, how's this . . .' Naomi rose from her seat and stalked around the room, explaining her thoughts to Rufus, who was watching her intently. 'Let's say the drug was ingested by both victims. If it's the same drug I think it is—' Naomi winced at that. She knew what it was called, but she couldn't bring herself to say it out loud. Nightmare — a synthetic with one of the most dangerous profiles she had ever encountered in her time as a police officer.

'Let's say Eleni and Varya take the drug. It's stronger than either realize and it kills them. The dealer — now murderer — tries to clean up the mess. Chucks the drugs, then the bodies, then . . .'

Well, what *then*? And how many bodies were set to appear? Would they all follow the same pattern? Was this one tragic event, or a calculated string of crimes?

Concern cornered Naomi's heart. Supposing more bodies appeared, supposing it was not premeditated. The clock was ticking. It was only a matter of time before the murderer melted into the crowd. And assuming Naomi was running out of time, so was Shannon Baines.

The problem with that assumption was it presupposed a chain of thought and action that didn't fit with what she knew about the victims. It was fruitless to continue with little more than two names and Sofia's word that Baines was involved, to say nothing of Baines's skulduggery, or their confrontation at the Marine Police HQ. Everything seemed speculative.

That rankled her too. The illicit drugs trade was worth roughly seven billion pounds a year. With that much money in the game, how could corruption within the force *not* happen? There had always been bent coppers, but only narcotics generated the kind of money that made the good ones turn the other cheek. Despite everything, Naomi still absolutely believed in the good fight — the essential necessity of her lifelong deployment. She couldn't stand it when the police themselves became warped and tainted.

Was *that* why she'd had help from the informer with the deep throat voice? The source behind the calls remained a mystery for the moment. Naomi racked her brains, considering those colleagues who believed in the good fight so completely, they'd use underhand tactics to achieve it.

She heard that voice again now, the computer-altered baritone. *Find out how they died.*

'I don't have anything.' Naomi was surprised to find she'd said this out loud. She couldn't move forward because all she had was the skeleton of a victim profile. She looked ruefully at Rufus. The cat's silence mingled with the rain outside. He padded under the desk and coiled his tail around her feet.

Naomi winced, and a decision fell quickly into place. She couldn't move forwards, but she could profile the police involved and work backwards. What if she focused her efforts on the one person who seemed most interested in Sofia's lab results?

Rufus shot away as Naomi pulled in her chair and opened a new tab on her web browser. She needed to find a way into the case. It was like trying to penetrate a fortress. One way in was to attack from all sides. Another was to storm the gate. It might be large and well guarded, with an obvious but treacherous path leading up to it. Or the way in might be hidden. A storm drain full of shit, covered with so much ivy you had to root around to find it. But it was always there. If you hunted long enough, you could always find a way in. Sometimes it was a piece of evidence found at a crime scene. Sometimes it was a witness. Sometimes events and logic and reasonable doubt did the rest. The very least she could do was discover what Baines was up to.

Her phone rumbled on the desk. *Withheld.*

Naomi's hand hovered over the handset. Then she answered. 'Hello?'

'*Harding, you're not looking in the right place.*' The hissing again. And that voice, guttural, as if someone had tarmacked a driveway inside her head.

'Who is this?'

More hissing.

'Answer me,' Naomi demanded.

'*PNC.*'

Naomi frowned. The Police National Computer?

'*Case number 82517.*'

Naomi grabbed a pen and jotted down the number. 'Why? What's there?'

'*That's up to you.*' The call ended.

Naomi wasted no time. She logged into the PNC and details appeared on the screen. An incident report for the drugs David had found. Below that was a real-time status update.

*Case closed. Authorized by Cmdr Roy Bishop.*

Naomi almost fell off her chair. What was Bishop doing closing the case? She cast her mind back to the last time she'd seen him — in the women's locker room of all places.

He'd come in wanting a private word. What had he said to her? Something about the drug squad suppressing overdose victims. Several dozen of them.

Curious. According to Bishop, Baines needed his help with her investigation. After that, Bishop had asked after David. *I hear a diver found a kilo of the stuff . . .*

Naomi ran her hands down her face. She had half-suspected Bishop was the person tipping her off, but if Bishop was helping Baines, who was behind the anonymous phone calls?

There was something here — she knew it. Bishop had told her something else. *If you see anything strange, or hear anything or unusual, call me. I'll make it worth your while.*

The phone was in her hand. The number already dialled. 'It's Bishop.'

'Roy. It's me. I'm sorry to bother you, I know it's late.'

'Naomi?' His drawling voice arrived on cue. It was warm, leisurely, like a trickle of molten gold. 'Not at all. I was just fixing a nightcap.'

'You told me to call you if I had anything,' Naomi said. 'Remember that hard case, the one divers found on Sunday?'

'I remember,' Bishop said. 'By David Cade, wasn't it? The sergeant?'

'That's the one.'

'Ah, yes. Met him briefly. Seemed decent. What about it?'

'There's a case file on the PNC. Closed today . . . You authorized it.'

'I did indeed.'

Naomi listened intently, but Bishop's voice bore no trace of hesitation or fault. 'Didn't you tell me Baines was trying to suppress the numbers of OD victims?'

'Do you know, I believe I did.'

'Then why did you close this case? It amounts to the same thing, doesn't it?'

When Bishop spoke again his voice held a playful note. 'Ah, Naomi. I'm glad to see the old skin still fits. You're quite right. DCI Baines is suppressing numbers, and yes, I closed the case myself.'

Naomi frowned. She didn't understand.

'But why—'

'I take it you have something else?'

'What?'

'Surely you didn't call to talk about a closed case?'

'No, but—'

'Then why did you call?' Down the phone, she heard him sip his nightcap. 'What led you to that file on the PNC? Out of curiosity?'

Naomi was feeling cold, but it was not the temperature of the room that had changed. Here she was, chasing a lead she didn't understand, and Bishop had rationalized his actions. What had seemed like a way into this particular fortress now seemed like a trick of the light.

'I'm sorry, Roy. I'm . . . not thinking straight.'

'Nonsense. You're a detective. Something led you down this road.'

'It's Baines,' said Naomi. 'I know you're working closely with her, but . . .'

'Go on. Speak your mind.'

'I found out she's been impounding the bodies we found in the river.'

'Indeed?' Bishop took another sip of his drink.

'Didn't you say the drugs squad are filing a lot of ODs?' Naomi asked. 'If that's true, then what makes these girls so special?'

Bishop hummed at that. 'It's a good question.'

'Has she said anything to you about it?'

'Why would she do that?'

'Sir . . . I thought you were working with Baines on this?'

'Alas,' he said, 'Baines hasn't reported in to me for days. Come to think of it, that does seem strange.' There was a mutual silence, as Bishop apparently pondered the situation. 'Humour me,' he began. 'Say the anti-corruption squad had their hands full. And a certain DCI was, say, behaving strangely. A commanding officer may advise an investigator to, well, investigate strange behaviour. Within one's power, of course. It won't do to risk destroying what remains of one's career with subterfuge.'

Naomi found herself nodding along.

'I can't thank you enough for bringing this to my attention, Naomi. It's always good to talk things out, isn't it?'

'Yes, sir.'

'You'll call me if there's anything else you find? My door is open.'

'Thank you, sir.'

Before he hung up, Bishop could be heard rattling the ice in his glass.

# CHAPTER NINETEEN

Upon entering the gents, David was met with the disquieting vapour of urine. The club toilet was clammy and windowless. Four squalid urinals lined up against the right wall. Amid the event posters were declarations of love and civil protest scrawled across the tiles, and phone numbers on sticky labels promising sex were peeling off the cubicle doors. The room was bare now that the band's set had kicked off. Everyone had gathered on the dance floor, unwilling to miss the opening song.

He scanned the three cubicles on his left. The door to the third was closed, and a shadow juddered in the light beneath the door. David realized he'd been holding his breath and let it out in a long, whistling sigh.

He backed away from the door. He launched forward for the second time tonight, and the door opened with a sickening crack.

Piers Larwood spun round, his hands flying up to protect his face, but his guard lowered as he took the measure of David. 'Sorry, mate. Thought you were someone else.'

David flinched at the thick public-school accent. On closer inspection, Larwood was in his mid-twenties. He was wearing a linen suit the colour of claret and a dicky bow that made him look like a foul and unsavoury cock-bird. The quiff was styled questionably high, though a few rogue hairs had fallen prey to gravity's pull. His face was gaunt, his eyes full, and his jaw looked sore and swollen from a recent fracas that could not have been a day old. His nostrils were blanched from caning coke up his nose. Remnants of white powder dusted the lid of the toilet.

'I'm looking for someone,' David said.

'Aren't we all.'

'A girl.'

'What — in the gents?' Larwood raised a smart-alecky eyebrow, and once again David wondered why Lex had fallen for this chinless lout. Was it the wealth, the age gap, or a combination of both?

David produced his phone and showed Larwood a screen-grab of Lex. He had taken it from one of the videos she herself had made. 'You know who this is?'

Either Larwood had connected David's voice to the phone call earlier that morning or there was another reason, but his face paled. An invisible tremor passed over his jaw as if a phantom pain had rekindled there.

'W-Who's asking?'

'Answer the question.'

Larwood's voice came dry and breathless. 'Look, we get a lot of girls in here. I see a lot of faces . . . but maybe she came in once or twice on the fake.' He straightened up, remembering himself. 'And if she had, I'd have thrown her out.'

'Did you sell her something?'

There was a pause — a second too long. The next moment, David grabbed Larwood by the collar and shoved him against the wall so his heels met the toilet bowl and he toppled backwards.

'Where is she?' David growled, crushing the dicky bow in his fist. 'Where did she go?'

Suddenly, Larwood's frown mutated into an unsympathetic grin, and David felt something connect sharply with the back of his legs. Pain ruptured as his knees gave out. Hands seized him. He was drawn level with a bouncer's face.

Then there was a kaleidoscope of lights and fists and he was lugged off like a rag doll in the arms of a toddler. It took two more bouncers built like brick walls to subdue him. David was strong, but he was not able to break the armlock he was in. Amid strobe lights and lasers, liquor stench and dazzling heat, he saw stars. They wheeled and burst until they were not stars but fireworks that domed the club's ceiling. Then, with the dim sensation of travelling like an arrow in the darkness, he found himself flung through a set of doors into the driving rain.

He crash-landed hard in the alley. Agony lurched through him as he tried to stand but collapsed on the wet ground. Nothing was broken, but his nose was streaming with blood. Through the rain, David saw the white Range Rover and Piers Larwood framed in the stage door, watching the scene unfold.

Survival instinct brought David to a crawl as the doormen advanced. He was outmatched. He felt a flurry of kicks and blows. Pain lanced his body, and his face contorted in a rictus of agony. A hand closed on the back of his neck. He was shoved forcibly into a large pothole flooded with water — and held there.

He forgot the pain. The sensation of suffocation tightened down in his chest like locking bolts. Black roses — the harbingers of asphyxiation — bloomed before his bulging eyes. But he didn't panic. This was something he'd felt many times before. Memory and time and the shapes of all he lived for danced in front of his eyes. If this was drowning, it wasn't so bad.

With a jolt and a rush of air the water flayed away from his face. His mouth fell open and filled his lungs with oxygen as his chest muscles unfastened themselves, and the black roses wilted into pricks of light in the dark.

When he could at last make sense of things, he saw that the bouncers had left and the stage door had firmly closed behind them.

132

There was no sign of Larwood. The white Range Rover was gone.

* * *

It was past midnight when David found his way home. He spent the journey in the back of a cab struggling to mask his pain, and he was filthy to boot. But the driver only had eyes for the road and the fare at the other end of it. David went ignored, barring a brief warning not to vomit in the cab.

He staggered through his front door (the spare key was untouched) and crashed out on the sofa. He felt as if he'd been fossilized in sheer rock. Every muscle in his body ached, and he needed to change out of his wet clothes. He lay there, on the edge of sleep. He'd been awake since daybreak the previous morning, and barely slept the night before.

When he came to, an hour had passed. Now his stomach growled. Adrenaline and anxiety had reduced his appetite to what felt like a grain of sand. But he had to eat. It wouldn't do to starve himself.

He hauled himself into the kitchen and shoved a ready meal in the microwave, then went to the bedroom. Inside, he was greeted by the sight of the aerial map he'd pinned to the wall the previous night. The line of the river had been filled with jagged blue marker, akin to a cardiac rhythm. Notes and arrows circled points of interest — the drugs from St Katharine Docks, the dead girls at Blackfriars and a question mark pending at the secret place. It was all he knew about Lex and her disappearance.

David cast back to what Larwood had said.

*She came in once or twice on the fake.*

That rang true. Lex even had mocked him for it.

*You drink and meet boys and do drugs.*

He ate quickly, trying desperately to forget the physical pain from his beating. Busying himself in the bedroom, he took his laptop from the bedside drawer and set it up in the corner. Soon he was picking through the contents of the

USB stick on the screen. There were fifty-four files in total. Fifty-four recordings from different cameras in the north-west corner of the club, covering a period of twenty-four hours, from Sunday gone to Monday morning. The smashed camera he'd found in the bar implied there was *something* here to find. Meanwhile, the empty folder on the club's server had supported the theory. So where did Lex fit into it?

It was a daunting prospect, but one that had to be faced. David clicked the touchpad, and a window launched. It showed an image with a time caption on the display: CAM09_21:42:16PM. It was a front-facing angle — not a part of the club he recognized. He scrolled through the file long enough to be certain it contained nothing useful, before repeating the process with the next.

By the sixteenth recording, he was beginning to feel defeated. He considered the map a final time. Then the weight of the night's ordeal got the better of him, and fatigue fell over him like a lead curtain.

# CHAPTER TWENTY

No one would have guessed, watching Piers Larwood strut indolently through the rain to the Range Rover, that he was a man with a desperate problem. The issues, he knew now, were greater and more complex than he'd realized.

He started the engine, nose-blind to the odour that seeped from the back of the vehicle. As Larwood's heart beat out a series of staccato notes, he took a last glance at the man who had been ejected from the club. How easily his thoughts circled back to Lex, as he stared back at the pitiful figure, the girl's father no less, lying crumpled on the wet ground.

*Why don't you just kill him?*

The voice was gleeful in its victory. How had he been tracked down? His operation was airtight. The police knew nothing about the plan. Yet here *he* was, looking for Lex.

*Kill him.*

No. He was no murderer. Not really. Not as far as he was concerned. Sure, he might think about it. But his sense of self-preservation always won out. It was not the first time he'd quenched the instinct to kill, and this was the way it always worked. When the compulsion was at its strongest, his fear of the consequences — real, hard-time consequences — rose up to build a wall around it. Any event, good or bad, could be turned around and made to fit. Dumping the bodies wasn't an admission of guilt. It was an extension of all he'd meant to do on the night they died — of all the promises he had made.

The urge fell silent for a moment and then began to howl, conscious of the trick he was trying to pull. He'd let it drive him on autopilot, allowed it to believe he'd lost control, but now he was taking the wheel again.

Larwood pulled onto the main road. With two girls still to dispose of, he felt strongly that the only reasonable reaction to this fresh and unsettling curveball was to get himself — and the evidence — as far away from The Pale Horse as possible.

The windscreen wipers worked double time against the storm overhead, which gathered strength and filled the night with thunderous drums. Meanwhile, dread was clawing its way up his trachea, with cold sticky frog hands. But it was not David, nor the bodies, nor his lengthening rap sheet, nor even the thought of things to come that shredded his nerves.

It was Lex.

\* \* \*

It had gone three in the morning by the time he had returned to the club. The drugs would have been at the bottom of St Katharine Dock by that time, which had offered a measly comfort. His thoughts had begun to fixate on the bodies he had to dispose of — with no idea how to do it.

Though the sun rose a mere hour afterwards, evicting the short summer night, Larwood knew only darkness that day. Later, he would ask himself if it was possible to grieve for someone you killed.

He recognized the feeling. One year after his father's death, he'd thrown himself at alcohol and Class A narcotics, and when anyone in the know had asked if he was getting over it, he would double his efforts to find the next big high. He didn't have a choice. Grief wasn't something you got over. Losing someone was like losing a limb. You adapt, rather than recover.

He had let himself in through the stage door, checking the main space to ensure he was alone. He'd reached the private bar and unlocked the door to four bodies lying as they had fallen, atop one another, in a terminal embrace.

Larwood had shut the door behind him and locked it. He had felt light-headed, as if part of him were somewhere else and dreaming of this, and he'd wake up to find that everything was normal. But when his eyes flayed open again, the bodies were still lying there in a grisly heap, and the reality had rushed back in a cold flash. He had stood there, heart beating too hard and too fast, until his phone had gone off.

'Is it done?'

At one time, the owner of the voice had consoled him at his father's wake, but nowadays it was coldly pragmatic.

Larwood had found he could only respond in a strident, tear-filled series of sobs. 'It's gone.'

'You're certain?'

'Threw it in the river.'

'All of it?'

'It's gone.' His arms had waved wildly, like the drowning man that he was.

'Were you seen?'

'Course not — what do you take me for?'

'Then it's done.'

'It's far from done,' Larwood had whispered, his voice scrawny and breathless. 'What about the rest?'

'What about it?'

'We have to get rid of the girls.'

'There is no *we*. This is your mess. I expect you to clean it up.'

Larwood hadn't managed a riposte before the call was ended. As his eyes had travelled around the room, weighing again the emptiness of his existence, they had met the broken camera. He had then noticed the subterranean map on the wall. He had stared at the map, until his heart had beaten a little faster and he knew what had to be done.

* * *

His thoughts swooped and spiralled as he drove across the city. He was thinking about Lex again. Of that night she had told him she was so happy she wanted to live in that moment for ever. It was when they were at the centre of things. Amid the gold rush of cool in this area of East London, everyone was afraid of missing out, no one more than her.

It had been a matter of weeks since they'd met, but it was starting to feel like they'd known each other a lifetime. He thought about her hair, permanently mussed and sweet-smelling — and her eyes, bronze and deep in ways he'd never known.

Somewhere, listed on a database, were a series of drug offences he'd stacked up selling gak at house parties. It had never been about the money. He liked the rush, was all. Balloons and cosmic chocolate were harmless enough. Anything harder than that was always treated with the respect it deserved. He paid good money to make sure it hadn't been cut. He wanted the rush, and offences like those were trivial anyway. People like him never went to prison for that.

They were not the worst offences, however. Some of his charges related to violence towards women. Larwood scoffed aloud at the reminder of it. He hadn't thought much of that night or its consequences. He'd paid the escort good money. He'd only got rough because she'd deserved it. The kink was give and take. He had even parted with extra readies to seal her silence, but it had not been enough to still her tears as she'd limped off the premises. It had not been enough to prevent the hotel manager from blowing the whistle.

It was only afterwards he'd discovered the escort had lied about her age. He had never managed to figure out how the gossip had reached his public-school circles, but he had suddenly found himself ostracized. His privilege had meant nothing. He had even felt his late father's disappointed stare from somewhere beyond the grave, as if it was not he that had failed his son, but the other way around.

That night with the escort, it was like a seal had been broken that could never be replaced. No. That wasn't it. A line crossed? No. That wasn't how it felt, either. It was more like the die had been cast, like he'd crossed a threshold of violence. And what scared him the most was how powerful it felt, *good* even — but the kind of good it is to press your tongue against the raw, exposed fissures of a torn-out tooth, knowing you shouldn't, that it will hurt you more, but you're not able to stop.

When he met Lex for the first time, she'd easily succumbed to a charm offensive. He chose to believe she'd not mentioned her age at first meeting. It scared him that, while he suspected how young she was, he was still tempted, and it hadn't stopped him from acting on it. He was scared to think of the notion she was unversed between the sheets — and yet he *liked* it.

He could have anyone he wanted, obviously. It was one of the perks of his lifestyle. When he had been part of it, before he'd disgraced himself, the Belgravia scene had allowed him to enjoy the affluent life, which came with a set of particular entitlements. Money couldn't buy everything, but it could buy pleasure in spades. When he inherited his late father's property portfolio, his network had expanded to other parts of the city. Perhaps it wasn't surprising that his coterie hadn't adopted a wilder, scuzzier lifestyle. A club in Shoreditch was quaint and small-time compared to Eden Rock.

Yet he found solace instead in the status he'd inherited. Running a club at this young age meant clout. Respect. All the things he'd never had. A trust fund was nice — it impressed the bourgeois girls — but it did not keep him warm at night, or whisper in his ear when he slept.

Lex hadn't cared about his past — or his money. She had been anything but bourgeois. She had been willing to worship him. And, truthfully, he enjoyed being worshipped. He craved it. It was why, in the beginning, they had held each other too close and too tight, with every limb and finger entwined. And while the elite boys and girls whiled away the time in overpriced docklands seafood restaurants, Lex had shown him where to mudlark on the foreshore. While Lex carefully combed for Tudor rings and wishbones, he'd kick the stones away, hoping he would find a Victorian cudgel or something equally sinister.

He would not be meeting her parents, or be absorbed into her life so completely as to become part of the furniture. He was older. He was an outlier. A risk. The sex was secretive, the encounters clandestine. He had taken her to Hampstead and she had shown him a secret place known only to her. The thrill was exhilarating, unknown to him in all his years living in Belgravia. When he was with her, his past — warts and all — were somehow out of the frame. If he squinted at the bigger picture he could almost convince himself the die had never been cast at all.

Lex was his future, shining back at him. But like everything in his life, between the sex and the booze-addled nights, the shine had begun to come off. It was not long before he'd started to sell coke at the club, and it was then that Larwood had sensed Lex slipping from his grasp. She was nervous enough candy-flipping — she wouldn't touch cocaine. The other night, he'd even slipped a gram in her backpack, just to see what she'd do.

Larwood massaged his jaw. It was still sore where she'd hit him. Suddenly the memory of Sunday night — was it not even forty-eight hours ago? — bloomed like an inkblot. She was not supposed to have been there. The evening was a last hurrah, a skim off the top, a down payment before he and Lex left the country. He was good for the money. There would be no shortage of interest, and you couldn't have a better asset than cocaine when you needed cash in a pinch.

Larwood pressed down on the throttle, the engine drowning out the memory of Lex screaming as the girls lay dying. He had hours to wait yet — better to dump the body in the dead of night. In the secret place.

He thought about Lex, and her father, and suddenly the compulsion to *clean it up* reawakened.

140

# CHAPTER TWENTY-ONE

THURSDAY 24 JUNE
Low tide: 02.09 (1.14 m) / 14.30 (1.63 m)
High tide: 08.29 (5.83 m) / 20.47 (5.75 m)

By morning the storm had passed, cooling the air and leaving a sky cratered with cloud-forms. A membrane of smog was already reforming its stranglehold on the skyline.

A steady buzz made its way into his dreams, and David woke, tired and sore. His watch confirmed it was just gone 7 a.m. For a cruel moment, he thought he heard Lex at the door.

His phone lay clamped in his right hand. He let his mind drift over his body, probing each bruise gently, until he remembered there was security footage to watch and his brain back-pedalled.

He grabbed his jacket — wet through from the night before — and put it on painfully, checking the spare key was under the mat before he departed.

Once outside, his thoughts dithered. He felt malnourished, unable to concentrate. He had to remind his legs to place one foot in front of the other. Focus returned only upon first sight of the river. The air was thick with petrichor, and cormorants were bothering the jetty. The sounds of the city dropped away as a feeling of unease swept over him. This was not the same as the baseline of dread that had followed him for days. It was more acute, like the moment before a tsunami when the tide rushes out, leaving sand and silence in its wake — an expectation of ruin.

Reaching the dock, he slunk inside and scanned around. All was still. It was nearing the end of the graveyard shift. Faint laughter echoed from the changing rooms, and one of the boats was missing.

David felt at a loss so he decided to see Lynch. The captain would wield strong words for the scene he'd caused on the foreshore the day before, but he meant to receive them sooner rather than later. So he traipsed towards the captain's office, down the long angular corridor. He slowed as he passed the glass partition.

Naomi Harding was inside riffling through drawers and paperwork.

David opened the door and cleared his throat angrily. 'What are you doing?'

Naomi leaped up, blowing a line of hair off her face as David closed the door.

'Well? What's going on?'

She narrowed her eyes, as if deciding whether to trust him. 'No one cares about the girls.'

'What girls?'

'You know what I'm talking about.'

'Where's Lynch?'

'Not here.' She studied his face. 'What happened to you?'

'Huh?'

'Your *face*.'

David realized how he must look to her. 'Never mind that,' he said. 'I find you snooping round the man's office — what does that have to do with the dead girls?'

Naomi held a hard look in her eyes. 'Squaddies have been on the creep ever since you found the Class A in the river. Now they're sniffing around dead people no one wants to identify.'

'So?'

'So — it's *odd*. Something is going on. Lynch steam-rolled me when I told him the same.'

David blinked mechanically, resisting the urge to agree. 'We pass the bodies on—'

'What the hell is wrong with you?' Naomi snapped, as if he were a toddler testing her patience. 'Are you blind? Something is wrong and I know you feel it too.'

David tried to speak, but no sound came.

'Fine. I get it,' she said. 'The Marine Police don't care about dead girls, so why start now? But neither, apparently, do the Criminal Investigation Department.'

'Isn't that their job?'

'Have they ever come down here before? In person?'

'No . . .' David trailed off.

'See?' she said. 'Makes no sense, does it? If the Marine Police pass the bodies on to forensic teams and wash their hands of them, why give a shit about them now? What does Shannon want with those girls?'

David quietly wished he had never sought out Lynch in the first place. Naomi seemed empowered by a frightening and intense energy. He set his teeth. 'If you're on first-name terms with DCI Baines, why don't you ask her?'

He must have struck a nerve because Naomi could not answer. She opened her mouth, but the only sound that came out was a sharp, high-pitched hum.

The tolling of the rotation bell severed the moment. With that, Naomi opened the door and swept from the room.

What had she been doing in here? What was she looking for? Did she think Lynch had something to do with it? But what was *it*? The questions shoaled in David's mind, then wheeled away to avoid a trawling angst about Lex.

He slumped in the empty chair and tried to square them away. Naomi had been a detective herself — and old habits die hard, he knew. She wouldn't find whatever she thought she was looking for because there was nothing to find. How could there be? Stephen Lynch kept his cards so close to his chest, you'd think his arms would concertina into his body. But David trusted him. A decade together in the Marine Police had seen their bond forged in fire. If something was amiss, Lynch would find it. The status quo hadn't changed overnight. Divers were always the last to know, but they were bound by the same rules as the rest of the Met. In any case, whatever Naomi was after, he couldn't see how it connected to Lex.

He returned to the dry dock. A group of divers were crowding around the relay system, a small irradiated box strangled by wires. Naomi had joined them and was speaking at the receiver. Her expression was grave.

David reached her. 'What is it?'

'They found another body,' she said.

*Another.* The word triggered him like the scent of blood to a shark. He sprinted across the dock to the RIB bobbing in its lane. Voices chased him, but all were lost, all but those four words. *They found another body.*

He yanked the outboard and the engine yowled to life — there was no time to change or tally equipment. When he turned to throw off the line, Naomi leaped onto the deck and met his eyes.

*They found another body.*

There was no time to argue. David threw the line off the cleat and opened the throttle. The boat detonated onto the river, horsepower stripping the surface of the water with a catcalling hiss. Not a word was spoken until they reached Blackfriars.

'There,' said Naomi, as the bridge hurled into view.

The Port Authority Watchdog was moored nearest the south shore. There was a commotion at the water's edge, but it was not circling as it had done on the morning they'd found the first girl.

David shepherded the RIB alongside the Watchdog, a feeling of dread rising in his chest. The skipper stepped to the aft of the Watchdog, and David's eyes swept the water. He couldn't see a body.

The skipper called out. 'They took it. I radioed in to stand you down.'

'*They?*'

The skipper pointed at the foreshore. David and Naomi turned together. A sudden rush of anxiety avalanched through his body.

There was the high-security van, visible over the river wall. The formidable shape of DCI Shannon Baines could be seen supervising a team of crime scene investigators. As they packed up, the van's panel doors were closed with a dull slam that ricocheted over the water.

Baines turned and watched them from across the way. It was impossible to interpret the expression on her face this far out, and nothing could be done from their position on the river.

David returned her gaze with flashing eyes, as stoic as a Queen's Guard in winter.

\* \* \*

David disembarked the boat and found Lynch blocking his path.

'You look like hell.' Lynch wasn't making it up. David hadn't bothered to check the mirror before he'd left, but if this and Naomi's reaction was anything to go by, his beating wasn't going unnoticed.

Lynch took him aside. 'When was the last time you spoke to your daughter?'

David faltered. He had not expected this. 'Why do you want to know?'

'Just took a call from the drug squad. Baines reckons you're insinuating yourself into her investigation.'

'That's wrong.'

'Is it?' Lynch had hiked his voice higher than was necessary for the benefit of the other divers. There had always been an assumption David was untouchable, thanks to his years of devotion to the job. This performance made it clear that this no longer applied.

'Listen,' David said. 'Baines doesn't know what she's talking about.'

Lynch rolled his eyes. 'Care to explain the record of your use of the PNC to look her up? Baines outranks us both. You know the rules. As your supervising officer, I have to take the allegation seriously.'

'There's nothing to take seriously.'

'You're butting in,' growled Lynch. 'Now it's spiralling and you've left me no choice.' He looked askance for a moment, a hint of regret at what came next. 'You should have come to me first.'

David frowned. 'I'm doing my job. There was another girl out there, I took Harding to check it out.'

'You had no reason to be there,' Lynch snapped back. 'If I put every senior officer that came down here in the chipper, we'd have no one left. Those girls are obviously connected and Baines is investigating. This is much bigger than you realize, Cade.' Lynch leaned in, plucking vowels like dark chords. 'Baines took the body off our hands. She did us a favour.'

'But she's hiding something.'

'Between this and the scene at Blackfriars yesterday, my hands are tied. You're suspended — effective immediately.'

'What?'

'You heard. We're done here.' Lynch trained his eyes on the doors to the street. 'Turn in your things at the station. That goes for you too,' he told a dumbstruck Naomi.

Naomi made to speak but Lynch was walking away. David kept pace with him, but the captain wasn't having it.

'Stephen—'

'Why are you still here?'

'You don't understand —'

'This conversation is over. Didn't you hear me the first time? Two weeks, with pay. Now both of you, get off my fucking dry dock.'

# CHAPTER TWENTY-TWO

Ten minutes later, David made for the street, one foot stalking the other, eyes drilling angrily into the pavement. It was flecked with gum and cigarettes, and his daughter's face.

Lex. Always Lex, ricocheting around his head.

As he turned a corner, he met an unexpected sight. Naomi Harding was waiting further down the street — and she was wearing uniform. She'd not worn No. 1 dress in his company before, but there she was: black suit, white shirt, black-and-white checked cravat, epaulettes on her shoulder.

*Holy shit. She's an inspector.*

He mentally catalogued every transaction he ever had with Naomi. Every word and slight. She'd told him she was a DI but he hadn't listened. He had assumed her rank had been stripped from her when she was sent to work for the Marine Police. What did this mean? Was she still a ranked police officer? Was she still part of a task force? If so, what was she doing in the Marine Policing Unit?

It was then he caught wind of another idea. Naomi could help him — make sense of all he'd seen at The Pale Horse. David didn't know why Baines had seized the bodies, but Naomi might. Maybe that was why she'd been snooping in the captain's office . . . David had to wonder whether she *would* help him, given he had got her suspended. If she refused, he would have to convince her somehow.

Naomi's back was to him. She had her eyes on her phone, and when the unmarked car pulled up beside her, he realized she'd booked herself an Uber. Wapping was a pesky part of town and a blind spot for public transport. She clambered in, and the vehicle veered away.

David sprinted into the open and splayed his own hand as Harding's car made its departure. A black cab passed by (mercifully frequent for the time of day) and David piled into the back seat. He tapped the glass. 'See that car? I want you to follow it.'

'Follow it? Do I look like Huggy Bear?' The cabbie's eyes were darkened by a flat cap, and he threw a glance in the rear-view mirror.

David slapped a pair of twenty-pound notes on the tray. 'Drive.'

During the short journey he fidgeted on the back seat, watching Harding's Uber through the windscreen. The air con was turned up high, and he was grateful for that. They were travelling west, along Upper Thames Street, which ran parallel to the river. They passed the Tower, Temple and Waterloo Bridge. At Whitehall Gardens, Harding's car turned off. The cabbie's eyes met David's in the rear-view as he followed.

'So, what's this about? You the nick?'

David said nothing.

'If you're the Old Bill, show me some ID.'

David held the man's gaze.

'Look, I don't wanna be an accessory—'

'Turn here.' David leaned forward as the Uber stopped on Dacre Street. He climbed out, feeling the heat immediately, and jogged towards Naomi. She was already walking away from her car along the street in the other direction.

'Hey!'

She span round. Her alarm quickly turned to anger. 'What are you doing here?'

'Just hear me out.'

'Fuck off, Cade.'

She swept up the pavement, shaking with apprehension and rage.

'I didn't listen to you before. I owe you an apology for that.' David had to walk double fast to match her pace along the street.

'I can't believe you followed me.'

'You're angry. That's fair. But can you give me two minutes?'

'I'll give you one.'

David gathered his thoughts. 'Something's happened, hasn't it? There's a connection between Bishop, Baines, the dead girls—'

'Everything all right here, ma'am?'

Naomi swivelled a fraction too quickly. A police constable walking the beat seemed to have magicked himself into being, right there on the street. David realized, with a ripple of alarm, that Naomi could say anything she liked if she didn't want him involved. Naomi seemed to sense it too, as her mouth slid open and the words tumbled out. 'We're fine . . . Thank you, Constable.'

'Ma'am.'

The bobby gave a nod to acknowledge Naomi's rank. Then he continued on his way, taking a moment to pinch a sweat patch on his shirt.

A thin wind rushed through the parched street, hassling Naomi's hair as she rounded on David. 'I don't need or want your help.'

'Are you sure? It all involves the river somehow. And you're no diver.' David cleared his throat. 'No offence.'

'None taken. But you didn't answer my question. What are you doing here? Why did you follow me?'

David's teeth clicked. He had already decided against mentioning Lex. There were still too many unknowns. 'I didn't listen to you, before,' he hedged. 'And something is going on that doesn't feel right. You see it too. I know you do.'

'So what — you grew a conscience?'

'No. I'm proud of what I do. If I help you wrap this up, I can—'

'Buy your way back onto the team?' she finished.

The wind picked up again, a reminder of time's slow march.

'I won't deny it,' he said. 'So can I help you or not? Tell me what's happening here.'

Naomi offered a calculating look, then seemed to nod inwardly to herself. David found it refreshing that Naomi had a clear mind, and her thoughts were marshalled tidily. 'Months ago, a psychoactive alkaloid came to London. That's not unusual — there's a reason the city's called the cocaine capital, but this was a new kind of synthetic drug, and its chemical make-up was more dangerous. It was cut with Nightmare.'

David frowned. 'Nightmare?'

'It causes hallucinations and muscle spasms strong enough to asphyxiate the user. It's cut with the cruellest profile imaginable, and it only exists to kill people.' Naomi's voice hardened. 'I discovered a consignment was being trafficked in via Greenwich Cruise Terminal.'

David seemed lost in thought.

'Nightmare was designed to tear a hole in the city's drug-using community,' Naomi said. 'Or in this case, annihilate the competition, paving the way for a syndicate to dominate the drugs market and rebuild the newly integrated supply chain with untainted product. I carried out a raid to destroy the consignment and cut the head off the snake. But—' Naomi paused, as if in memoriam. 'You know the rest. My failure cost the lives of three police officers. That's how I ended up at MPU. In the last week, Baines has recovered overdose victims, and Roy Bishop's taken a sudden interest in the Dive Team . . . It's no coincidence.'

David nodded agreement.

'I need to prove the girls were deliberately poisoned with this alkaloid, and to do that, I need to trace the supply back to its source.'

David waited until Naomi had finished before adding, 'I guess if you do that, the Met will have to exonerate you.'

Naomi blinked. David took a moment to consider all she had said. 'How do you plan to prove the Jane Does were poisoned?'

Naomi's eyes flashed. 'We have to find them first.'

Her gaze ranged up the sun-baked walls of New Scotland Yard. She led the way around the building to the entrance with its impressive glass pavilion. She nodded to the armed officer manning a turnstile at a staff entrance. Beyond that was a compound forecourt full of incident response vehicles.

David heard Naomi's voice in his ear. 'We do this my way. Clear?'

He nodded, not wishing to speak.

Naomi approached the officer at the turnstile. 'Afternoon,' she said. 'I need to see Shannon Baines.'

# CHAPTER TWENTY-THREE

On the top floor of New Scotland Yard's operations area, DCI Shannon Baines paced her office, pondering her need for revenge.

It had been an eventful morning in Major Crimes. The investigation relied on every necessary precaution, not to mention secrecy, but it seemed that everyone was vying for a slice of the action. She was in a precarious position. Naomi Harding and David Cade were getting too close for comfort, more involved than due process should allow in the normal course of things. But there was nothing normal about this case, so that was the price she had to pay. She was having to walk a tightrope to get to the root of a dark and dangerous problem. If she played her hand too soon, everything would come undone. The target would crawl back under a rock, mothballing the case, and her with it.

But although she needed David, his expertise, and his recklessness, he was starting to cause her headaches. Silver and black coronas were forming in the centre of her vision, as if someone had cracked the glass she used to look out onto the world.

Shannon circled the desk and hunched in her chair. Her free hand opened the bottom desk drawer, which contained its own private pharmacy, and took out the box of codeine. She shook the packet, ignoring the stark black letters: *MISUSE OF NARCOTIC MEDICINE CAN CAUSE ADDICTION, OVERDOSE OR DEATH.*

The irony was not lost on her as she pressed two pills out of the packet and white residue powdered the palm of her hand. She wondered, idly, why codeine produced more dust — then she wondered if she was losing her mind. It was her experience that drug abuse caused the most damage to society. Drugs were the cornerstone of her birth mother's many addictions, which had left her impoverished and unwanted. Even as a teenager, Shannon had never experimented with drugs. She wanted to fight the problem where it lived. It had proved hard work to defy her adoptive parents, who were mortified by her decision to join the police.

She managed the trauma with her own addictions: to the police, and the gym. The rest was history, with the accolades framed on the wall to show it. She stared at them now, admiring the SCO19 Firearms Training certificate, which she considered the crowning glory. Shannon was well aware that given the chance, a therapist would say this spoke of rage safely channelled into something useful. She scowled at the notion. Too many child therapists in her life had tried to cross-examine her, pondering the true meaning of the shadow dogs she'd make with her hands. As she leaned back and let the codeine work, she let the thought of therapy drift away. Drugs would have to do.

Workplace success did nothing to lift her mood. She hated the office. She wasn't made for it. She wanted to be out there, kicking down doors. But for now, it was vital to keep up appearances. Everything — *everything* — depended on going undetected.

'Whatever it takes,' she muttered under her breath. The motto reminded her of Alexis Cade, but she cut through the thought as easily as a blade through silk. It was one of many necessary evils that circled back to figures. Her Majesty's statisticians (in their wisdom) wanted one hundred drug arrests each year and no more. One hundred, in a city of nearly nine million people. This could be achieved in a matter of days, targeting street-level scumbags alone. Proper dealers — the real villains — could be tracked down and arrested in a few weeks with the right approach, but the brass were only interested in the numbers. No sooner did the drug squad reach a hundred arrests, she was told to back off.

It was not what Shannon had signed up for. She'd had to watch the police change from being a crime-fighting force to a crime-management system built on a business model. The Home Office simply did not understand real people: their lives, their needs, or their habits. It was beyond the pale to imagine the human suffering, and what it did to families, siblings — children. The reality of a trade characterized by violence and debt bondage meant criminals walked free more often than not, because the higher-ups in the police were busy chasing vote-winning figures. Most senior coppers, as far as Baines saw it, were now more concerned about surviving their careers than reducing crime.

Real systemic change wouldn't happen overnight. There had to be education and treatment — and Shannon couldn't wait that long. She needed to catch someone out. And she was close, a hair's breadth . . .

Retribution did not follow a straight line. In the wake of Naomi Harding's failure, a new path had revealed itself. Shannon's grudge against the Met was a rock that resisted erosion, building layers of sedimentary meaning. She only needed to detain one target to hold the entire rotten system to account. That was all that mattered to her in the end: bringing the system that had failed her countless times to its knees.

The drug squad comprised herself, several senior investigators, a handful of PCs running errands, and a surveillance team. It was expensive. Authorizations for every aspect of an investigation had to be obtained by a division commander or a superintendent, both of whom had to be regularly briefed. Yet no one would cooperate. To record drug crime was to admit the city had a drugs problem. No recorded crime? No problem.

It was why the mandarins hated her — and why she didn't flinch when Roy Bishop walked in without knocking.

'You look awful,' he said.

'Morning to you, too.'

Bishop unbuttoned his overburdened suit jacket and took the neighbouring seat, which groaned under his weight. 'You're working too hard. A break might do you good.'

'Need something, sir?'

'Makes a change, doesn't it? Me wanting something.' Bishop allowed a smile to complement his customary drawl. 'You've not sought an authorization in weeks. Isn't there a dealer to arrest, a crack den to clamp down on?'

Shannon noticed Bishop's smile had not reached his eyes.

'What are you up to? I hear you're impounding human remains.'

'I can't talk about counter-drug activity,' Shannon replied. 'As you well know.'

'So there *is* an investigation.' Bishop stroked his tie. 'Who are you reporting to these days?'

'The Super.'

'And you didn't think to inform me?'

'Wasn't aware it was necessary.'

Bishop's expression changed. It was warmer now, more calculated. 'Baines, you're a big girl. You're free to do as you wish. I may be talking out of school here, but I've always done my best to accommodate your needs.'

'I don't disagree,' said Shannon.

'So let me wet my beak. I'm the one handling the press with the assistant commissioner on leave. I run the show. The least you could do is defer to me.'

Shannon looked at him shrewdly. Bishop was poking around the fringes of her plan. If he learned too much, it could spell the end of everything.

'Whatever happened to recusing yourself?' she asked.

The man scowled. 'Need I remind you that it was I who came to you with information? I'm the one that pointed you to the nightclub in Shoreditch.'

'And I appreciate it. Remind me again why that was such a cause for concern in the first place?'

Bishop changed tack. His scorn and frustration disappeared, and the saccharine, media-trained smile formed a half-moon on his face. 'I am merely asking for an update.'

'You've asked me to share confidential information about an ongoing investigation.'

'My dear Shannon, I'm not asking you to do anything!' Bishop clapped his enormous hands together. 'I'm only interested in the greater good. But at the moment, I'm at a loss. I'm meeting senior management within the hour, but if you won't give me anything, what am I going to say?'

'The super will take care of that,' Shannon said brightly. She wanted to savour this moment, having played Bishop at his own game. She folded her arms to hide her shaking hands. The codeine was having little effect. 'You're a gifted orator, Roy. Buttering up the brass has never been a problem for you.'

Bishop grimaced, and she registered his disappointment. He had never forgiven her for canning Naomi Harding. She was his favourite, always had been. It was unfinished business, but it would have to wait. It was imperative she kept things to herself.

The landline phone warbled, and Shannon answered it gratefully. Someone at the front desk informed her Naomi Harding was asking for her. She glanced at Bishop, wondering if he had something to do with this unexpected visit. Not for the first time she felt a desire for revenge to renew its furious resolve.

She replaced the receiver. 'We'll have to do this some other time.'

Bishop held the door for Shannon before he skulked off into the bullpen, and she gathered speed as she forged a path to the lift. Unseen, she felt her chest heave and release a pent-up tension the codeine could do nothing about.

The doors pinged open, and Shannon's eyes locked with Naomi Harding's. It was a bizarre sight to see her in uniform again.

'What's this? Halloween party?'

Naomi said nothing, but stepped aside to let David Cade out of the lift. Shannon was startled to register the state he was now in. His eye had ripened to a delicate shade of maroon, his face was covered in scrapes and cuts, and he limped slightly as he stepped towards her.

They stood there in a triangle of silence.

David made to speak, but Shannon shook her head. 'Not here.' She led the way back to her office, all too aware of her chest tightening once again.

## CHAPTER TWENTY-FOUR

Naomi looked out at the bullpen as they passed. It was plain to see that the unwritten rule among the rank and file, that overtime solved crime, was still in force. The operations area was crowded, the air stale and close. Police often worked shifts in excess of sixteen hours to tackle the sheer statistical challenge of sifting through the thousands of crimes committed in the capital every day.

A group of squaddies stood at a whiteboard with what looked like a map of the capital. On the map, several blue lines had been highlighted. But the scene passed her line of sight as they reached Baines's office.

Baines showed them inside and closed the door. No one sat, so she rounded the desk, feeling like a headteacher calling truants to the block.

David spoke first. 'Where's the body?'

'If you're talking about the remains of the young woman I fished out of the Thames, rest assured it's taken care of.'

'Meaning?' Naomi said.

'It's part of an ongoing investigation.'

'Let me guess. You can't discuss it.'

'Swatting up on protocol, I see.' Baines folded her arms. 'Shame your gifts weren't put to use sooner.'

'Why did you take the girl?' David asked.

'Why do you care?'

'It's my job to bring up the bodies.'

Naomi flinched. She hated those words — his rote recital made her wonder what was left of his soul.

'But you *don't* bring them up,' Baines said coolly. 'These girls surface, don't they? You know I can't discuss any of this. So why are you here?'

'I have reason to believe someone's trying to sweep a few dozen overdose victims under the carpet.'

She struck a nerve at that. Baines's eyes flickered from Naomi to David.

'Look, David. I know why you're getting involved. You think your daughter has something to do with it.' She paused there, as David's face grew pale.

'How do you know about Lex?'

'I can't tell you that.'

'Are you saying she is involved?'

'I'm saying there's an ongoing investigation.'

'Hold on,' Naomi cut in. 'What are you both talking about? What does Lex have to do with this?'

'Do you know where Lex is?' David pressed.

'It's complicated.'

'I'm all ears!'

'*Enough.*' Baines raised a hand, glancing between them. 'What I'm about to tell you stays in this room. I don't have to defend my reasons for keeping overdose victims quiet. Least of all to you, Harding. But if I felt that a defence was needed, I might say this. I'm a copper trying to catch a criminal . . . That's where your daughter comes in.' She turned to David. 'A few days ago, I found out Lex was put into police protection.'

The words hung in the mildewed air.

'Impossible,' David said at last. 'Lex is a minor. You'd need my consent.'

Baines just shrugged, and Naomi had to wonder why she was content to duck the question. There had to be a reason for it.

'By all means shoot the messenger,' Baines continued. 'I can only tell you what I know.'

'Who told you this?'

'I can't say.'

'When did you find out?'

'I can't tell you that, either.'

'You're lying,' David snapped.

Baines's face was carefully impassive, as though she were unwilling to deny the accusation. Naomi searched for the involuntary movement that would give Baines up as a liar. But she saw nothing. Either Baines was telling the truth or she was an extremely gifted liar, and Naomi couldn't tell which it was. It was sinister to imagine Baines was willing to lie about something as serious as consent.

Baines held David's eye. 'I take it you haven't consulted your wife about this?'

'Ex-wife,' David corrected testily. 'And yeah, I spoke to her. She would have told me if she'd been approached.'

'*Would* she?'

'I have a right to know.'

'That doesn't mean she'd tell you though, does it?'

Naomi felt distracted. Whether it was true or not, she needed to understand where this rabbit hole led.

'Why would Lex have been offered protection?' she asked.

Baines looked at her. 'Why else?' she replied. 'To catch a criminal.'

'Lex doesn't know any criminals,' David said.

'Doesn't she?' Baines feigned surprise. 'How well do you know your daughter, David?'

'I want to know who she was talking to. I want to know why. I'm her father, I should be allowed to know.'

'You're right, you should be.' Baines crossed her arms. 'But if she's a protected witness, it means she needs protecting.'

'Not from me,' David spat.

'Well,' Baines said, 'that's up for debate, isn't it?'

Silence fell.

Naomi spoke up again. 'Say you're right. That Lex has information, or she's seen something she shouldn't — at least tell us who it involves. How did the police get to her in the first place?'

'I don't know that, either.'

'You don't know or you can't say?'

'A bit of both, pick your favourite.'

'Do you know *anything*?' David was struggling to control himself.

Baines barely moved. 'It's an ongoing investigation I'm not privy to. I'm sorry. I don't have anything else.'

Naomi felt the weight of these words. Next to her, David seemed to be reeling from them. She imagined the questions that would race through her own mind if the roles were reversed and her own daughter was missing. 'How do you know she's a witness?'

'The information was passed down. You know how undercover investigations work.'

'So she is alive,' David said.

That seemed to give Baines pause for a moment. 'You tried to report her as a missing person?'

'Yes.'

'And?'

'There was a conflict on file,' he said bitterly. 'The request was denied.'

'Then the case is ongoing.'

'What does that mean?'

'We can't have someone this close to the investigation helping to investigate it. If your daughter was in that kind of danger, it would forfeit the case.' Baines tried to meet his eyes. 'There's every reason to think she's safe.'

Naomi stifled her impatience with the situation. She'd only come here to find out why Baines was suppressing the numbers of overdose victims, but was beginning to understand Sofia's warning. Just not for the reasons she'd thought. Things were moving too quickly. 'We want the same things,' she coaxed, not quite believing it herself. 'We can help you.'

'How?'

'For god's sake, Shannon, we need each other. Put your pride to one side for once.'

Baines rose quickly and towered over Naomi. 'It's not a matter of pride. I don't *trust* you, Naomi. The men from the Firearms Unit were friends of mine, and if it wasn't for your incompetence, they would still be alive. You were sent to Wapping for a reason. Frankly, I think even that was too good for you. I only allowed it because Bishop defended you. *Bishop*, of all people.' Baines caught herself and simmered for a moment, before turning to David. 'You, on the other hand. We can work together. I'm not your enemy.'

'Looks that way from where I'm standing,' he said sullenly.

'Looks aren't everything.' She gestured them to the door, but David gaped helplessly from his chair.

'What am I supposed to do now?'

Baines offered a shrug. 'That's not up to me.'

# CHAPTER TWENTY-FIVE

Naomi kept her eyes open as she led David back to the lift. Though she'd not been party to the operations area for months, she knew the bullpen all too well, every nook and crevice. It was why, during this particular visit, she had noticed something unusual.

The function rooms that broke off from the bullpen were generally set aside for surveillance equipment. Yet now all the rooms had been ransacked. There was no sign of the equipment anywhere. It was possible a large surveillance operation was underway, but that wouldn't require all the tech to have been moved off-site. Could it be connected to the undercover investigation Baines was loath to discuss?

The doors peeled apart with a ping, and they stepped out of the lift into the ground-floor lobby. Naomi tugged at David's sleeve and motioned to an unmarked door. He followed her through it. They were now in the middle of a large steel stairwell with a landing winding down to the basement levels.

'What are you up to?' David hissed at her.

'Going off-piste. What do you think the uniform was in aid of?' Naomi took the stairs down to the lower levels, David trailing behind. Considering it was his second infiltration in as many days, David was strangely calm. This one was far less fraught than the first.

'Where exactly are we going?'

Naomi made to answer, but her head snapped to the landing below. She silently shoved David to the wall, so that they were both concealed by the spandrel.

One floor below, a security guard walked across the landing and tapped a code to open a security door. Naomi waited just long enough for the guard to step through. Then, lurching forward, she wedged her fingers in the gap before the door closed. She offered David a mischievous glance as she pulled it wide and beckoned him through.

Soon they were traversing a series of corridors that routed to various departments. For the moment, Naomi's uniform seemed to do the trick. No one tried to stop them. Staff were going about their day. Eventually they reached a corridor and passed a glass partition, on which were etched the words *Pathology Unit*. Beyond that was a larger steel door.

'The forensics lab,' Naomi told him under her breath. 'This way.'

Naomi kept her voice level, trying not to reveal her disquiet. She hated this side of police work, and the autopsy suites in particular. She'd never managed to get used to the underlying smell of antiseptic, or the harsh light bouncing against polished metal surfaces. Inside the lab, all was sanitary-sheened chrome. It was staffed by a handful of forensic scientists, although the lab was currently empty but for one figure.

Sitting at a workbench, sifting through a wad of paperwork, was Dr Sofia Pérez.

'What the hell are you doing in here?' she demanded when she caught sight of Naomi.

'We need your help.'

'And I need a week on the beach. You can't be down here! Have you any idea how much trouble you'll cause?'

'We came to see DCI Baines. She mentioned I should pay you a visit.'

Sofia looked less than impressed. 'I warned you not to get involved, Nay.'

'I can't get anything done based on one bad feeling.'

Naomi cast her eyes about the laboratory. Neither she nor Sofia paid any attention to David. Sofia was too busy trying to decide what to do with her bewilderment. 'I'll give you ten seconds to explain yourself before I call security.'

Naomi smiled. 'I just figured, since we're passing through—'

'Oh no. Forget it.'

'But it'll only take ten minutes.'

'I won't have you contaminate—'

'We'll contaminate *nothing*,' Naomi assured her. 'It's below minus fifty in there. Anyway, I thought you said there was no case to contaminate?'

Sofia pressed a finger and thumb to her nose. Naomi understood her concern. Strangers poking around remains was a serious breach of protocol, and the consequences involved if they contaminated evidence were severe. Moreover, custodianship of the bodies was personal for Sofia. The victims were now under her protection, and the indignities they'd been subjected to were over. They had been silenced — forensic evidence left behind was how the victims spoke. It gave them a voice in the matter of their death.

Naomi waited patiently for Sofia to remember that she was no stranger, that she was still a police officer. Perhaps David's mere presence was enough to give Sofia pause. There were cuts and bruises scattered all over his face, and he had the look of someone haunted by anxieties too numerous to account for. Sofia was eyeing him suspiciously.

'This is David,' Naomi said. 'We work together.'

'You're down in Wapping?'

'I'm a frogman,' David said.

'He's a sergeant,' Naomi corrected, adopting her most solemn face. 'Do you have a pathology report yet?'

'What if I do?'

'Sofia, this is really important. Come on. Let me see it.'

After a moment's hesitation, Sofia handed over a file from the paper tray on a nearby desk. She didn't resist as Naomi steered her by the shoulders to the door. 'Why don't you take an early lunch? I'll have it sussed in ten minutes.'

'Five,' warned Sofia.

When the coast was clear, David looked quizzically at Naomi. 'Why was that so easy?'

'You're not the only one interested in those girls. Anyway, we're here now. Enough questions. Try doing some actual policing for once.'

Naomi crossed the room and stared through a plate glass window. There was a sign screwed to the door beside the window: *COLD STORAGE. STAFF ONLY.* The area was comprised of a pair of chambers, and the first resembled an industrial kitchen. Long steel benches laden with microscopes lined the walls, all of which were tiled by light screens.

Naomi looked back at David, then thrust open the cold-room door. In this heatwave, they were not accustomed to the cold. Naomi's breath plumed like fog. The room had an eerie metallic smell that made the air taste like a penny under her tongue.

A bank of lockers dominated one wall of the chamber. Each drawer had a number and a temperature gauge, and a longer number on a slide label for further identification. Where to begin?

David approached a drawer and pulled the handle so a locker slid away from the wall. A pale face launched itself into the room. Then shoulders, and a torso. The man's eyes had glassed, and his skin was duck-egg blue. A white sheet veiled him from chest to ankle and was tethered to grooves on the tray. The effect was strange: as if the dead man had been tucked too tightly into bed with a mesh curtain for a duvet.

Naomi noticed the shudder course through David's whole body as he stared into a dead pensioner's face. 'What's wrong?'

'Nothing . . . just . . .'

Somehow, Naomi perceived what it was. He'd seen countless cadavers in his life, but there was something about seeing them in this cold, glazed state. She knew he was used to fishing people out of the river, their bodies broken and bitten, and that it was easier to forget they were human. But this man was neither of those things. His remains seemed closer to life.

Feeling goosebumps raise on her arms, Naomi pushed the locker into the wall. She opened another, and the air bulged in her throat. It was one of the dead girls from the river.

They both stared silently at the remains, now surrounded by murdered human beings. People with lives and jobs and loved ones. The chances were high that they'd done everything right.

The hush of the room hung over them, but as Naomi went to speak, the look on David's face silenced her. She knew what he was thinking. She would have been thinking the same. What if it was her standing in front of these lockers, praying she wouldn't find her daughter's remains? Naomi could well imagine David was conjuring a picture of Lex in his mind, and she remembered her standing in the alley smoking. The last time they had seen her.

Without warning, David crossed the room and reached for a handle, and a locker slid from the wall. Naomi couldn't see the corpse as his back blocked her view. The chill she felt was not from the cold. 'David?'

As she drew close, she caught sight of flaxen hair, and realized what he was looking at. The second girl from the river lay dead on the tray. She was tall and elegant, and her skin was the colour of alabaster. The gemstone in her left ear had been removed so both lobes were now bare, and the sheet shrouding her had replaced the dress they had found her in.

David was leaning over the girl, studying her meticulously, a visible compassion to his movements that had been absent when Naomi had watched him lug the girl out of the water two days ago. Naomi stared to see what held his attention. It looked like icicles in her hair. This was the same grit they'd found on every corpse to date. But where that had come away in his hands, this had somehow petrified.

David wrenched a pair of nitrile gloves from a container on the wall and pulled them on. Unlatching the sheet and folding it to access the girl's left side, David took her hand and turned it over gently. It revealed the phantom shape of a stallion.

Naomi felt a wave of sadness. 'That's two.' Mindful of the time, she opened Sofia's file and found the lab results. 'Both women are confirmed overdose victims,' she said. 'Credit where it's due. You called it when we found them.'

'Where's the third girl?'

Naomi looked around the room.

'There were three of them,' David said. 'Where's the one that Baines stole?'

Naomi wasn't sure if she liked the accusatory tone to his voice — it was hardly accurate to say Baines *stole* the corpse. But when her eyes met a gurney in the corner of the room, and the long, still object concealed beneath a plastic sheet, she swept that thought aside.

She nodded to David, and together they approached the body. David pulled the sheet carefully away, revealing the mottled corpse Baines had requisitioned that morning. She was doll-like, with cropped, straw-coloured hair and that stallion stamp on her hand. Like the others, the same grit was encrusted in the girl's hair, and remnants had flayed away as he'd prised off the sheet. Some of the residue had caught on the blue plastic of the gloves he was wearing.

'She overdosed too,' Naomi said, quietly relieved it was not David's daughter, 'according to the file.'

'Think they all died together?'

'That or they were dumped by the same means,' she said. 'All three were found on separate occasions over three days. That's not a coincidence.'

'Someone must be dumping them,' David muttered. 'Trying to cover their tracks. Make it seem as if—'

Naomi stopped him. 'Later.' She walked to the steel door and opened it. 'We have to go.'

David clocked the urgent look on her face. As they passed through the lab, Naomi placed the pathology report back in the paper tray on Sofia's desk.

Reaching the door, she turned to David to make sure he was following, and was surprised to find him zipping his jacket up to his neck. She didn't think it had been that cold, and the heat of the day would do for it.

She led him out of the room, hoping her incursion would trouble Sofia no further, and wishing that she could thank her.

# CHAPTER TWENTY-SIX

Naomi took David back to the turnstile, feeling hot with pressure. Sofia's pathology report had offered answers to her questions, but now she was torn about who to trust. On the one hand, there was Roy Bishop, a man whose intentions baffled her. On the other, there was Shannon Baines, who seemed to be playing her own game.

But the person who chases two rabbits catches neither. If it seemed impossible that neither of them had blood on their hands, then it probably was. That meant there was someone else involved, someone invisible to her, dumping the bodies and getting away with it.

Naomi's thoughts turned briefly to her friend. Sofia had risked a lot giving them access to the lab results like that. And the results themselves had proved very revealing indeed. She recalled Sofia's angst.

*'I've got a bad feeling about this . . . I've never been asked to withhold information . . .'*

It still felt like it could go any which way. Sofia had seemed unmoored by Baines most of all, but after meeting with Baines in her office, Naomi still could not say why.

It was only when they had walked down the street a little that Naomi spoke again. 'You realize we're in deep shit.'

'Story of my life.' David continued to walk.

'There are cameras all over the building, it won't go unnoticed how many rules we just broke.'

David slowed, looked at her. 'I guess when the end justifies the means, there's nothing you won't do.'

Naomi stared at him. This deception was not why she'd joined the police, and it was certainly not in keeping with the good fight she'd convinced herself she'd been fighting all her life. But gains had been made. They'd found the third girl, and identified the same clues. The pathology report confirmed they had all died in the same manner.

She relented. 'All right. Call it water under the bridge.'

'We need to get out of here,' David warned.

They returned to the main road, and it took a few minutes for the Uber to arrive. When it did, Naomi climbed in the back and David confirmed a Wapping address with the driver.

* * *

David checked that the spare key hadn't been moved from under the doormat before opening the door with an identical set. He stepped over the threshold, without prompting Naomi to follow. She lingered in the hallway. The fact was she didn't know David very well, and she knew better than to go into some strange man's flat alone. It was something you learned quickly. All the same, David was a colleague and he wanted the same things as her. And her allies were few and far between.

She followed him in and looked around curiously. It was a peculiar place. There were no ornaments, no photos, no home comforts of any kind. Sunlight cascaded through large windows, blanching every surface with a sinewy glow, but that was the only warmth she could find.

Tower Bridge drew Naomi's eye to the picture window, and she walked to it. 'How can you afford this place?'

David grunted, apparently unwilling to humour her. She heard a zip being pulled, and when Naomi turned around, David was fishing the forensic report from his jacket.

'You *stole* the lab results?'

'I didn't steal anything. These are just printouts. It's all backed up on the internal servers.'

'That's not the point.'

'Seems to me it is,' David said. 'If Baines wants a copy, she can print another one.'

'But this is confidential information, David!' Naomi paced angrily. 'Sofia is going to kill me. You shouldn't have taken it.'

Even as she spoke, Naomi could feel her mobile phone buzzing in her pocket, the telltale sound of Sofia's angry messages.

David had turned away. He was already dialling his own phone and pressing it to his ear.

*Hi, it's me. If that's you then talk to the beep.*

David's aspect changed. He threw a glance at Naomi.

'What's the matter?'

'There was no ring this time, no click.'

'So?'

'She's switched off her phone.'

Naomi understood what David was saying. Either Lex had turned her phone off, or someone else had done it for her.

'Don't rush to conclusions,' she said. 'Baines told us she's under police protection.'

'That doesn't mean she's safe,' he snapped, ending the call. 'And we both know Baines could have been lying.'

'She gains nothing by doing that,' Naomi insisted. 'Look, I can't tell you what to do, but if the police got consent and it wasn't from you, maybe you should call your ex-wife.'

'I spoke to her already,' David said. 'She would have told me, I'm sure of it.'

'You're sure?' David didn't seem so. He stared down at his phone, and Naomi assumed he was trying to determine the answer. In the silence of the moment, she considered the question of safety. It was true — police association did not guarantee Lex was protected by them. Among a wide majority of decent and dedicated serving officers were a small minority of thugs who joined to coerce and control, whose aggressive behaviour was sanctioned and protected. The truth was often twisted to better suit the public narrative.

Naomi tried to distract herself by rereading the lab results. Now that she had time to study the file carefully, more detail jumped off the page.

'Look.' She beckoned him over. 'The girls *were* poisoned . . .' She trailed off.

David sensed her disquiet. 'What is it?'

He took the report and read the note to the coroner. Autopsies uncovered no obvious cause of death. Sofia had sent muscle from the left thigh of each cadaver, along with a liver sample, to forensic toxicologists. The thigh muscle was the most stable tissue in the body, making it a good place to find traces of poison. The samples had then been tested using mass spectrometry. The toxicologists had provided a graph showing the levels of different chemical compounds present in the liver samples from both girls. They contained traces of strychnine metabolites, formic acid, and a metallic element forming a number of poisonous compounds.

'Arsenic,' David read aloud.

Naomi grimaced. 'That report proves they both died of a haemorrhage at the point of ingestion.'

David read the section over. The gruesome chemical make-up was enough to make him feel sick.

'This is Nightmare? The synthetic drug?'

'You've scratched the surface of what it contains. In the past we've found trace amounts of ricin, paraquat, brodifacoum . . .'

'Arsenic works faster than all that.'

'True. But like I said,' Naomi finished. 'It only exists to kill people.'

'Is it the same for the third victim?' David asked.

Naomi double-checked the results but knew the answer already. 'The autopsy showed no obvious cause of death, same as the first two, but there hasn't been enough time for toxicology to come back on the body fished from the river this morning. But if the results come back with the same, that would certainly be an intriguing development.'

'So, they didn't overdose at all.'

'Not in the conventional sense,' Naomi agreed. She studied the results again, and noticed something else. 'They've actually written "Jane Doe" here for both, but Sofia had their names. She gave them to me. There's no reason not to have identified them in the coroner's report. If the names aren't here, they must have been redacted.'

David frowned. 'Maybe she got the names wrong.'

'But why redact the names at all? It's an internal document.'

Naomi kept her eyes fixed on the words 'Jane Doe'. She'd been loath to admit that Sofia had already given her the names as a lead. Nonetheless, David had raised an important question. 'There must be a confidentiality issue. Same reason Baines wouldn't tell us anything: the same undercovers are working the case.'

'The undercovers Lex has been talking to, you mean.'

'No. Don't put words in my mouth.' Naomi watched David stalk around impulsively. She wished he'd sit down. She preferred the religion of technique, sitting quietly to square information away.

'Where do we start?'

'With what we know,' she insisted. 'Three dead girls in the river, but they didn't drown. They had been dead for several days, but they hadn't been in the water long. Same cause of death, based on toxicology — assuming the third one follows suit.' Naomi paused.

David stopped pacing, as he waited impatiently for her judgement.

'Yes . . .' Naomi nodded to herself. 'That tracks. Haemorrhages imply they all died quickly.'

David bothered a stain on his thumb. 'I reckon they're being stored somewhere before they get dumped in the river. That's why all the victims turn up at Blackfriars. They've been dumped around the same time, maybe even at the same place, on consecutive evenings.'

'What makes you say that?'

David turned to her. 'You asked me why that body landed at Blackfriars, when usually we dredge remains at river bends.'

She remembered.

'It's a dead straight,' he confirmed, 'so either they're getting dumped nearby, or they're surfacing around there.'

Naomi contemplated what he was saying. She knew David had come to doubt the religion of technique, but careful investigation was all they had at their disposal. It had never failed her before. But technique was no substitute for experience, and David's instincts didn't lie. It meant he could see things she couldn't. But he relied too heavily on instinct without interrogating it with careful reason. 'Is it possible they were dumped further upriver?'

'It's only as far as the tide carries the cadavers, before the Port Authority find them.'

'Why Blackfriars? Why not at Hammersmith or the Isle of Dogs?'

'My guess is they're being jettisoned further downriver.'

'Don't guess,' Naomi warned. 'Tell me. Why Blackfriars, and nowhere else?'

David riddled it out. 'The tide slacks hard around Blackfriars, and the current will slow them down.' He quickly shook his head. 'No, that doesn't make sense. If the girls didn't drown, their cadavers would only have been a day old, not much more. Otherwise the cavities would have filled with gas . . .'

'Which meant they wouldn't sink,' Naomi chimed in.

David nodded. 'If the victims were being ditched further west from that point, we'd have known about them sooner: there's no way a body floats along the surface of the river as far as Blackfriars without us knowing about it.'

'And there's no way they were ditched further east and . . . I don't know, just lingered in the water somehow?'

'No,' David said decisively. 'There isn't. If they were dumped further east, the tide would have carried them away from Blackfriars and we may never have found their bodies. Chances are they'd have been washed out to sea.'

She nodded at the logic of this, relying on his knowledge of the river's behaviour. 'If we keep finding them at Blackfriars, then we should start at Blackfriars.'

David faced the window. He seemed unhappy with how the jigsaw was coming together. Between them, they had the edge pieces, but it felt like a picture of the sky at night with a missing piece thrown in. He snapped out of his reverie and noticed Naomi was watching him.

'Let's go down there,' he agreed.

'Sure. Wait, you mean *now*?'

'Why not?'

'Tide's coming in, isn't it?'

Naomi checked her watch. It was coming on for mid-afternoon and the window of opportunity had passed. The momentum of the last few hours would have to wait until the next ebb tide. She could tell what he was thinking. If someone was dumping bodies, and if Lex was involved . . .

'We should pick this up when the tide slacks.' David studied the bedroom door, thinking of the camera footage he had still to sift. He'd decided he wasn't yet ready to tell Naomi about that.

'Agreed.' Naomi got to her feet. 'Tomorrow.'

'Need a ride?'

Naomi hesitated. 'It's fine. Tube's not far.'

'Please,' David said. 'You'd be doing me a favour. I, um . . . I could use the distraction.'

He had already reached the door.

# CHAPTER TWENTY-SEVEN

David led Naomi to the tired Nissan Sentra parked in a bay adjacent to the apartments. As they started for the main road, Naomi squirmed in the passenger seat. The drive was fractionally easier than the Underground at rush hour, but he needed to busy his mind, and she felt sorry for him. She found herself thinking about Amy. It wasn't difficult for her to imagine what was going through David's head.

They were heading north towards Bethnal Green, and it wasn't until they hit their first set of traffic lights that Naomi broke the silence. 'Can I ask you something?'

David nodded. They were passing Weaver's Fields, leafy and flecked with sunshine. The carefree were out in force and frisbees sailed over the grass.

'We keep getting told not to care. Bring up the bodies and pass them on. Even you told me not to ask questions.'

'Sounds about right.'

'So what changed?'

He drove through traffic lights, then onto Queensbridge Road, before he could summon an answer. 'You've been right all along. No one cares about the girls.' His eyes were fixed on the road ahead.

'You know the chances that Lex will show up in the river are—'

'I know that,' he interrupted. 'But there's still a chance.'

They veered to Kingsland Road and continued to criss-cross the streets.

'Let me ask you a question,' he said. 'Do you trust Baines?'

Silence filled the car, fermenting the accusation.

'Are you asking me if she's bent?' Naomi kept her voice soft. He didn't respond at first, and she looked out at New North Road, wondering how to respond. Another thought had complicated the answer — she still had no idea who had tipped her off, masking their voice to remain anonymous. Could it have been Baines, doling out prompts that could so easily be lies?

'It's difficult to say,' Naomi said at length. 'Either way, we all want to solve the case before more people die.' She changed the subject, buying herself more time with the question she'd wanted to ask David since day one. 'I take it you haven't always been a diver?'

If he was caught off-guard, he didn't show it. 'Why do you want to know?'

'We're working together.'

'But why do you care?'

Naomi chose her words carefully. 'I'm trying to decide where we stand.'

A pedestrian struck out in front of them. David pushed hard on the brake.

'You don't need to hear my story, Naomi. We all make choices. Mine came down to a frog-suit and a mask, or a hard hat and a hammer.'

'There's more to it than that. Weren't you in the marines?'

At the Highbury Corner traffic lights, he turned to look at her. Naomi reimbursed his stare with a clairvoyant gaze. 'I did some digging around. You're on the internet. Call it a duty of care.'

David exhaled and faced the road. Tension idled in the air like debris as the car moved on, but she stubbornly refused to do so. 'So you don't dive because you have to,' Naomi figured.

'Why are we still talking about this?'

'There's a reason you choose to do it.'

'Do what?'

'You spend half your life underwater.'

'Because it beats the half I spend up here.'

The car swerved onto Holloway Road. Naomi sat back in her seat like a card player sussing out her opponent. 'All right, David, have it your way. Just tell me this one thing. You ignored me when I told you about the girls. Why are you listening to me now?'

David decided he was willing to tell her. It was the first time he'd recounted the tale — of Lex, The Pale Horse, Piers Larwood. It was a relief to explain it, although he decided to withhold his discovery that Larwood and Lex were more than friends. He still flinched when he thought of it.

Naomi listened with fierce interest as the car wound deeper into the suburbs. She already knew about Lex, but David's infiltration of the club and finding clues in the private bar made her raise her eyebrows. By the time he'd finished explaining, they had reached their destination.

'Turn here. You can park anywhere.'

He pulled in beneath the shade of a large tree, one of many that lined the rows of affluent Georgian town houses.

David was caught by surprise. Naomi lived here? It was that or she'd taken him down a garden path for the sake of privacy. Perhaps she lived several streets away. She didn't seem inclined to divulge the information.

Naomi stepped out of the car, but as she did so, the front door of an adjacent house creaked open, and a young girl called to her from the stoop.

'Mum — come and see!'

Naomi seemed flustered. 'Be there in a minute.' Then she dropped her voice, and leaned down into the cab, partly to speak to David, partly to obscure his line of sight. 'Listen. I'm not going to trivialize what's happened, but it's important to put it into perspective. Baines told us Lex was under police protection. I don't see what she stands to gain by fabricating the truth. If anything, she'd pervert the course of justice by doing so. And I don't think Baines would do that.'

'How can you be sure?'

'I can't be sure. Just a feeling. I don't think Baines is playing us, or that she's lied to us about Lex.'

'But she's been missing for three days,' he said quietly.

'You don't know that. If they had an e-fit, they'd have released it by now.'

'And what about the open police file?'

'That doesn't mean she's missing. The police have files for everything, you know that. And if she really was in danger, then it's the Met's duty to tell you as next of kin.'

*Unless they don't want me to know.* David tapped the steering wheel with a finger. 'Why won't she answer the phone?'

'She's a teenager,' Naomi answered evenly. 'Have you ever thought it might be out of spite? London's a big playground for a girl her age.'

David stared out of the windscreen, prospecting the empty road.

'Or you could blame it on the Underground,' she added. 'That's what I do when I don't want to take a call. Lex is stuck in a tunnel and there's no signal down there.'

'For three days?'

'You're welcome, Naomi. Thanks for letting me talk it out.' There was a sarcastic trill in her voice.

Absorbing that, David presented Naomi with a faint smile. 'You're right. Thank you . . . Tomorrow, then.' He searched Naomi's eyes. He was surprised by the genuine care behind her words.

Finally she shut the car door and walked to the house. David pulled away, not wishing to invade the privacy she'd so carefully guarded.

On the main road, at a set of traffic lights, he touched the bruise below his right eye and considered his next move. Naomi's words were still echoing around in his head, batting back and forth like a metronome.

*Blame it on the Underground.*

180

# CHAPTER TWENTY-EIGHT

FRIDAY 25 JUNE
Low tide: 03.03 (1.24 m) / 15.32 (1.69 m)
High tide: 09.38 (5.78 m) / 22.10 (5.79 m)

He swam through infinite space, to the place where Lex lay floating with her arms outstretched.

He could hear his breath catching like a wounded animal. He could smell chlorine. He reached out, made to drag her out of the pool. But she was snagged on something he couldn't see, and when he tried to pull her free he saw the whites of her eyes. Lex looked like she was on the cusp of a scream. But her cry was drowned out by his father's voice, telling him of the truth, resentment and bitterness radiating from him . . .

*You're nothing. Less than.*

David woke in the pit of the night, driven awake by fear of the dream. He pressed his hands to his ringing ears. But only silence remained, save a soft ticking of the clock on the wall and the residual hum of the city.

He tried to recover from the details of the nightmare and how it had started. The image of Lex on the edge of the pool testing the water with her toe, then a flash of her sprawled on the tiles and him trying to resuscitate her. The pain of Audrey insisting it was his fault, and Lex believing he was abandoning her. It mingled with the very real pain of knowing she hated him for it. But he hadn't known how to be there for her, without putting her in harm's way.

*You are the harm.*

Leaving was the only way he knew how to be a father to her. The only way to keep her safe . . .

He checked his watch and realized he'd slept hard for four hours. He tried to stretch, his joints aching with the effort. Each bruise felt like anvils pressing the vessels in his body. He sat up on the sofa. He didn't remember how it was he'd managed to fall asleep, but Naomi's ideas about Lex, about her status as a protected witness, had left him feeling frazzled and confused.

He dragged himself to standing, and did a lap of the apartment to check he really was alone before entering the bedroom. The detritus of his investigation — the mess of notes, photos and plans, and the blow-up map of the capital — were still laid out, but the most important parts of a human life — the emotions, the character, the experiences — were conspicuous by their absence.

*How well do you know your daughter, David?* Shannon Baines breached his thoughts.

His gaze settled on the laptop in a low-power state in the corner of the room. He wouldn't sleep again, so he decided to kill the hours till daylight by gutting the forensic reports. He started by taking the photographs of each victim and tacking them to the wall alongside the blueprints and layouts. Every photograph of human remains looked like hell's own pin-up, but the madness helped him to focus his thoughts.

Finally, he turned his attention to the laptop. There were still fifty surveillance files to sift through. He launched a video and scrolled swiftly through the footage. When he was satisfied it held nothing of note, David closed the file and crossed it off the list. And so it went, for a long time.

A thought crossed David's mind, and he paused the slider to focus on it: one of the parting shots Naomi had left him with. *Blame it on the Underground.*

He stared through space, letting that thought permeate. Then he noticed the time signature on the display was 19.01 . . . He rooted around the footage, but in the end, there was nothing to see.

David rubbed his eyes. His mind was beginning to wander, and he heard Naomi's voice. *Blame it on the Underground.*

He looked down at his hand. He'd been bothering the stain on his thumb again. His eyes ranged up to the map of the City. To Blackfriars.

Amid the lines and the scrawl, there was a line he hadn't seen.

He fumbled for a pen, traced the line, and took a step back. He'd created a blue vein from the north of the map to Blackfriars Bridge.

It was the secret place. The one that only they knew about.

And suddenly, it all made sense. The static that had been interfering in his brain disappeared, and he was left with a clear signal.

David tore the map off the wall. Snatching his keys, he left the apartment and raced to the car, leaving the surveillance footage on the laptop screen to play out.

So the file continued to run.

\* \* \*

David had his foot on the pedal, flashing past billboards and neon lights. In the short summer night, the omens of life were nothing to him. The street-lit roads were bare, save for the occasional minicab or night bus trundling along its route.

Reaching Blackfriars Bridge, David stomped on the brake and the car came to a sudden stop. He checked his watch. 2 a.m. The capital was domed with light but remarkably there were no people. The place seemed poised at the edge of a knife.

David left the car with its hazard lights ticking over, and he hurried to the bridge's pier. Though the bridge was lit, the river layered on the night, black on black. Even with the tide nearing its lowest point, he knew that current well. The fresh-water areas of the Thames could still run up to seven knots, faster than an Olympic swimmer. If he tried to swim across in a straight line, he wouldn't make it. He would go down fast. And that was not the only danger to think about. Despite the summer heat, the water would only be about twelve degrees — cold enough to cause an immediate shock response.

Nerves twanging like violin strings, David made a snap decision. He couldn't rely on the Dive Team now. He descended the stone steps to the foreshore, took one deep breath . . . and walked into the water.

It felt like razor blades stabbing at his legs. Already the shock provoked rapid breathing, increasing his heart rate. Though David knew this feeling, he needed to immerse him-self carefully and slowly. If the muscles in his arms and legs got too cold, he'd struggle to coordinate them into a swim-ming stroke. He could go into spasm. If that happened, there was nothing stopping the river from dragging him away from the bridge altogether.

David checked his feet, invisible under the water writh-ing around his knees. They felt numb and hard. He thought about how strange and pale and corpse-like his feet would look under the water, and for the briefest moment he could smell the antiseptic from the forensic lab all over again.

Taking another breath, he waded further out. Then his gasp reflex kicked in, the blood vessels in his capillaries already beginning to constrict.

He knew he had to fight it. He took a third breath, and, exhaling, swam out. He let out a yell. Every nerve from the tips of his toes to the roots of his hair was alight with adrenaline.

The current dragged him towards the bridge. He was heading straight for one of its pillars, vast and wide in the channel. He braced for impact, trying to keep his body as rigid as he could. He must not swim: that was the first rule of cold-water shock.

*Whatever comes next, I must not swim.*

His body lanced with pain as he collided with the pillar, and he managed to find a groove in the ironwork to hold on to, the water nicking him like the bills of nesting seabirds. He needed to wait it out — let the shock pass. Use the river's strength in lieu of his own.

He let out a laugh at the idea, high and giddy. This was madness. But it was too late now. Here he was, out here in the open, the river up to his neck. It was both terrifying and exhilarating.

The dancing black stars began scattering from his vision, and then he could see things clearly. He took in his situation. Ignoring the original pillars, he set his sights on the second leg of the bridge. The first leg was some ten feet across open water. He needed to reach it. There was a thin channel on the Thames Walk side, nestled between the dark selvedge of the river wall.

The current below the surface lugged at his lower half, and he renewed his grip on the pillar. He could not swim, but he wouldn't be able to reach the channel if he didn't. He would have to aim for it.

*Aim?* But that was impossible. He was ten feet away from the channel.

But he couldn't stay here.

To aim was madness. To stay would tempt hypothermia.

David looked to heaven to psych himself up. The Thames would fight him every inch of the way. This would take every ounce of his strength.

A cocktail of endorphins rang in his brain. A fresh swell of euphoria. Of calmness . . .

He shot off over the water, spun his body so the current pushed his legs askew. He kicked hard, lungs burning with breathless effort, and with arcing arms, his hands collided at last with the next pillar.

He hauled himself close to it and took an enormous breath, grateful for the depleted strength of the ebb tide. Carefully, he began to orbit the pillar using the arch of his back to steer himself in the water, until the current ushered him into the channel.

There — a grille yawning out of the stone.

David's fingers met the jagged surface. The grille itself was enormous. He dared to look inside. The mouth of a tunnel yawned back. Its maw was thin but wide enough, and despite the gaping darkness, he could see it was vomiting dank water. A torrent spewed suddenly out of the tunnel, so strong that it saturated his outstretched arms.

David explored the grille with his hands before trying again with his legs, whereupon he discovered empty space beneath the surface of the water. At least three or four feet — enough room for a corpse to pass under it.

He hooked one arm through the meshwork and used his free hand to caress the grille. Beneath his fingers, composites crumbled as a hard powder. His palm was now the colour of ancient industry. *Impossible.* Iron was a corrosive metal — how could it survive the ravages of the Thames?

He looked more closely at the grille itself, fossilized by a layer of clay. Déjà vu stronger than the freezing water lashed out at him. The answer was right here.

Now he needed to escape the water.

Somehow, he managed to reach the rungs on the river wall and pull himself out. He was immediately aware of the post-swim high — the ecstasy of it was drawing his attention away from the evaporating water dragging down his body temperature. His sopping clothes had warped to his skin. Meanwhile, the walkway above was deserted, so he clambered up. He jumped on the spot, relishing the bracing air, then sprinted this way and that to warm up. In the relative darkness of the walkway his breath rose as a long, rattling heave. He was caked in mud and residue, like Swamp Thing had emerged from the bog.

Despite the chill from the river, the night air was sultry and close, and he began to warm up. He took a moment to rest, noticing his hands were stained a deep shade of russet. The strange powdery deposits had washed away, but his hands were swarthy where they had blemished on his skin. It was the same colour he'd noticed on each of the victims he'd dredged.

He needed to get home. Tell Naomi all he had learnt. Everything was connected now. The momentum of it was rendering him insatiable, like a mountaineer hungry for the utmost point. He took the stairs back to the bridge and his car came into view.

He suddenly ducked back with a jolt of panic, heart pounding in his chest. Kneeling behind the stonework at the top of the steps, he chanced another look.

Someone was circling his car.

The hazard lights were tick-ticking in the lamplight. The driver's side door was open. Hadn't he locked the door behind him? David's eyes were fixed on the foreboding shape of a person as they stooped to investigate the cab.

The figure stood again at full height. Piers Larwood circled the vehicle, head cocked in tense deliberation. He was wearing dark street clothes and chukka boots, and a Glock was sheathed in a pancake holster under his jacket.

David swore under his breath. He cast about for a sign of the Range Rover. If Larwood had driven here, the vehicle was out of sight. Though traffic trawled the empty roads that lined the river, the bridge itself was otherwise deserted.

Larwood showed his back momentarily as he leaned into the cab again to switch off the hazard lights. He shut the car door, and the sound filled the empty air.

David watched Larwood edge to the stairs on the other side of the bridge. His back was turned again as he peered down at the river. Slowly, he walked down the steps out of sight.

Seeing his chance, David crept out from the stairwell on the opposite side and made for the car. He had barely managed to reach it when Larwood returned to the bridge, scowling at the water spots on the tarmac.

He crouched by the rear alloy with his limbs tucked in behind the wheel. His heart was thudding wildly in his chest.

He could hear the *chuk-chuk-chuk* of Larwood's boots on the tarmac. He didn't dare breathe. His ears were pricked, his whole body tense.

More silence, followed by more footfall, as Larwood made for the opposite set of stairs.

David thought of his car keys zipped inside his pocket. It was torture to drag the zipper down and take them out without jangling them. He quietly began to snail around the front of the car, until his hand met the door handle on the driver's side.

Quick as a whip, he opened the door, threw himself into the seat, and shoved the key in the ignition.

The engine roared to life.

When he looked up, Larwood was emerging from the stairwell, feeling for his gun.

David slammed his foot on the gas pedal, and the car lurched forward with a jolt. Larwood flashed by in a blur . . .

Then he was gone.

# CHAPTER TWENTY-NINE

As the car sped past Old Billingsgate, heading east across the city, David tallied the perils ahead. He felt as if his mind was coming loose from his body, such was the strange and formidable mission he now faced.

He could not go it alone — that much was clear to him. It was also true that the task ahead could not be carried out without proper equipment. This realization came with an overriding problem: he was suspended from duty.

Another key point had also become blindingly clear. He knew Lex had been liaising with the police in some capacity, but he had no idea *who* she'd been talking to or why. He didn't know if it was true, but if it was, he should have been consulted. Lex was under sixteen. As Baines well knew, the police would have needed to seek consent from a caregiver, and required the presence of an appropriate adult in an interview situation. It didn't feel right to him that Audrey could have given consent without telling him, much less deliberately kept it from him. And supposing Lex was in league with undercover officers — what were they hoping to accomplish? None of it made sense.

David tried to decide if he was a fugitive in the eyes of the Met. He had trespassed on a business premises and stolen sensitive information from Scotland Yard. If they wanted to prevent David from decisive action, they would come looking for him. But his instincts told him that the police (and Baines by proxy) were not the main concern. If they really wanted to stop him, they would have. It was child's play to trace a vehicle — security cameras were everywhere. Even on foot, police could catch up to him without difficulty. No, it wasn't the Met he had to worry about right now.

There was a killer out there, murdering women, dumping their corpses. David wasn't certain if Larwood was behind the crimes, but why else would he be stalking around Blackfriars in the middle of the night? But as the car swerved through central London, the fact remained: he needed gear. There were too many risks to investigate without it.

He thought about Naomi. He knew exactly what needed to be done, and how to go about it, but convincing Naomi to abet him was another matter entirely. He wasn't certain he could sway her on this. Their task would be completely illegal, and pardoned only by the threat of the greater evil at hand. Informer or not, Lex could still be aligned to this grim chain of events.

Not long after, David arrived back in Wapping. The night was cool and still, and a dog was barking somewhere. He left the car on a side street and crept stealthily towards the Marine Police building.

Reaching the warehouse doors, he caught sight of Connor Beckett's primitive shape smoking a cigarette on the kerb, silently absorbed by a gambling app on his phone. David slunk along the wall of the neighbouring wharf building and slipped unnoticed into the alley. A chill lanced through his empty throat. This was where he'd last seen Lex. David gave himself a mental shake, urging himself not to dwell. He edged past the bulging rubbish sacks and opened the fire escape.

The dry dock seemed deserted. The Ribcraft boats were bobbing in their slip lanes, and the hangar doors were wide open as usual. The river was lapping at the landing stage with a series of wet slaps.

Voices caromed down the hallway from the locker room. 'Hey, Connor! Are you playing or what?'

David ducked away as Connor walked across the dock, shoving his phone in his pocket. A far door closed, and the sound carried. After that, all was still as a church.

David assembled a short inventory in his mind before stepping inside. If anyone crossed the dock they would notice him, and that would be the end of it. He'd have to move fast.

He grabbed a loading trolley and wheeled it to the rows of equipment, where he heaped pairs of neoprene membrane suits, masks, aqualungs, demister bars, bailout tanks, and flashlights onto the trolley. He added two ballistic vests, black with fluorescent strips and ornate with police insignia. He also took a charting watch, with target detection and navigation aids on its interface, and added that to the pile as well. In less than a minute, he'd procured everything he needed.

David's ears pricked at the sound of footsteps. He abandoned the gear and hurtled silently back to the fire exit. From his hiding place, he saw Lynch appear on the dock. The captain cut a forlorn figure as he made for the open hangar doors.

To David's surprise, Lynch ignored the trolley completely. Perhaps he assumed it was the detritus of an earlier rotation. Straining to hear Lynch's movements, David checked his watch. Time was of the essence. He inched the door open, the better to keep Lynch in his sights. But the captain remained motionless. He seemed to be staring out at the river, lost in thought.

'Going somewhere?' Lynch turned to David. For a moment, neither moved.

'I take it you've found something,' Lynch said.

David blinked, mystified. 'Yes . . . I mean, I did.'

'You're certain?'

Lynch latched his fingers. Wind slid through the space between them, and David had the prevailing sense of being a character in a John Ford Western — but he did not know which side he was on.

If he'd expected Lynch to move one hand to his shooting hip, he was disappointed. 'The bodies you dredged amount to one crime,' Lynch told him. 'Scotland Yard don't know what that is. They only know that you're onto it.'

'How do you know?'

'I don't. But it makes sense.'

The men stood there, weathering each other's silence. Lynch, for his part, seemed to be considering his options. Perhaps he knew that he shouldn't help David, much less allow him to leave with the equipment. The reason he did was what allowed David to bend the rules.

David's instincts were always right. He had never been wrong, not once in twelve years. That was long enough to command respect.

'So what now, Stephen?' David asked. 'You turning me in?'

Lynch shrugged. 'How can I? You were never here.'

* * *

Thirty minutes later, David was back in Highgate. The streets were still and quiet, swathed in a peace he did not feel.

He reached Naomi's front door feeling apprehensive. Having tried calling, her phone had rung but there was no answer. He genuinely had no idea how Naomi would react to his coming. With his battered face and tired eyes, he was an increasingly unwelcome presence to most anyone.

The porch light blinked alive as he traipsed up the winding path. Drawing a nervous breath, David pressed the video doorbell. It chimed, and he stood there waiting, trying to ignore the nagging sense that there was no time and he could not wait.

Naomi's face appeared on the screen above the doorbell. She cursed him. Then the video switched off. It took another moment for her shadow to fill the front door's leaded glass panel, rippling in a kaleidoscopic burst of shapes. A lock unlatched from inside. The door opened an inch, and he saw Naomi's face again.

'David. It's the middle of the night. What are you—'
She paused. The shock in her throat softened her voice to a whisper. 'You're wet through. What happened?'

'We can catch him. You and me. Tonight.'

'What?'

'I figured it out, Naomi. I understand everything.'

She paused again, cogwheels turning as she decided what to do. Eventually, Naomi let the catch off the door and opened it fully.

He sensed her unease almost immediately. Perhaps she'd anticipated Shannon Baines standing at the door, or had decided that David had finally cracked.

Naomi did not switch on a light, so the entrance hall remained cloaked in darkness. She quickly dragged him over the threshold, but as David stepped forward, something small and matted with fur shot through his legs and scurried up the stairs with a yelp.

Naomi clacked her teeth at the cat, latching the door behind them as quietly as she could. Wheeling David around, she jabbed a finger in the direction of the kitchen at the end of the hall.

He had barely taken a few steps before he heard a sound from the stairs.

'Mummy?'

David felt his insides churn as he looked up at a little girl's face watching him through the bannisters.

'Who's that man?'

Naomi's dismay was palpable. 'What are you doing out of bed?'

'Take a wild stab in the dark.'

The cold baritone belonged to the man descending the stairs past the little girl. He paused on the bottom step, as if this somehow meant he could claim the high ground in the altercation to come.

'Why are you all wet?' the girl asked.

'I . . . went swimming.'

'In your clothes?'

David didn't know what to say. This wasn't part of the plan.

'Sweetheart, it's time for bed.'

The girl ignored her mother and continued to inspect him, then said, 'You're kinda gross.'

'*Amy*.' Naomi shot David an apologetic look, then glared at the man, her mouth forming a straight line. 'Miles, can you take her to bed for me, please?'

Without waiting for a response, Naomi turned her attention up the stairs to speak to the girl. 'It's OK,' she said gently. 'This man is a police officer.'

'Like you?'

'Exactly — like me.'

'It's three in the morning,' the man growled.

'I know,' she snapped, flicking the light switch. 'But this is important.' She looked at David, jerked her head at the man on the bottom step. 'This is my husband, Miles.'

David offered a weak smile and raised his hand to shake.

'Hi. Um . . . Sorry it's late.'

Miles did not take his hand. Throughout, the girl held a silent vigil.

'Let's talk in the kitchen,' Naomi told David. 'Miles, take her to bed, please.'

The girl wore a disgusted expression — this was far more interesting than bedtime. For a fraction of a second, David sensed Miles sharing the girl's disappointment, but the man proved far trickier to read.

Naomi offered a rueful look, and Miles gave David a wary glance before rounding back up the stairs and prising the little girl away from her vantage point.

Naomi marched him to the kitchen and switched on the light. 'This had better be worth it. Why are you in my house in the middle of the night?'

194

# CHAPTER THIRTY

'Well?' Naomi urged. 'Come on. What are you doing here?'

'I know why the bodies are turning up at Blackfriars.' The words tumbled out of David's mouth in a mad rush. 'There's an underground river and—'

'You're talking about a sewer?' Naomi eyed him evenly from the other side of the breakfast bar. The room was spacious and brimming with personality. A flash of red, a circle of yellow, statement tiles, rainbows on the fridge. Trinkets of the girl on the landing.

He took a breath to steady his thoughts and placed his palms on a stool. 'How much do you know about the old waterways?'

'Only that the city is full of them. They were covered over in the nineteenth century.'

David nodded. 'Someone is using the Fleet to ditch the victims. There's a tunnel at Blackfriars Bridge that empties the Fleet River into the tidal Thames. That's why we keep finding bodies at Blackfriars.'

David flipped his palms to show her the discolouration. 'Look at this. We found the same on the victims, didn't we?'

Naomi frowned. 'Where exactly have you been?'

'At the outfall. The grille under the bridge. Don't you see?'

Naomi didn't.

'Iron corrodes in water, but this is mixed in London clay — which is rich in iron oxide. That's why it's not washing off in the water,' David explained. 'The clay has hardened around the grille, which is what's stopping it from corroding. The residue we've found on the cadavers is what happens when the bodies hit the grille and they're ejected into the river.'

Naomi left a long silence, not quite buying it. 'There's any number of reasons the victims could have grit in their hair, and countless ways it could have got there. How can you be sure it came from an underground river?'

'Because I've seen it before. There was a map of it on the wall.' David explained about the backlit map he'd found at The Pale Horse. He then reached for his pocket, took out his own map, and flattened it out on the breakfast bar.

The sudden appearance of the map and the mention of the one at the club triggered something in Naomi's brain. 'There was a map just like this back at the bullpen.' It was her turn to explain, so she told him about the squaddies hunched over the map covered with the blue lines.

'There's more,' she recalled. 'Major Crimes retain investigatory communications as a security measure. Relevant evidence, surveillance tech, it's all kept close to home. But when we passed the function rooms, all the equipment was gone. The rooms were empty.'

David didn't know what to make of that.

'It doesn't make sense.' Naomi's thoughts had circled back to the underground rivers. 'They were covered up. They're not traversable anymore.'

'The river mouth to the Fleet River is,' said David.

'How do you know?'

'There's more than one entrance to the Fleet. This is a secret one.' He tapped a dirty finger on the map's upper section. 'It starts here — in Hampstead. See the headwater there? It feeds Hampstead Pond to the outflow.'

Naomi's eye was drawn to a large green expanse veined with blue lines. To the right was a smaller blue shape. It looked like a deep cut from a medieval dagger.

'I'm guessing the bodies are being dumped there,' David finished. 'There's time at the river mouth if you can get away before the tunnel floods. *Here*.' He jabbed his finger at a place on the map where two veins met.

Naomi crossed her arms. 'If it's so secret, how does our man know about it?'

David faltered. He'd not mentioned the secret place before, nor the video of Lex showing Larwood the hole in the ground. He'd omitted that when he'd shared the story.

'I think he and Lex were . . . together. Or something.'

Naomi's head snapped up. 'Isn't she a minor?'

'She's fifteen.'

'But he's clearly an adult.' Naomi's expression became a mask of utter disbelief. 'You're saying that she was . . . with *him*?'

'Yes,' David said feebly. 'It's easier if I just show you.' He used his phone to log into Lex's Instagram using the iCloud keychain, and found the video of Lex and Larwood exploring the entrance. 'I used to take her up there. When she was a kid . . . She's obviously told him about it.'

Naomi watched the video, not quite able to shield her disgust.

'Do you have a picture of him?'

'I can go one better.'

On the phone, David launched his daughter's Facebook account, but when he tried to click through to Larwood's profile, a message blipped on the screen.

*Sorry, this content is not available.*

'Damn.'

'What?'

'His profile's been deactivated.'

Naomi frowned. 'Could it be he knew you were looking?'

At David's blank stare Naomi went on. 'He may have blocked you,' she said. 'On some of these sites, you can view the search-engine terms and . . .' She fell short, realizing her efforts to keep her own daughter safe on the internet may not be a welcome topic of conversation at this particular moment. She took out her phone, found Larwood's Instagram profile. 'This him?'

David grunted.

She grimaced at the quiff and the dicky bow.

'Don't ask me what she sees in him because I don't know,' David said.

'He looks rich,' Naomi noted. 'He's older. Trying hard to be a bad boy.'

'Look, there isn't time for this now.' David seemed flustered. 'I can explain all of it to you on the way.'

'Hold on.' Naomi wasn't listening. She was staring down at the map, attempting a calculation. 'The Fleet runs from the southern edge of the ponds all the way to the Thames. That's got to be three miles at least.'

'Four,' David corrected.

Naomi threw up her hands. 'You want to search four miles of subterranean river?'

'We don't have to. The bodies wash through to Blackfriars via the irrigation system — it regulates water, so the ponds don't drain into the Fleet. Surface run-off is discharged at intervals timed perfectly with the Thames floodtide.'

'So all we have to do is search the river mouth,' Naomi finished. 'But what about the floodwater? You've seen Soho after a storm. London drains can't handle excess rain — and it pissed it down the other night. Are you certain that water runs off?'

David made to speak, but Naomi interrupted. 'And it's a pretty long-winded way to ditch a corpse, don't you think? Why not bury them? Weight them down in the ponds themselves?'

'Come on, Naomi,' he coaxed, 'you've collaborated with Forensics. You know how hard it is to hide a body. Anyway, this is quick, as far as it goes. Think about it. When we find the corpses, we assume they're suicides, don't we?'

'Yeah, so?'

'So, *he* assumes he'll get away with it. I've told Lex all about this stuff.'

'What — suicides?'

'Yeah, she loves it.' David lingered, conscious of how that might sound. 'Kids love true crime. The gorier the better. She must have told him about it, too. Of course — it all makes *sense*.'

Naomi rebuffed him. 'You're making a lot of assumptions, David. Why go to such lengths to cover your tracks?'

'Because he doesn't want to get caught. Argue all you want. Fact is the Met haven't figured this out. And as for the floodwater — we won't know what we're up against until we get there.'

'We?' she trilled. 'No. Stop. No way. We call backup, set a perimeter, do it properly—'

David threw a glance at his watch. 'We don't have time for all that. It's half three. We've got two hours.'

'We can't do it ourselves!'

'Who else is there to trust?'

'I am not going down there.'

'Why?'

'Let's count the ways, shall we?' Naomi was struggling to keep her voice level now. 'For one thing, I don't like the sound of catching a killer, in a sewer, in the middle of the night, with just you as backup. For another, your daughter was trying to help the police catch the bastard — so let *them* take it from here.'

David's face morphed into a scowl. 'Fine. I'll go alone.'

He made to walk out, but Naomi stepped around to stop him. 'Listen. You've convinced yourself the killer has drawn the same conclusions you did — which isn't the same as proving criminal intent. If there's even the slightest chance we'll catch him red-handed, we need more time.'

'There *is* no time,' he hissed. 'He doesn't know the bodies get flushed out. He's got no idea we're on to him. If he did, he'd have stopped dumping them this way. That's why it has to be now.'

'You can't investigate assumptions, David.' Naomi craned her neck to the ceiling, wishing this was more straight-forward. The moment you wanted to believe something, it undermined an investigation. And yet, there was no denying David's insight. *What if he's right?*

Resolve burned in David's eyes as two beacons of flame. The rollercoaster of the last few days surpassed coincidence by any reasonable measure.

*The simplest solution fit the facts.*

Naomi searched his eyes. 'Do me a favour . . . Wait here.'

* * *

Naomi returned to the hall. From where David was standing, he could hear her arguing with Miles in hushed tones, as if he'd been eavesdropping from the hallway just beyond the kitchen door. There followed a clomping upstairs, and a door closed on the landing above.

He decided he shouldn't have come here. He was wasting time. If Naomi couldn't help him, so be it. He would do this on his own.

David made his way back to the hall. He was about to open the front door when he noticed an open door to the playroom. A towel had been left to dry on an airer. David felt his heart quicken. The towel was covered in handstitched swimming badges, and they reminded him of police insignia for a brief moment, before his thoughts skirted back to the smell of chlorine and the sounds of screaming children, and of Lex lying listless in that pool. A lump formed in David's throat.

From the landing there came a sharp rejoinder that he couldn't quite make out, and Naomi marched down the stairs.

'Let's go,' she said without ceremony. In the hallway, she grabbed a blazer jacket off the rack and took a key from its pocket. She unlocked a drawer on the sideboard to retrieve a can of self-defence spray, along with a pocket Swiss Army knife. Then she opened the door and marched out of the house, without so much as a backwards glance.

David hurried out and closed the door behind him. He had a thousand questions — about Miles, her daughter, life, the universe and everything — but Naomi maintained her silence until they climbed into the car.

'Naomi, I'm sorry.'

'What for?'

'I shouldn't have come. You never told me about all this.'

'What exactly would I have told you?' she snarled. It was a shot across the bows. She buckled her seatbelt and composed herself. 'So — what happens in two hours?'

'Huh?'

'You said we have two hours. What happens after that?'

'You really want to know?'

'I'm asking, aren't I?'

David collected his thoughts. 'An underground cistern regulates the river and collects rainwater until it's pumped out.'

'And then?'

'The tunnel floods.'

Naomi became very still. She aimed her gaze straight ahead.

'Drive.'

# CHAPTER THIRTY-ONE

The gravel crunched beneath the tyres as Piers Larwood came to a sudden stop. It was the fourth trip he'd made out here in the dark, and this was destined to be his last.

He checked the time on the dash. Half three. He didn't want to waste any more time tonight. He was hell-bent on getting it done. It was with that resolve that he left the engine idling, lights on, keys in the ignition, as he stepped out to open the boot.

He was unfazed by the sight or smell when he opened the tailgate and rolled the corpse towards him. If anything it was met with relief — he'd begun the week with four dead girls to dispose of and he'd whittled that down to one.

Larwood shifted his weight and dragged the body out of the vehicle. It was easier to bear the full weight now the bloating stage had passed. The first bodies had been stiff with rigor mortis, but he'd left this one so long it was pliable again, and he was able to bear the victim in a fireman's carry.

He elbowed the boot lid, kicked the tailgate shut — he'd grown quite adept at this ritual. It was irritating he'd not been able to dump them all at the same time, rather than having to carry out this gruesome work over a series of days and deal with the difficulties that arose from putrefaction.

Larwood made a sinister little scoff in the darkness. He wished he could tell Lex all about this. He was ditching the girls at the secret place after all — he had her to thank for showing him where it was. There was no way to tell if the bodies were being recovered, but he'd felt the need to visit Blackfriars to make doubly sure. He was reasonably sure they hadn't been found there, but if they had, the trail had not made its way back to him yet. This was especially fortuitous, given he had failed to deal with Daddy on the bridge. Larwood had wondered about that — what was *he* doing there?

Larwood tried to put him and Lex out of his mind. He was still smarting at how he had not seen her for days. He didn't even really know if they still had a chance, or even if he could convince her to leave. He wasn't sure what he would do when he found her. He suspected she was in too deep if she'd gone to the police, and that the only way to cover his tracks fully was to do what had to be done.

One task at a time, however. There was plenty of time for all that. Once he was finished here, he would go looking for her. And when he found out where she was hiding . . .

The first time he'd come up here, on Monday, he'd left the Range Rover behind and struggled to find his own way to the hidden entrance Lex had shown him. The dead weight of the corpse had made him almost want to give up. Tonight, he hurried on as fast as his legs would carry him through the trees to the ponds. Once or twice he lost himself in the darkness and had to regain his bearings. But soon he found the tree, and lowered the dead weight into the ditch with relief. It landed in the headwater like a paperweight in the dark. He took a moment to catch his breath, then pulled a Maglite out of his pocket, ducked beneath the fallen tree and dropped down into the ditch.

As he waded into the sewer, Larwood dredged the events of the week. Once the notion of how to ditch the girls had lodged itself as a logical possibility, he'd set about without delay. Monday and Tuesday had passed without incident, though he had fallen badly in the tunnel and banged up his leg. Despite that, he'd started to think he might pull this off. For the super-rich, as a rule, did not wander the Heath at night, preferring to steal themselves away in the high-walled strongholds that scattered the surrounding area, caught up in their own self-centred existence, paying little attention to matters of the world around them. Thus he had been able to conduct his business quickly — and quietly. But on Wednesday, events had conspired against him, and the fear he might get caught had ricocheted round his brain.

It had begun with the phone call early that morning. He'd managed to fob off Daddy, albeit clumsily, but had decided that he needed to be seen to be acting normally so as not to attract further attention. The Pale Horse was closed Mondays and Tuesdays, but Wednesday night he'd gone to the club, as if his mere presence at work would afford him an alibi for everything else that had happened.

Then the storm came, and worse still, Daddy had tracked him down. Larwood had deemed it too risky to visit Hampstead on that particular night. Shaken by the call and the encounter at the club, he had lain low, locked in his Belgravia flat, popping the few pills he had left. He had also been in contact with a vendor on the dark web selling decommissioned firearms under the counter, along with the kit and instructions to restore the gun. He'd frittered away the daylight hours watching YouTube videos, teaching himself to use the Glock in a pinch.

Now as he slung the corpse over his shoulders and entered the sewer, a cold drip landed cleanly on the back of his neck. Larwood shivered. He thought about how many shallow graves there were in Hampstead, and whether he should have made life easier for himself. He wondered if he'd weighted the bodies down and tossed them into the ponds, whether the police would ever have found them. But shallow graves were easily found. Bodies in ponds still surfaced.

In any case, the ordeal was reaching its end. By now he'd watched three girls vanish into the culvert, the arched tunnel that flowed beneath the city. He'd done this with the satisfaction of a man who knew he was getting away with murder. But he wasn't doing it to protect himself. He was doing it for *her*.

Yes, he told himself, that was the real reason for all of it. Larwood wanted to start again and he wanted to do it with Lex in tow. And he wasn't going to take no for an answer.

He shone his torch into the secret place, and not for the first time tonight, Larwood was reassured by thoughts that held no remorse or sentiment for the dead.

This was the last time. Then he'd be free.

# CHAPTER THIRTY-TWO

Naomi's eyes trained ahead, the drive to Hampstead stirring the disquiet beginning to simmer in her mind.

She was busy considering Sofia's words again, pondering the possibility their true meaning was unveiling itself to her at this exact moment. That her impulse to do the right thing in the hour of need, to prove to herself that the good fight was more than an egoistic crusade, meant she had been doomed to end up in this car, speeding towards a dangerous and uncertain reckoning. Perhaps she was about to discover who she really was.

'There's gear in the back,' David said as he drove. 'I, um . . . dropped by the dock.'

'Did you now.' There was a caustic edge to her voice.

David let the dust settle on that before he spoke again. 'So, Miles. He's your—'

'Partner.' She dispatched the word without fanfare.

'Is he happy about . . . ?'

'What do you think?'

Naomi turned her head to gaze out of the window.

'I am sorry for dragging you into this. For what it's worth.'

'You're not sorry at all. The least you can do is be honest about it.'

She was right of course — all roads led to Lex. And unlike David, Naomi didn't think of herself as a hero. She wanted to do things by the book. But whether she liked it or not, David *had* dragged her into it, and she *had* been convinced by his argument. She only hoped they were not too late.

'Miles didn't want you to go with me. Am I right?'

Naomi drew air through her teeth. 'Yeah, well. Fuck it — he doesn't make the rules.' And she meant it. Miles had asked her not to go. Actually, he had demanded it. That was the catalyst in the end.

David pursed his lips. 'I know you're angry with me—'

'Of course I'm angry,' Naomi spat. 'You had no right to come to my house.'

'I get that.'

'No you don't, David. You haven't the first clue.' She paused. Softened her voice. 'How long have you been with the police?'

'Twelve years.'

'Then you're ugly enough to know what happens to women in the Met. When I first started out, if you had child-care issues, you were bunged on a desk job quicker than you can say "equal rights for women". I keep my personal life separate for a reason. You've no idea the sacrifices I've had to make to uphold it.'

Naomi ran out of breath. She turned over the argument with Miles, still fresh in her mind. No one, not even her husband, had the right to tell her what to do. She was tired of trying to make the men in her life understand that, and having to explain it to them over and over again. Privilege was like air. Hard to see when you're free to breathe.

Naomi yawned, and her jaw cramped painfully. She checked her watch. 'Just gone four. Let's make this quick.'

They were on the approach to Hampstead, having circled the Heath to avoid undue attention. Now they were driving along The Bishops Avenue. The wide street was lined with derelict mansions and Naomi caught herself counting the gargoyles astride steel gates, glowering like deities in the gloom.

They headed south around the Heath's lush green borders, and down a narrow lane that atrophied the edge of the Heath. When they reached a gravelled car park, David cut the engine. The Nissan's headlights went out, and though the moon was concealed by clouds that hung spectrally in the sky, they could make out their surroundings, soft-edged in the gathering light.

They noticed the headlights from the vehicle on the other side of the car park, and heard the sound of an engine ticking over.

David clambered out and nodded at the white Range Rover. 'That's Larwood's car.'

The headlights were dazzling, but the early morning light did for the beams before they could reach the trees. David popped the boot of the car, located a pair of flashlights and a set of diving gloves, and pulled them on.

Larwood's vehicle had displaced the gravel as if it had arrived at speed. Through the glare of the headlights, it was almost impossible to determine whether there was anyone in the cab.

Naomi reached for the knife and spray concealed in her inside pocket. The small car park was near silent, save for the crunch of the gravel underfoot and the Range Rover's engine humming in the dark.

David didn't hesitate. He marched up to the SUV and yanked open the passenger's side door with one gloved hand.

The cab was empty — there was no sign of the driver.

Naomi approached, wearing gloves, and a warning look on her face, signalling that David shouldn't touch anything else. Gingerly, she sniffed the air and peered in through the back window. On the backseat was a set of blankets stained with brown smears. There was something sodden about them, something blemished.

She inclined her head to the boot of the car. David followed her to it, and she tried the switch with the tip of one gloved finger. The boot lid yawned upwards.

The stench was overwhelming. Pine-scented air fresheners mingled with the ammonia tang of decay hadn't fooled the blowflies. Naomi could feel them flash past her face with their distinctive, irritating buzz.

David covered his mouth as he peered inside and shone his flashlight at the tarpaulin on the floor. It was encrusted with dried blood.

Something shimmered in the light of the torch. A gemstone lay on its side, between a crevice in the canvas.

'It's the earring,' he whispered, aiming the torch so Naomi could see. 'The first girl we found was missing one.'

Naomi gave him a significant look. She moved to the front of the vehicle, opened the door to aim her light into the cab. The keys were in the ignition. Her stomach muscles tightened. 'Why would he leave the keys?'

'Because he's coming back,' David guessed, a note of warning in his voice.

He examined the keys, and the stallion-shaped key ring winked in the light. There was an address engraved upon it.

*The Pale Horse, 666.*

'David—?'

He wrenched the keys from the ignition and slipped them into his pocket before joining Naomi, who had since doubled back to the tailgate. She was already shining her torch onto the ground, where the gravel had been strewn aside. She frowned. 'These marks can't have been made by the car. They're far too wide and irregular for tyre tracks, right?'

It was then she noticed the marks trailed across the car park and into the trees like snakes.

'We'll lose them in the treeline.'

'Doesn't matter.' David met her eyes. 'I know where he's going.'

* * *

They changed into their gear, saddled up and struck out into the early twilight. Though the Heath was rugged and rough-hewn, their equipment did not slow them down.

It was too early for dawn, but the short night was ending. Birds unsettled them with elegies through the mosaic of shrubland. When the trees parted, they saw Parliament Hill rising as a whaleback in the gloaming. The sky smouldered with an urban glow. London's skyline stretched out, dotted with aircraft lights.

Naomi followed David to the lagoon at the foot of the hill. Its two-stream valleys had been dammed to create a dozen ponds, and one pond's southern end revealed the source of the Fleet, which was draining into a grille half-submerged by the water.

'There's no chance anyone could get in there,' Naomi whispered.

'He's looking for the secret place.' David edged past her, along the side of the pond.

Soon they came upon a tree. Its gnarled roots lay cruciform on the ground, petrified where lightning had once felled it. David recognized the scene, not from the video Lex had made, but from scores of old memories occluded in the background of his thoughts. It was a risk to use the torch, but he needed to see for himself.

Sure enough, beneath the deadfall they found a ditch gurgling with the sound of headwater.

Naomi crept to David's side, and stared into a hole in the earth. It seemed to pulsate with a foul phosphorescence that rose to greet them. The stench was so strong it made her neck hairs stand on end.

David aimed his torch at the mouth. It was a lesion in the earth, swathed in silt and lichen. The torchlight could not penetrate the darkness within. It did, however, circumnavigate the pipe that led to the Fleet. It was almost tall enough to walk in — if you arched your back.

The only sound was babbling water. The rest was eerie silence.

Through the darkness, Naomi heard David whisper solemnly in her ear. 'He'll kill again. You know he will. I understand if you don't want to go in there — I'm not going to force you to do anything. But I don't have a choice. I think he means to kill my daughter, that is if he hasn't already. We both know he's not going to stop there.'

David couldn't be sure that his words had any effect. He knew this was insane. Of course it was. But if there was even the slightest possible chance he could save a life — not least his daughter's — then that was what he was prepared to do. It had taken them less than ten minutes to reach the secret place from where the vehicles were parked. There wasn't any more time to waste.

Self-consciously he patted down his vest, checking his gear was in place. Belt. Knife. Umbilical wire. At last he heard Naomi's response in his ear. 'Have you ever done this before?'

'No. Let's go.'

Then he climbed down.

# CHAPTER THIRTY-THREE

A shriek filled the tunnel as something fat and furry whipped through Naomi's fingers.

David trained his beam on her before shining it over the pipework and further into the tunnel. A cluster of tiny blinking lights blazed back at them. Only they were not lights at all. They were eyes.

The rats screeched and scattered with a slap of water as David trudged over to her.

'You good?'

Naomi nodded with a shudder, then checked her watch. They had just thirty minutes before the cistern released the irrigated water. When that happened, the water level would rise. There was no way of knowing if they would escape this place when that happened.

They tentatively began to pick their way ahead, their eyes straining into the gloom. David shone his torch down the tunnel, its features bare and exposed. The bright beam stripped out most colours, washing everything with monochrome shades. It was difficult to tell in the darkness, but under the glare of the flashlight, the tunnel was wider than expected, though their path looked thin and uneven.

Naomi stumbled, her heel catching on something splintered underfoot. She heard herself give a tiny laugh of surprise, bitten off before it began. She had stood on a femur bone. Its remnants were riding off in the waste water streaming at the base of the pipe. 'This is insane. Let's go back.'

'We can't.'

'Fine. Let's stay here. There's only one way out, right? He has to come back sometime.'

'What if there's another way out?'

'What if there isn't? You have to accept this is cra—'

A shadow caught her eye on the wall ahead, and David swung his torch away to quickly kill the beam.

Naomi did the same, and felt him clasp her arm. 'Down there.'

A light hovered up ahead. It was almost shapeless, a reflection in the shallows of the water. Then the light moved, as if it had been somehow jimmied off-course.

They both heard it at once. A crack. Naomi held her breath, her ears ringing.

Nothing. Then another crack. Was it the broken rhythm of footfall? She couldn't tell. Naomi stood stock-still as she sensed David's movement behind her. Before she could do more than begin to turn her head, he had forged past her.

'Hey — *wait*.'

But he did not wait.

Naomi set her teeth and crept after him. It was now pitch black in the pipe. Her short time as a diver had not numbed her to darkness, and this was like the inside of a snake as it devoured you alive. She imagined sliding wide-eyed down its throat.

Then she heard a groan. Not a human sound. Something altogether worse, as it travelled up the spine of the tunnel. She shone her torch at David. The water was now deepening up to her shins as it poured through ducts in the tunnel wall. It could only be the surface run-off from tributaries feeding the Fleet.

Her breathing grew heavier as she sloshed after David. And that was when her torch went out. Now there was nothing. Only rushing water, the cold, and the aqueous smell of death.

Naomi lost her footing. With a cry, she slipped into empty space. A biting chill swept over her as she fell.

Down.

Down.

Into nothing.

\* \* \*

'Naomi!'

David retraced his steps back to where Naomi had been, calling her name over the crashing water. Reaching the place where he had last seen her, something brushed up the side of his boot. Something hard and heavy. He knelt down and pulled Naomi's torch out of the water.

The bulb had smashed.

Gingerly he caressed the walls with his light as the tunnel forked into a junction. The second fork was narrower, funnelling downward, and it was a source of rushing water. David must have missed it by dumb luck.

'Naomi?'

His voice sashayed in the tunnel, splitting off down each of the forks, as he cast his eyes ahead for a glimpse of the rogue torchlight. Sure enough, he saw it gambolling in the dark, before it vanished, as if a firefly were snuffed out.

He steeled himself, taking a breath to replace fear with a helpful high alert earned through military training. His entire body pulsed with adrenaline. Though the element of surprise was blown, David had the advantage: he was right now standing between the killer and the way out. And, even if there was another escape route, he'd taken Larwood's car keys.

With a quickening heartbeat, he threw the light at his watch.

*Twenty minutes left.*

David cupped his hands and called out for Naomi. He strained desperately to hear her voice, but there was no sign of anything beyond the river's tumult. He listened to the water cascading down the throat of the tunnel. What followed was a rumble at the edge of hearing, of run-off spilling into the Fleet.

Then a new sound reached his ears. A groan swelled to a roar as water gushed through surrounding grates. In a break between surges, he hurried back down the tunnel, muscle memory seizing control of his body. He was the one who had convinced Naomi to come here. He was damned if he'd let her die for him.

The pipe levelled out suddenly, and he stepped into empty air. David dropped several feet before landing on the floor of a damp stone passage that curled off to the left. His legs buckled with a wet thud.

He straightened up. He was now slick with slime from the waist down. The water here haemorrhaged from grilles — it belched its way into the channel of water flowing along the curved passageway. The darkness here seemed penetrable somehow. His eyes were slowly adjusting, so that shapes formed outlines and monstrous shadows.

One of these shadows moved.

David froze, muffling torchlight with the palm of his hand. His lungs throbbed painfully but he didn't dare to breathe as he watched the shape ribbon up the wall. There could be no shadow without light. It had to be the killer's torch — the shadow's owner must be lying in wait. David pictured Larwood waiting to pounce, but he couldn't know for certain if that was who awaited him. He was sure of one thing: if he advanced, he could be walking into a trap.

But there was no way back now. There was only forwards.

A sound like an amplified whip-crack pierced the empty air. David recognized it as the sound of a gunshot ringing out. Its echo filled the passage and swept over his head. His ears rang with the sound.

David ducked on impulse. It took several moments to acknowledge he hadn't been hit. The gunshot must have come from somewhere up ahead.

There came a pattering and a splashing that grew into a rumble like that of an infantry charge. A large black mass surged up the passage towards him. The rats scurried and screamed at his sight. They parted like the Red Sea as they clawed up through the grilles on either side of the pipe, dislodging globules of waste that fell into the water.

Suddenly, a freezing hand shot out and clamped over his mouth.

David cried out, but the hand muffled the sound. As he wheeled around, Naomi's face emerged through the gloom, her face grey in the stark light. She had the index finger of her free hand pressed against her lips. Slowly, soundlessly, she lowered the same finger and pointed.

There was a cavity up ahead. It was a kind of yawning space in the ironwork, a baroque wormhole. The space beyond dropped down again, and opened out into what appeared to be a vast and dimly lit chamber.

'Down there,' she breathed.

David didn't look back, concerning himself with Naomi. 'Are you hurt?'

She shrugged with one shoulder. A glance at her left arm and a scrunch of her face implied the injury wasn't serious, though it looked to him like a dislocation. Before she could say anything, a thunderous crack rang out, followed by a hail of rubble, as a second gunshot struck the wall up ahead.

'Come out, come out. I know you're up there. Show yourself.' It was Larwood catcalling them from somewhere in the chamber.

David locked eyes with Naomi and found himself caught between fear for their lives, and what it would mean if he didn't confront—

'Show yourself!' Larwood's voice came again.

Naomi read his thoughts and shook her head wilfully. 'David — don't you dare.' She clawed at his shoulder using the hand of her good arm, but David peeled away from her grasp.

Her voice swelled as loud as she dared to raise it. 'You fucking idiot, get back here.'

But David wasn't listening anymore. A red mist had descended, and his gaze was fixed on the space and the drop down into the chamber. He crept silently towards it, gauging Larwood's position before he stepped down and finally entered.

The space beyond was cavernous and murky, yet somehow the dark was incomplete. Where was the light coming from? The whole place danced with an iridescent glow like moonlight viewed through carnival glass, yet there was no source of light to be seen. He was unable to account for the chamber's size or the pillars of stone that disappeared into a high ceiling. Gnarled walls bore the avatar of Old Father Thames, the river god's flowing beard and hair like the water itself. The Fleet, meanwhile, was busy spewing into a large black pool. Stone borders diverted the run-off from a tributary that seeped into a culvert.

Movement drew his eye to something trenched in the wall on his right. David looked up in amazement. It was not a cistern that released the irrigated water. It was a wheel.

The pillars created countless blind spots, and David studied the few feet between himself and the nearest pillar. If he dashed out, Larwood might chance a shot. Yet there was no sign of him nor any sound but for the headwater now gathering in the chamber. Why had Larwood made no move to attack?

The nerves in David's body tingled. He'd relished showing Lex hidden things like the secret place, but he had never been foolhardy enough to actually *enter* the tunnel.

It was startling to think of how Lex and murder now seemed to occupy the same thought. She existed in the past tense now, as if she was already dead. For a moment, his courage was caught up in premature grief.

David came to his senses, narrowing his eyes, searching for the smallest sign of movement. But there was nothing.

Rooting around for rubble in the water at his feet, he fished out a loose stone and quietly lobbed it into the chamber. It plopped loudly near the culvert.

There came a second splash.

His eyes shot to the place where the stone fell. Nothing. He edged round the pillar, until the place he thought Larwood might be hiding ranged into view.

Over his shoulder, he heard a chamber load.

'Don't move.'

Recognizing the public-school accent, David raised his hands and turned around.

He found himself staring down the barrel of a Glock semi-automatic.

# CHAPTER THIRTY-FOUR

David looked carefully between Larwood and the outstretched gun, calculating whether he could disarm Larwood
from where he was standing. Larwood himself was gaunt like
a starved dog, nostrils red-raw from cocaine abuse. The swelling on his jaw had not gone down from where Lex had dealt
him her fierce blow.

That did not stop the smile spreading across his chapped
lips, or the glee that burned in those dark and wretched eyes.
When Larwood finally spoke, his voice was husky and tight.
'Come alone?'

David nodded. The distance from the chamber to the
entrance of the tunnel was long, but he scarcely believed
Larwood hadn't heard him searching for Naomi.

He kept his eyes fixed on the man in front of him,
not daring to glance back to where she was hiding. Larwood
seemed to accept his response, but more than once David saw
the man's finger tighten on the trigger.

'That was you on the bridge tonight, wasn't it?'

'I just want to talk.' David began to circle away from
Naomi's position with small sidesteps, adrenaline reanimat-
ing old muscles. Larwood's gun arm hinged with each step,

shifting the weapon's axis away. David felt those desperate eyes tracking his every move.

'*Talk*? I don't even know who you are.' The cut-glass derring-do had all but disappeared. His voice jangled with something akin to panic.

David stared. This was not what he'd anticipated. He had assumed he was being manipulated — that this was part of a plan devised by a criminal mastermind. Larwood's use of the Fleet confirmed it. Hadn't it? David had been convinced the moving parts were the sum of something greater. He'd decided as much when he found the case at the dock. Naomi's story about the land grab and the raid had cemented the idea that a higher power was involved. Yet facing down this man-child made it impossible to believe. Larwood had the look of someone floating in the gut of a nightmare. There was an eerie, fevered expression on his face. His mouth hadn't formed a smile so much as a crack. The hollow of his throat was panting fast, and when he spoke, his voice was crooked and coked-up.

'You followed me here.'

'No,' David answered.

'Don't lie to me.'

'I found your car,' David said. 'I told you, I just want to talk.' It was an effort to keep his own voice steady.

Larwood's eyes flicked away for a moment before snapping back to David. His gun arm straightened, and David watched the muzzle, its black point just visible in the gloom.

'This wasn't my fault,' Larwood trilled through ragged breath. 'They wanted the coke. Begged me for it. It was just a bit of fun.'

David winced at the words. 'Listen to me,' he said. 'I'm a police officer. I can help you . . . and there's no chance of getting out of here with that gun trained on me. You know that.'

'I can't go to prison,' he snarled.

'I hear you.' David tried to focus on the eyes behind the barrel. It was difficult to master his adrenaline with Larwood waving the gun about like a toy. A gun he knew how to use.

'You were there,' croaked Larwood. 'At the club. Night of the storm. You worked it out.' He sounded more interested than angry.

'Not all of it,' David admitted. 'Not then.'

'I never thought Lex would get hurt.' Larwood flinched at her name. 'She wasn't supposed to be there. I need you to believe me.'

'Who wasn't supposed to be there — Lex?' David's nails dug into his palms. 'Where is she now?'

'I wanted to keep her safe.'

David took an imperceptible half-step forward. 'You don't need to do this. We can help.'

'What does it matter?' Larwood shook his head. 'It's gone too far.'

David could hardly believe the gall of what he was saying. Larwood's eyes shone in the relative gloom, but it was hard to tell whether they flashed with tears or another symptom of his madness.

'Those girls overdosed,' David said. 'That's how they died. Right?'

Larwood nodded.

'So you didn't kill them. It's not first degree.'

'I'll still go to prison for manslaughter . . . Hey!' Larwood had noticed David step forward, and raised the gun higher. 'Stay where you are!'

'All right. Just keep calm. I'm worried for Lex, same as you.'

'Shut your mouth.'

David had miscalculated. He realized relations were deteriorating, and added a note of agency in his voice. 'You can still turn this around, Piers.'

Larwood faltered at the recognition of his name. 'I can't. It's not that simple. You don't understand.'

'Make me understand it, then.' David waved his upraised hands, coaxing Larwood to lower the gun. 'We want the same thing right now. Think about Lex. She loves you, doesn't she?'

Larwood stared. He tried to take a deep breath but his chest was heaving.

'Well, doesn't she?' David pressed. 'If you love her back, then come with me. If you won't do it for yourself, at least do it for her.'

Larwood's face twisted. 'It *was* for her!' he screamed. 'All of it. I did it to protect her. What was I supposed to do?' He was making frantic, fitful noises halfway between grief and laughter. David saw in Larwood's eyes the same faraway, puzzled expression of a soldier in the last seconds before their knees gave out and they fell sprawling to bleed out on the ground. Perhaps Larwood had realized there was nothing good in his past that could be rescued, and nothing in his future that was worth trying to save.

David ran frantic calculations. How far he was from the gun now, the rounds left in the magazine, if Larwood had it in him to pull the trigger. How much time he thought they had left before water came rushing into the chamber . . .

'Son. You have got to tell me what's going on,' he insisted. 'Please. Tell me where she is.'

'You're too late.' Larwood blinked once, his eyes now brimming with tears. He stepped aside.

Behind him a human form lay in the shallows, a mane of bleach-blonde hair roving about in the water.

# CHAPTER THIRTY-FIVE

A bomb went off in David's chest.

The body lay face down, so that all he could see was the back of the victim's head. By some cruel trick of the light, it looked as if she were breathing.

*Don't let it be her. Please, don't let it be her.*

He waded towards the shape, feeling as he did so as if he were sinking. He took a slow and steady breath, imagining himself underwater, trying to summon the nerve needed to dive into the blackest black.

He reached the body. Under his gloved hand, the hair swam as the victim sloshed onto her back with a wet thump. David's eyes clamped shut, until, with an effort of will, he was ready to look. He gazed into the glassy eyes.

They did not belong to Alexis Cade.

'You're too late.'

He heard Larwood's voice come at him. The words were wretched, as if it were an entirely reasonable remark, and there was no evidence of remorse in those eyes. This girl was the fourth to have perished by Larwood's hand.

It seemed incredible to David that, only days before, her remains would have meant nothing. She would have just been another Gucci to him, another find. But his apathy had disappeared. He tenderly lifted the hair away from the cold face, then closed the dead girl's eyes with his thumb and forefinger. Her features were still and lifeless, and all the more desolate because she was young. A pendant floated around her neck, the rose-gold letters bunched up in the hollow of her throat.

Zosia. Her name was Zosia.

David turned slowly back around to face Larwood, unmoved by the madness he saw in those eyes. 'You,' he said, 'are going to tell me whether or not you've killed my little girl.'

The words bounced off the walls. His voice sounded strange to his own ears as he appraised the killer with fresh eyes. Any question of leniency had been shot to pieces. A killer was all Larwood was to him now: no more than a murderer brandishing a gun. Four lives ended too soon because of him.

'Where is she.' It was not a question. David stepped forward. He was only a few feet away now. The shaking gun was still out of reach, but he could move fast, disarm the little shit, break his arm and then he'd—

'I could just shoot you,' breathed Larwood. 'No one knows you're here.'

'Why haven't you?' David already knew the answer, and why Larwood hadn't taken a shot when David had first arrived. It was one thing to brandish a gun, another to actually use it.

Larwood quickly wiped the drug-addled sweat off his face with his sleeve. 'She hated you. Never had a good thing to say about Mum and Dad. She wanted to leave with me, you know. Leave London for good.'

'Where is she?'

'She said she didn't love you. Guess she saved it all up for me.'

'Stop talking.'

'She said she hoped you'd drown on the job. At least then she could live off you.'

David stepped forward, but Larwood raised the gun higher.

'I asked you a question,' David snarled. 'And I'm not going to ask you again. Where is my daughter?'

'You think I *know* that?' Larwood roared, his own anger bubbling up like lava. 'You should be on your knees. Begging me not to kill you.'

As Larwood waved the gun, David saw his chance and lunged — but Larwood's free hand came down hard and collided with David's face. Brightly coloured sparks of light fountained in the darkness. Beyond them, Larwood was laughing. 'Get on your knees.'

David lowered himself carefully, the cold water lapping at his lower half. He took the opportunity to lower his hands too, the better to steady himself. Beneath the waterline, his gloved fingers felt for the knife on his belt.

'Now beg.' Larwood was trembling like an electric wire with too much current running through it.

'Kill me first,' growled David. 'What are you waiting for?'

'*No.*' Larwood's wheeled the gun around like a compass-needle. 'You're going to beg me not to tell you what it was like with her. How much better it feels with a virgin.'

David's fingers closed around the knife handle, inches above the inlaid blade. He meant to disarm Larwood with it, drag him out of the tunnel by force if he had to.

He caught movement. Naomi closing in on Larwood from behind. His pulse quickened. He wanted her to back off, to insist that he had his hand on the knife.

Larwood ducked back, seeming to have sensed her, causing her to misjudge the blow. And suddenly, as his gun arm sprang back up, another gunshot rang out.

# CHAPTER THIRTY-SIX

It was as if an electric plug had been pulled out of the wall. David met the gun barrel and raised it high. The punch from his free hand broke Larwood's nose, and the pain of impact spread across his knuckles with a sickening crunch.

But Larwood fought back, hurling himself at David, and with a jolt — and a shock — he landed on David's knife.

Larwood never heard the deep *throom* quake through the chamber. He never saw the wheel begin to turn, or water retch into the pool and swell all around him. The last thing he saw was the hilt of David's knife slide out of his abdomen as he staggered away from the blade.

David watched with horrified triumph as the Glock folded through Larwood's fingers and crashed into the pool. Larwood blinked, unbreathing. Then he fell backwards into the rising water. He vanished before David had a chance to react.

Bile thickened suddenly in David's mouth. The knife had been self-defence. Even as he conjured the alibi, the word rang like a bell in his mind: *Murder.*

The truth felt like a finger dulling the knife still in his outstretched hand. He'd defended himself, and in so doing, he'd allowed the worst to happen.

David frantically searched the water around him. The dark shape loomed into view, but it was steadily catching an eddy forming in the water. David thrashed his way to it and grabbed the shape with both hands. Larwood's eyes were wide open, motionless in death.

David panicked. They had to get the cadaver out of here. Zosia's too. It was all the evidence they had to defend themselves.

But the chamber was dark, and the water strong. It was pulling Larwood's corpse further away in a gruesome tug of war.

*Throooom.*

'David!'

He wheeled around to Naomi behind him. She had made her way back to the raised opening of the chamber.

'We need to—'

'There's no time!' she barked. 'Get up here now.'

David didn't listen. He spun back to the body. He was still holding the lapels of Larwood's jacket with his hands.

Asked later why he did it, David could not have produced an answer. It made sense in the moment to take the phone and the bulging leather wallet from the inside pocket as if that were a consolation prize. The phone itself was retrofitted with a waterproof case — one of those fully enclosed with a seal clip. It was all David could do to hope the device was still operational. Slipping it inside a waterproof membrane pouch in his suit, David averted his eyes as he let go. The corpse was absorbed by the current so fast, it may as well have been swallowed by a hole in the earth.

*Throooom.*

'David!'

He turned back to Naomi and thrashed his way towards her. The rising water was spilling over into the culvert now, and when he cast his eyes around the chamber, David saw the film of slime on the walls where water had slicked the chamber's full height. His heart began to race. If they did not get back to the raised tunnel, the whole chamber would flood around them.

*Throoooom.*

Somewhere far away, he heard Naomi's anguished yell.

The water was gathering almost to his waist. The eddy current at the Fleet river mouth was much stronger now, writhing and twisting as David fought his way in Naomi's direction.

She'd managed to hoist herself up into the tunnel, and was reaching for David's hand. His attempt to grab it failed as rushing water threw him off-course. Suddenly their hands collided. Naomi howled at the shock to her shoulder, as he hauled himself to his feet, and quickly met her eyes.

'Your umbilical,' she hissed. 'Give it to me.'

David did as he was told. He prised his ballistic vest apart to reach the Arvest underneath, and the umbilical wire pleated in a pouch.

Naomi snatched it. She laced it out to its full length so the wire was unencumbered. Taking her own, she tied them off. Then she met his eyes for an awful moment.

*Throoooooooooom.*

'Brace yourself,' he said.

Suddenly, with an almighty groan, the wheel spun through its axis, and a solid wall of water charged into the chamber below. The level rose so fast, it surged towards the chamber's opening until the culvert sucked it out of the chamber again.

It was all they could do to wade back up the tunnel as the flume flowed down in the opposite direction. Once or twice, Naomi staggered against the force, and David had to prop her up and push her on.

The last thing he saw as they hurried back up the tunnel was the face of Old Father Thames emerging from the waterline, absolving him with moist stone eyes.

# CHAPTER THIRTY-SEVEN

Dawn had broken with a blaze of red fire by the time they reached the car.

Escaping the tunnel had brought them onto the silent Heath just as the night waned and shadows were forming up. It wouldn't do to take Naomi home, or even to the Royal Free Hospital nearby. There would be too much explaining to do. Besides, David needed her, now more than ever — he knew what had to be done.

He drove at speed through the streets, empty but for the night buses and early joggers, and made it back to Wapping without incident. There was no one around as he hurried her into the building and helped her up the stairs.

Once they were inside his apartment, David lowered her to the sofa. Naomi's face was the colour of a day-old bruise. She hadn't spoken a word during the drive, but now looked at him with a fixed and fierce expression. He fetched a blanket, a tube of Deep Heat and a first aid kit from the bathroom. Returning to her side, he caught himself reaching for the knife sheathed in his belt. He went to retrieve a kitchen knife instead and cut Naomi's vest away from her upper body.

Naomi played with the edge of a blanket as he examined her shoulder properly. It had the chemical smell of the bleach Lex used to dye her hair.

'That shoulder's dislocated,' he told her. 'I need to pop it back in.'

Naomi looked askance.

'It's going to hurt,' he continued. 'You might black out. But once it's done—'

She nodded once before turning away. 'Do it.'

David repositioned himself beside her and took the wrist of her injured left arm. He needed to guide the ball of her arm bone back into her shoulder socket and there was no way to do it without . . .

He tugged, *hard*.

Naomi groaned through clenched teeth. She had just time to catch the apologetic look in David's eyes. Then she passed out.

David checked her heart rate before doing anything else. He tied a sling with hemp from the first aid kit. Then, repositioning Naomi so that she lay on her side on the sofa, he raised her arm carefully into the sling.

Afterwards, he washed up at the kitchen sink. Tending to Naomi had aggravated the nicks on his hands. His lips drew back in a grimace as he watched thin threads of blood swirl down into the drain. He allowed himself a moment to relish the warm water. The heat was comforting, and steam rose slowly up into his face. Despite the torrid warmth of the night he'd been seizing up where the wetsuit had clung to his skin — to feel something other than that discomfort was a genuine novelty.

He meant to leave Naomi to rest, but felt he had to check for open cuts. After all, they had spent a night wading around in what was once the Fleet ditch, a notorious cesspit of disease. Gently, taking care not to jar her injured side or cross any boundaries, he determined Naomi had no other wounds. Her wet suit was soaked through however, and he needed to keep her warm. He used the kitchen knife to cut the suit away from her top half. He replaced it with a dry T-shirt and covered her legs with the blanket. Finally, he went to the bathroom to peel himself out of his own suit, which held fast to him like a second skin.

He ran a shower and stayed under the water until warmth returned to his bones. The trauma of the night refused to budge from his brain, curling around him with the steam that filled the bathroom. How long would it take for divers to dredge Larwood's body? Would Shannon Baines requisition Zosia's corpse if they found it as well?

What worried his conscience most was the notion that finding Lex was becoming a faraway dream. He felt no closer to tracking her down. The idea that she might be safe — despite police involvement — was starting to slip away from the high shelf in his mind.

He hadn't meant for Larwood to die. Death was too good for him. He'd deserved to serve out his days in a cell. David had only wanted to disarm him, drag him out of the tunnel, force him to take him to Lex. But it seemed like Larwood really had not known where Lex had gone. If that were true, it meant pieces of the jigsaw were still missing. *She* was still missing.

He stepped out of the shower, pulverized with exhaustion: a pale imitation of the man he once was now staring out of the mirror. He changed into dark jeans and the top he was wearing on the day Audrey had come to the flat. He dumped the scuba gear into the bath before returning to check on Naomi.

Sunlight was streaming through the window by now. The chop of an India 99 police helicopter fanned the landscape as the aircraft spiralled overheard.

David took out his phone. He didn't expect it to work after his ordeal in the sewers, but his membrane suit had done the job of protecting it. There were no messages from Lex, so there was nothing to keep his eyes on the screen. David put his phone down on the coffee table, then unzipped the pocket of the membrane suit to retrieve Larwood's device.

*Not Larwood's anymore.*

It was strange to perceive the limits of your own guilt. It was like a concussion catching up to his brain.

Had he killed Larwood simply by holding the knife? But the victim was himself a killer. Where did that leave him?

David didn't know. He would face the truth about Larwood's death later.

He unclipped the seal and pulled the handset out of the sleeve. Although the case was cracked, the phone still seemed to be working. He realized now that it was a popular device for Britain's criminal element. It used an instant messaging service so heavily encrypted, any message caught in transit couldn't be deciphered. David grimaced. He'd need a digital forensic scientist to crack the phone, and a gifted one at that. It was a tantalizing notion that information on the device might reveal his daughter's location.

Although the phone seemed to work, there was no way to tell if it had been damaged by the water. To be on the safe side, David found a mixing bowl in the kitchen, placed the phone at the bottom of the bowl, and emptied a full packet of rice over it. The phone had been through a great deal, and he'd need to pass it on when the time came.

David paused. What now? Wait for Naomi to come round? Wait for the police to show up? If the detectives had continued their investigation, and considered Lex an asset they could not afford to lose, it was likely that he'd incriminated himself with his actions. Baines could charge him with anything she liked — there was an embarrassment of riches at this point.

A soft groan sounded from the sofa as Naomi stirred. David looked out at her. *I should have taken her to the hospital.* Of course — what was he thinking, bringing her here? Would Miles have tried to call? Would he have contacted the police himself? Would Shannon hear of it if he did? It all felt like a chain with too many links.

David idly flipped through Larwood's wallet as he mulled it all over. There was nothing much in it except for a mangy tenner, several bank cards and a driving licence.

The premier bank cards, including a Coutts account, were all registered in Larwood's name. That card looked like it had been used recently, but not for financial transactions. A long white skid stretched along its rim — the hallmark residue of recreational drug use. David studied the licence. The headshot was years old, but all the same, Larwood's quiff had risen to the occasion.

The image was suddenly replaced by a vision of Larwood's face as he fell away into the water. David felt sick, remembering that final moment, that he hadn't managed to rescue him, and worst of all, that the answer to his questions had died with Larwood.

*Where. Is. Lex.*

The fleeting hope she was alive and safe crashed against his fears as he thought about everything that had happened over the past three days. He looked down at his hands.

The discolouration. Somehow, it was still there. And beneath that, the smudged shape of a stallion.

*She's dead, and you know it.*

The voice was no louder than the flap of a humming-bird's wing.

*She's gone. It's over. You have nothing left.*

David laced his fingers and pressed them to his mouth. Tears channelled new veins on his cheeks. He stumbled away from Naomi's sleeping form and into the bedroom, where he could weep. Away from it all.

Inside the room, pale light from the laptop flickered its ominous glow. The laptop's fan was spinning loudly, filling the room with noise. The CCTV footage he had left behind was still running. Playing out, in real time.

Now he remembered: he'd not switched it off when he'd left to recruit Naomi. He peered at the image — at the private bar of The Pale Horse. The display in the left of the frame read:

*C000346_Pale_Horse*
*QFD_QFD_VIPBar.mov*

The time was 01.15. David strained to remember what time it had been on when he left the flat. 19.01 — that was it. Six hours had passed. In that time, everything had changed.

On-screen, a hard case lay open on the floor, and one brown parcel sat in the middle of the oval table. It was torn open. Cocaine had been cut on the surface of the glass, beside a tumbler full of cocktail straws.

Four girls surrounded the table. The flaxen-haired girl on the left was wearing a black cocktail dress. The second girl was taller, also blonde, also in a cocktail dress. David had last seen the third girl supine on a gurney in the forensic lab at Scotland Yard's Pathology Unit. Zosia's rose-gold necklace was just visible against the grain. As he watched her take a straw from the tumbler, David's stomach rose to somewhere just above his heart and hung there, knotted like a wet rag.

He was about to watch them die.

# CHAPTER THIRTY-EIGHT

*The private bar was warm. The ornamental bracket lamps were turned down low, though the bar itself was festooned with a blaze of light. The assembled party put out a good deal of heat themselves, cheered on by the booze they had drunk, and the perfume of spirits and cocktails lingered heavily in the air. There was a good deal of lounging and draping but the girls took no notice of the temperature, not even when it shot up as Alexis Cade entered the room.*

*'Get up! Get out of here!'*

*Lex circled the table but the girls howled with laughter in their intoxicated state. Their host was paying their rate and then some to have a good time — who were they to argue?*

*Piers Larwood followed Lex into the room.*

*'What's that?' Lex jabbed a finger at the cocaine on the table.*

*'Just a bit of fun.' Larwood adjusted his dicky bow for good measure but the gesture had the reverse effect on her.*

*'Are you serious right now?'*

*'Oh, will you give it a rest?' Larwood kicked the door closed behind him. 'I didn't ask you to come here tonight.'*

*'Why wouldn't I?' she spluttered. 'You're supposed to be my boyfriend.'*

*'You really don't have to give it a label,' purred Larwood. He was already settling down and draping an arm around a girl.*

'Don't touch her!' Lex shouted. She felt confused and angry, but wasn't sure what to do about either. Instead she danced on the spot.

'I said relax,' Larwood insisted in a mocking tone. 'Why are you even here?'

'Fine. You want to know? I'm done.'

'No, you're not.'

'Aren't you listening? This is too much, it's not what I want.'

Larwood laughed. A high, cold laugh that shocked even the party guests. Only Lex seemed unmoved by it. 'Come on, don't be like that.'

'It's not a joke, Piers. I don't want to be with you anymore.'

'Where would you be without me?' Larwood growled. 'Whatever happened to getting away from it all?'

'Like I'd do that, now I know what you get up to when you're down here. Do you think I'm impressed by it all?' Lex was waving her arms around the room. 'How long has this been going on?'

'What does it matter? It doesn't mean anything — hey, where do you think you're going?' Larwood sprang to his feet as Lex reached the door and pressed his palm against it. She resisted, and he grabbed her and shoved her backwards into the room.

Lex gaped at him. She had to work hard so as not to reveal the extent of her fear. She didn't want to give him the satisfaction. Nevertheless she was afraid — and not for the first time.

'Get out of my way, Piers.'

'Why? Where are you going?'

'Where do you think? I have to go get tested. You've been paying for it all this time, I need to make sure you haven't given me something.'

'Sure — like it won't be the other way around.'

'Fuck you.'

'Excuse me?' That had done it. Glowering madness reflected in his eyes. 'Watch your mouth. This is my club. You don't get to talk to me like that.'

'You've been cheating on me and paying for it. I'm not doing this with you. Let me go — please.'

One of the girls at the table spoke up. 'Yeah, let her go. We can still have a good time.'

'I'm not paying you to talk,' Larwood barked.

The girl shrugged. She nodded at the table to show him they had finished cutting the coke. She was busy handing out straws. 'Let us know when you're done.'

'Help yourself,' Larwood told her before he turned back to Lex. 'Now then. You're not going anywhere until you apologize.'

'Apologize?' Lex looked at him in utter disbelief. 'What did I ever see in you? I don't even know anymore.'

'Well, I know what I saw in you,' Larwood said through a smirk. 'Shall I tell you?'

'I want to leave. Move away from the door.'

'No. I want you to say sorry. I want to hear you say it—'

With a sudden burst of rage she'd no idea she was capable of, Lex got right up in his face. 'I'm not going to ask you again,' she snarled. 'Fucking move.'

But Larwood didn't. His face had blanched into a mask of horror.

A wrenching, choking, gurgling sound rose behind Lex. The girl who had spoken before was beginning to convulse. The others had started to scream. The next instant, they all began spasming with the same gruesome violence, thrashing about as if mauled by an invisible force.

One of the girls met eyes with Lex. Blood was gushing from her mouth and nose like a ghastly crimson projectile.

Lex covered her mouth in a silent scream. Bile rose in her throat as she watched the full scale of the horror unfold.

Lex had no idea how long it took for three of the girls to crumple on the floor. She didn't understand how it had happened at all. She only knew that they were dead. She could see it in their eyes, the light in their pupils shrinking to pinheads before they vanished altogether.

The fourth and final girl — the one with the rose-gold necklace — was barely alive. She was caked in blood and mucus, and when she tried to stand, her knees gave out. A final macabre second of life ticked by. And then she fell. She was dead before she hit the floor.

Lex was sobbing. The events were already burning themselves on her mind like cattle brands.

Larwood was standing unevenly in the centre of the room, his back to Lex. His bravado had dissipated. In fact, he was paralyzed

237

*by the display before him. He had his back turned, so Lex couldn't see his face.*

*But she could see the door.*

*She had to get away. To the police, to her mum, to the clinic around the corner.* Anywhere *but here. She scrambled to her feet and made a mad dash for the exit.*

*She heard him, felt his hand on her as she ran down the corridor. In a whirl of frenzied panic, she span round, threw her weight into her arm, and struck Larwood across the jaw. Then, with a burst of strength, she broke free of his grip.*

*And she didn't stop running.*

\* \* \*

The chilling reproduction was over.

In a matter of minutes, David had seen everything unfold. The time signature was coming up on 01.19. His heart beat a loud tattoo in his chest. The only way to calm the sensation was to remember this had all happened days ago. He couldn't change the past. The only justice he could promise the dead was the knowledge they were not Jane Does.

One question rattled through his brain. Where had Lex gone next? To the police?

On the screen, Piers Larwood returned to the room, kneading his jaw with his hands.

*Of course.* The memory shot across David's thoughts like an arrow. His finger scoured the touchpad, raising footage he'd already bookmarked. A window shot open. There was Lex in the hallway, spinning, punching Larwood before running off.

David felt a pang of pleasure as the puzzle pieces fell into place. This footage was giving him the same moment from a new angle. There was Piers wandering the room in a panic. Taking a phone — the encrypted phone — from his pocket, dialling a number, pressing it to his ear.

David paused the footage. A strange sound was coming from the front room.

It was a bowl of rice shuddering on a worktop.

# CHAPTER THIRTY-NINE

The bowl rumbled with dogged insistence, the ringing phone causing grains of rice to jerk about on the surface.

David glanced over at the sofa, but Naomi didn't stir. The bowl was sidewinding across the worktop and teetering close to the edge, and he lurched forward to catch the bowl with both hands. He fished about, skittering rice grains over the floor as he pulled out the handset.

The name on the screen sent a shockwave of stunned surprise up the full length of his spine.

David thought fast. If the call finished ringing through, he wouldn't be able to unlock the phone again. He couldn't miss the opportunity. This new lead could be his last chance.

David snatched his own phone from the coffee table and opened the recording app. Then he answered the call.

'*Piers?*'

The caller spoke quietly, collusively. '*You there? Answer me.*'

For a moment, it was as though all the air had been sucked out of the room. The caller's face drifted to the front of his mind like a spectre.

'*Where are you? You haven't been at the club . . .*'

David made sure to breathe heavily into the phone.

The caller seemed to lose patience. '*I don't have time for this. Call me when you're ready to talk.*'

The call ended. The phone locked itself, and there was no hope of accessing it again without help.

When he was sure the caller would not ring back, David ended the recording and made a backup to be sure.

Now the front room was still again, David felt a trickle of dread caress his heart. Though Naomi lay on the sofa in front of him, he forgot about her completely. He took a pen from a drawer in the table, replayed the recording he'd made, and scratched notes into the skin on the back of his hand.

\* \* \*

Naomi opened her eyes. Sunlight shimmered like a polished shield as it spilled through the blinds. She snapped her eyes shut again and lay there, listening, easing recall into her body. Her arm was twinging with surplus pain.

She opened her eyes fully, coming back to her senses. The events of the night before rushed back into her thoughts, as if an invisible dam had been blasted apart.

She thought of Miles, and wondered how she'd ever explain it. That thought brought another kind of pain. She had gone into that tunnel by choice, and the desire to catch a criminal had not been the sole reason. But in the process, she had forgotten about the one person in her life that really mattered: Amy. She didn't want to even think about what would have happened if things had gone badly. Or any worse at least.

Naomi brimmed with shame, finally comprehending the true meaning of Sofia's warning: that she would always act before she stopped to think. Tears sprung in her eyes where emotion quarried the pit in her chest. As she reached to wipe her face, surprise registered as she touched the cotton surface. She was wearing a white T-shirt she didn't recognize, and it was several sizes too large. She paused, sniffing the fabric. Was that aftershave?

Her fingers slipped under the shirt — David had left her thermal underlayer intact. That was a relief. While she was out, David had put her arm in a sling. As for the rest, her membrane suit had been cut off down to her waist, and he'd tucked the blanket about her legs. There was a first aid kit open on the coffee table in front of her.

She must have passed out from the pain.

Hauling herself to a sitting position, Naomi glanced around the room.

'David?'

Her voice carried, and there was no one there to receive it.

She groggily brought herself to standing. She was still wearing the lower half of the wetsuit. She wondered if he'd brought her clothes up from the car, and whether she'd be able to get out of the bottom half of the wetsuit one-handed.

She carried herself to the bathroom and discovered David's scuba gear piled up in the bath, as if he himself had melted down to a puddle. But David wasn't here. There was no one here at all.

She returned to the living room, drawn by the noise from behind the bedroom door. A dull, thin whine, almost below the threshold of hearing.

She was aware that David had left her alone, and though she was in an unfamiliar place, that had to mean that he trusted her. Was she now about to violate that trust by investigating the bedroom?

The noise continued, and curiosity got the better of her. With an intake of breath, she twisted the doorknob.

The door crept open.

The room inside was an assault on the senses. It was a floor-to-ceiling mirage of pictures, printouts and photos. The bedroom itself was dark, but blue light bathed the walls, and the air was close and thick.

The laptop continued to whir loudly in the corner of the room — there was a written checklist beside it, with numbers crossed off in red pen.

Naomi stared at the wall, transfixed by the blueprints, notes and arrows. Dozens of photographs were pinned everywhere, and she recognized the faces: DCI Shannon Baines, Commander Roy Bishop, and even Captain Lynch himself was up there.

She also recognized Lex, in a Polaroid frayed at the edges, fastened to the wall in such a way that drew everything to its orbit. She vaguely recognized the photo as the one David kept in his locker.

In her mind's eye, Naomi imagined the police breaking down the door to the apartment. They would find this room. This shrine. David's heart for all to see.

For the first time, she felt she understood him. David had taken his daughter's disappearance as seriously as any criminal investigation, and it showed — the work he'd done here was *astounding*.

She thought of Amy again and wondered what was happening. Why hadn't Miles called her? He should have been on the phone by now, making frantic calls to friends and family and the Wapping Police switchboard. It was either that or he'd finally given up on the idea that she could be trusted.

She didn't like that. She should do something about it. But she stayed where she was, staring at the wall. This room was proof that she and David had been of one mind all along. That his own impulse to come through at the hour of need, perhaps to demonstrate devotion, was something she understood better than most.

This was who he really was.

As it transpired, they'd both had something to prove. By identifying the victims and proving how they died, she'd meant to weight the scale of justice in her favour. David had taken the baton and run with it. But the lack of discipline was plain. There were too many assumptions and not enough craft. There were Post-it notes everywhere, covered in theories. The links he'd drawn were mostly tenuous, but his questions had a foundation in truth. What was clear was that he hadn't quite managed to pull it all together.

A cursory look at the wall told her she could join the dots, complete the image for him.

*A quick look*, she thought. *Just a peek. Then I'll call Miles.*

David's laptop glowed with an anaemic image she knew to be closed-circuit camera footage. It showed a room she'd never seen, in a place she didn't know.

But she *did* recognize the four girls lying dead on the floor. And she knew the man standing over them, with a phone pressed to his ear. The on-screen display had the time paused at 01.19.

Was this proof?

She wasn't sure she was prepared to watch women die. It felt like a reconstruction too far — like viewing it would make her complicit in the violence. The coercion felt too close and familiar. But she had to. She knew she did. She felt sick, even as she thought it. They were not people, they were *victims*. Their bodies were *evidence*. She hated herself for dehumanizing them, but it was the only way to be sure.

Naomi's finger pulled the cursor back, and the image began to move.

# CHAPTER FORTY

Naomi watched in horror as the security footage played out on the laptop screen.

Larwood now had the phone to his ear, silenced by an inaudible response at the other end of the line. He was pacing, saying nothing. Whoever was on the phone seemed to be building back Larwood's confidence, because his body language switched from flustered floundering to swaggering reassurance. That notion held when Larwood kicked a victim's outstretched hand away with his boot. The young woman's life, along with three others, had ended a matter of minutes earlier, yet it seemed Larwood lacked even the barest shred of remorse. He was now pacing in such a way that revealed his attempt to compartmentalize the problem. Naomi had seen detectives behave in a similar fashion when they were confused by a case and hoped movement would knock their brain out of neutral.

She watched as Larwood faced the doorway and stared at a backlit painting. It took a moment to twig — he wasn't looking at a painting at all. The distinctive serpentine line that ran across its centre could only have been the Thames.

At once he turned and looked right at her. Fright flared in her heart and rose up her throat — except, of course, he was staring into the eye of the camera. She steeled herself, but it proved impossible to ignore the tremor that continued to course through her bones. Something about the way Larwood moved seemed *wrong*. Puppet-like, as if acting upon instruction, or possibly blind obedience.

Naomi decided the person on the phone had devised a set of actions. Larwood was obviously ill-equipped to cover up manslaughter. He was lurching around the room, running his hands obsessively through his hair, before finally checking his watch, and then . . .

He sat down.

*What the hell is he doing?* Impatience heaved in Naomi's chest until it dawned on her that Larwood was waiting for someone to arrive.

She nudged the cursor. The footage leaped forward.

And someone arrived.

She watched the story play out in mortified silence, until events reached an abrupt crescendo, when a large hand rose up to meet the camera lens. With a blow, the image quivered then went black, just as if a light had been turned out.

Naomi understood at last. The whole picture was right here on this tape. And assuming David had watched the same footage, there was no question of where he had gone.

She exhaled, mentally checking herself, as she always did when faced with a straw in the wind. Almost before she had determined her next move, her phone was in her hand, her fingers punching the buttons.

* * *

There was no question the end was in sight.

Larwood's corpse would have swept down the Fleet by now to crash out into the Thames. The sun was climbing in the sky, and it was only a matter of time before the divers picked him up. It seemed likely that when Larwood's failure was discovered, his accomplice would try to adulterate what remained of the trail.

The surveillance tapes proved Lex had managed to escape. That didn't mean she was out of danger, but David was making his next move in the blind faith that she was safe for now. He hoped, in some naive nook of his brain, that the good cops had got to her first. She had, after all, been witness to a terrible crime.

He drove towards Tower Bridge and joined the traffic there, anxiety swelling in the hollow of his throat. For all that, he was starting to feel sanity return to him at last. It was a strange thing, sanity. When it was taken away, you didn't know it. You only really knew when it was restored, like the first dawn chorus of spring.

Because suddenly he *knew*. He understood what had happened — and knowing it rose in the middle of his mind like a column of flame.

Reaching Scotland Yard, he flashed his warrant card and parked in the visitor's bay. It was 8 a.m. — still early, but the area bustled with the parry and thrust of foot traffic.

David lingered on the pavement. He could feel the shape of Larwood's phone in his pocket, which he'd sealed in a freezer bag. In the other pocket, there was the small, flat card with Bishop's phone number. The man's voice echoed in his head. *If you see anything strange, call me. I think we can help each other.*

The last four days felt lifelong, like a nightmare he was only now beginning to stir from. David hoped he was making the sane choice. It was the only rational idea in his head.

'David?'

He spun round with a start. The commander had pulled up in a Mercedes and was beckoning him to the open window.

'Bit early for you, isn't it? You're on suspension, I hear. You should be making the most of it.'

'Sir, I need to talk to you.'

Bishop nodded. 'Yes, thanks for calling. Get in. I need to park.'

David walked around the car. Taking the passenger's seat, he was suddenly conscious of his appearance.

246

'Good god, man. Are you all right?' Bishop had noticed too. 'Who gave you the shiner?'

'Long story,' David said. 'I'll tell you upstairs.'

Moments later, they were driving down a ramp into an underground car park, to a reserved space. The staff lift was manned by a guard, and Bishop greeted him jovially.

*Of course they're on first-name terms.* He should have expected that.

Bishop had David show his warrant card, then motioned him into the lift. They were followed inside by a handful of arriving personnel.

David was all too aware this was the third infiltration he'd carried out in as many days. But standing beside Bishop, surrounded by police officers, and feeling the pull of the rising lift, it didn't seem to matter.

\* \* \*

'I must say, this is a nice surprise.'

Bishop seemed eager to make what felt like small talk as they stepped out of the lift. 'Last I heard, you and Lynch had a spat. Terrible business. I take it you squared it away with him?'

David nodded, straining to play down the limp in his leg as he trailed Bishop across the operations area. He remembered Naomi saying something about the off-site surveillance equipment, and he noticed the function rooms remained empty. The bullpen was otherwise bustling to a comforting degree, dotted with tableaus of coppers getting on, and brimming with the smells of breakfast sarnies and cups of coffee.

David risked a glance over his shoulder, but the door to DCI Baines's office was closed. There was no way of knowing if she was aware he was here. In any event, Bishop was drawing him further away, to a corner office on the other side of the bullpen.

'This is me.' He smiled as he unlocked the door.

The office was bright and airy, and very tidy. David was conditioned to encountering the hallmarks of a workhorse copper: the overburdened paper tray, fat stacks of outstanding files, platoons of unrinsed coffee mugs. With the plant, the mahogany desk, and the expensive coffee maker, this felt more like a film set that had been recently dressed. Through the blinds, the river glittered in the sun.

David entered gingerly, as if testing a surface layer of quicksand, and took the offered seat. Bishop closed the door, quelling the office din. The blinds were down, the door was shut. The outside world seemed far away. Moments ago, the Criminal Investigation Department had supported life, but now it was as if its occupants had been erased from existence.

David noticed he was holding his breath. The ball of air escaped his lips.

Bishop took a capsule from a jar and popped it into the coffee maker. 'You look like a man that could use a cup of the strong stuff.'

David looked around nervously.

'That shiner of yours,' Bishop continued, 'is there a good story to it?'

*That word again*, David thought. *How easy it is to slip into the sliding scale of police-speak, where cars become 'vehicles' and crooks become 'perpetrators' and family members become 'suspects'. And in this particular case, actual bodily harm had become 'that shiner of yours'.*

'It's nothing,' David answered, absent-mindedly padding his pockets. 'Thank you for meeting me.'

'Nothing doing. I don't sleep much,' Bishop said. 'Time of life, you see. You'll find out soon enough when your best years are behind you. You'll be getting up three times in the night for a piss.'

David frowned at that. These words were all so . . . meaningful. It was as if Bishop knew what was about to happen. Until now, David had been working to secure the man's attention. It was beginning to feel like the tables were turning, and that Bishop had brought him here by design.

The coffee was placed on the desk with a dull *thunk*. 'Drink up,' said Bishop. 'I hear you divers don't take milk.'

David didn't touch the coffee, but Bishop paid that no mind as he circled the desk to his seat.

'I'm glad you called. Appreciate you keeping an eye. I knew I could trust you.' Bishop offered that saccharine smile of his. 'So, what do you have?'

# CHAPTER FORTY-ONE

David's battered eyes darted about the stifling room, look-ing for a reprieve from Bishop's waiting gaze. He suddenly wished the windows were open. The whole place felt close, like the inside of a car on the hottest day of the year.

'So?' Bishop said. 'You mentioned something about DCI Baines?'

The commander's smile was as pleasant as David remembered, his voice charming in an ersatz way. Bishop was apparently unfazed by the temperature in the room.

David felt for the mobile phone in his left pocket before he began. 'The thing is . . . I lied when I told you that. I don't have anything on Baines. But I do have something on you.' He pushed the coffee aside, fished in his right pocket, and placed the freezer bag with Larwood's phone on the table. 'Recognize that?'

Bishop said nothing at all. His eyes came to rest on the phone in the bag.

'I take it you thought the messages would be erased by the burn-on-read feature, but Digital Forensics can recover what's on here.'

'David, I'm not sure I—'

'That was me on the phone this morning.' David recited the conversation from the notes on the back of his hand.

He looked up, bracing himself for the outburst. Instead there was a look of confusion rendering on Bishop's face. When the man shook his head, neck flab rubbed against the pristine collar of his shirt. 'I'm afraid I don't know—'

'Save it. I've seen what Larwood did. And I know my daughter went to The Pale Horse that night.' David kept his voice low and level. 'So I'm going to ask you where she is one time. Because I think you know, and you're going to tell me.'

'I'm sorry, I don't follow.' Bishop's face was a picture of innocence.

'She's fifteen years old. Missing for four days. I know you have something to do with it.'

'With what?' Bishop's voice was courteous, but if his puzzled expression was a ruse, it was impossible to tell. 'I'm sorry to hear about your daughter,' he added, 'but this is the first I've heard of it.'

A cold silence filled the room, each man waiting for the other to draw first blood.

'Did you talk to missing persons?' Bishop said.

'They wouldn't let me file a report.'

'She'll turn up.' Bishop nodded. 'This day and age, it's difficult to disappear. Fifteen, you say? She's a teenager, she'll be using her phone. She'll take cash out at an ATM. Hell — someone's doorbell will have picked her up. Probably going to a skatepark or god knows what kids do these days. Come on, David — we all know what teenagers are like. She's obviously ignoring you.'

David felt the anger bubble up in his throat. 'She went to the club that night. She saw it happen. I've seen it too.'

Bishop frowned. 'What do you mean?' A note of impatience hovered around the question. 'Are you quite all right, David? Because you don't look it. Pardon my French, but you look like shit warmed up. Have you slept at all this week?'

251

David felt the air go out of him. He was suddenly exhausted. He hadn't known what to expect, but he'd not predicted gaslighting like this. 'Enough. This isn't a game. Four women have been killed. I came to you with a smoking gun. The least you can do is be honest with me.'

'I completely agree,' Bishop said. 'Where would you like to begin?'

'Don't think I haven't worked it out,' David spat. 'I've seen the footage, and I found the drugs myself. It all comes back to the consignment.'

'What consignment?'

'The one Naomi Harding was after — back when she worked for you. That's why you asked me to keep tabs on her. You knew things had gone awry — why else would you have come to the dock? You knew, after I'd found that case, making Naomi a diver was the worst mistake you could have made. She only had to prove the girls were poisoned by the same drug and everything would point back to Larwood. And the voicemail proves you were complicit in all of it.'

'Does it?' Bishop's mouth coiled into a thin smile. 'How do you figure that?'

'Because that's your voice on the phone,' David snarled.

Bishop received the accusation gracefully. 'A fine story.'

'It's the truth.' David jabbed a finger at the phone. 'You called him.'

'Yes. I called him.' Bishop's revelation dropped through the air like an anvil. 'But you need to understand, Naomi Harding's failure put lives at risk. Three men from Specialist Firearms Command lost their lives. We've been working round the clock to pick up the pieces ever since.'

'That's a *lie*.'

'Is it? Larwood was in debt to bad apples. He knew we were on to him. He'd forfeit the debt with his life, so he came to us for a plea bargain.'

'I don't believe you,' David insisted. 'Why would he willingly turn himself in?'

'Because he had a police record. Drug offences. Violence towards women. Underage sex. It's been getting longer all the time.'

David shuddered at the mention of this. He thought about Lex again.

'So you see,' Bishop finished, 'when he came to us offering information, we couldn't afford to turn it down. He was going to tell us who he was working for and who had sold him the narcotics. We were going to climb the ladder all the way to the top.' Bishop's smile coiled even higher up his face. 'Perhaps now, you understand my concern. Should anything happen to him . . .'

David gawped into space, unable to believe it. The empty seconds hung in the room like a zeppelin.

'No,' he said at last. 'This isn't true. He would have told me himself, before he—'

'Where is Piers now?' Bishop's eyes were brown and deep-set like a bloodhound.

David didn't answer. He closed his eyes.

'Well? Is he all right?'

Dread was rising up from the black pit where his stomach should have been, sensing Bishop forming barely plausible lies, just enough to buy time . . .

He opened his eyes. Bishop had the freezer bag in his hand. It rustled in his grip, and the phone inside was now leaning precariously into a corner of the plastic.

David leaped up, but Bishop stepped back to make space. 'Where did you get this?'

'Give me the phone.'

'It's inadmissible as evidence, you know. Larwood's a deniable asset. It would be an unlawful extraction of data.'

'You're lying. You've had your hands in this from the start.'

'And who would believe you, David?' Bishop spoke softly. 'In case you didn't notice, you're alone here. You have no tangible proof. No one cares what a frogman thinks.'

Actions seemed to play out in slow-motion. Bishop opened the freezer bag and casually tipped the phone into his open palm. When the commander looked at him, David could see the man's eyes were now sunken, glittering points. He was suddenly aware that no one knew he was here. He was confident he could take on Bishop and best him if it came to that . . . but then what?

Bishop seemed to know it too. He was already prising the phone apart to pluck the SIM card from inside. When he'd retrieved it, David could only watch as he pinched the chip with both hands and snapped it clean in half.

David quashed the impulse to pounce. If a fight broke out, all would be undone. Bishop would claim he was assaulted by an officer, and leniency would follow. He forced himself to remain where he was, looking on impotently as Bishop took the landline and pressed speed-dial. 'Security to Major Crimes, please.'

He replaced the receiver, then turned around. He looked more like an accountant caught with his hands in the till rather than an accessory to murder. 'I'm sorry, David. It's over.'

Bishop's mouth twisted into a smile that went nowhere near his eyes. David stood motionless as he opened the door and stepped through it.

Almost immediately, Bishop stopped in his tracks. Naomi Harding was marching towards him with a calm expression on her face. Accompanying her was Shannon Baines, flanked by a group of officers who filled out her squad.

'What is the meaning of this?' Bishop trilled.

Naomi didn't answer. She didn't have to.

David stepped into the bullpen, and a pair of security guards jostled in. Baines immediately ordered them to stand down. The background noise of the office grew louder, its personnel failing to ignore the unfolding drama.

As Baines closed the ring around Bishop, David produced his mobile from his left pocket. Pointedly, he offered Bishop a view of the screen.

The voice-memo app had been running the whole time.

# CHAPTER FORTY-TWO

Hours later, Shannon Baines settled the remains of the tale in her mind, which Naomi had seen play out on David's laptop.

Bishop had arrived at the nightclub and ordered Larwood to clean up, without so much as a thought for the dead. Minding the camera, he'd shrouded the lens with his hands. Digital Forensics would extract the data, and with any luck, trace DNA found at the club would match the victims' remains. All cameras had been seized from the premises. Even if the built-in mics couldn't pair the audio, David's voice recording would do for Bishop, whose mistakes now showed on his face in lines so deep, they told of a darkness that had been roaring through his head ever since his luck had run out.

The endgame had always been the commissioner's epaulette. That dream had soured when, after four decades of climbing, Bishop had been pipped to the post — by a woman of all things. He had painted himself in his mind as a victim of a politically correct, policy-driven world, destined to be forced out with the next round of compulsory redundancies. That was how the shadow had fallen across the Bath star — not completely black, but enough to make it hard to see.

An office search found stacks of red-bound enforcement warnings, late-payment letters and credit statements locked in a cabinet, the better to silence obscene phrases like 'missed repayments' and 'enforcement by distraint'. After the borrowing and the equity release, wages alone did not satisfy fruit machines and online casinos. With his life's ambition out of the question, the outlook had filled with deepening shades of grey.

The directorate had been skimming off the top for years. One superintendent had even told him about an officer running a firm that laundered cash for criminals. Bishop's cut was little more than a commission in the eyes of those involved. He was not the only one doing it and he would not be the last.

But profit came little and often, and he'd needed more than chicken feed. He'd needed a score large enough to settle the debt quickly. That chance arose when the drug squad seized sixty grand in cash. It was a quiet sting — heaven forbid London had a drugs problem — and Bishop made a skim off the top. The road had become clear.

It was easy. The police persecuted whistle-blowers all the time, creating a climate in which dishonesty and malpractice flourished. It had been a cinch to convince the overzealous Naomi Harding — the squad's then-captain — to go after the cash. There was enough money running through the city that there was always a trail for her to bloodhound her way down, leaving him to strim just a little for himself. Meanwhile he'd kept his hands in quality assurance and performance development reviews, while officers abused their roles via bribery and fraud, and the Met drew fire for its mishandling of sexual misconduct. By reporting the wrongdoing of others, the brass paid Bishop no mind. He'd made partial restitution with the bank by then, but cases for cash seizures took months to build. He couldn't wait. Nor could the debt.

He discovered Naomi had woven a spider's web of intelligence around Greenwich Cruise Terminal. When she'd told him what the consignment was worth, he had greenlit the operation himself. The deputy commissioner had held him to it following the events of that night. Assurances had to be made. So he'd offered up Naomi's head, certain she'd resign as a result.

In the meantime, Bishop had acquired a co-conspirator in his nephew. Larwood was the moistest drip the world had yet produced, but thanks to a dynasty and a trust fund, he had a controlling share in a nightclub. He was also a recreational drug user. Bishop usually abstained from such hedonism, but one bottle of Hennessy cognac was all it had taken for the lad to forget about the cameras. In the morning, there was enough compromising footage to make a deal: Larwood would sell gear in the club and split the readies with his uncle. He'd needed little encouragement — he was welcome to sample the merchandise for himself. Bishop meanwhile took every precaution. He'd installed cameras to cover private and public areas, the better to blackmail the shadier dealers, and Larwood himself if it came to that. He'd reasoned that if a police raid ever did take place, he would be there to intercept the files. He'd insisted Larwood only ever communicate with him using an encrypted phone.

At work, it was easier still. He'd introduced an evidence lock-up for Major Crimes' sole use, an enterprising, much-lauded initiative. After all, evidence was easily tampered with when it was far from reach, and anyway, the police needed to be able to study criminal evidence to help secure their convictions. He'd only had to walk in and doctor the inventory sheet.

Bishop made no concession to guilt of any kind, for in his eyes, these had been victimless crimes. Dead escorts were nothing to him. But there had been a loose end. A witness. He'd had no contingency for that. Nor had he prepared for that witness to be on the police's radar. The hunt for Alexis Cade had locked him out of the National Computer. Bishop had had a vague memory of what a 'conflict on file' meant, but by that point he'd had a bigger problem on his hands. Divers had dredged narcotics from the docks — and he'd needed to cover his back.

He'd remembered Harding's obsession over the purity of the drugs. And she was in prime position, swimming about with those frogmen. Seeking her out, he'd given up Baines as a red herring, doubling up on the ruse by attending to Baines himself. He had to be seen to be helping her. It was why he had brought the club to the DCI's attention, recusing himself on the grounds of Larwood's plea bargain.

Finally, he had reached out to Cade. It was useful to have a fall guy he could easily manipulate, and who better than a diver he could hold cheap?

The whole affair had been knottier than it had any reason to be, but Bishop had had no choice.

He'd hated the odds, and the players even more.

# CHAPTER FORTY-THREE

David stood outside the entrance to Scotland Yard, holding the phone to his ear. Despite Bishop's comeuppance, he
still didn't know where his daughter was, or if she was safe.
Every time he asked, he was rebuffed or asked to go over his
statement for the umpteenth time. Now he had a moment,
he decided to leave her a message.

He expected to hear an automated voice announce that
Lex had diverted the call. There was no bracing himself for the
sound of her voice on the answer machine this time. Everything
he'd meant to say rolled out of him like tumbleweed.

Baines approached, and he offered no indication he was
struggling to keep the emotion down.

She peered into his face. 'I need you to come with me.'

David blinked again, but didn't speak. There was no
reason to stay here. Naomi had gone to the hospital to see
to her arm, and Bishop had been entrusted to the custody
of the anti-corruption branch of the Professional Standards
Department. So he followed her to the unmarked car.

There he sat in the passenger's seat as Baines drove.
They were heading east, skirting the river's north shore. It
was no coincidence that, as they passed Blackfriars Bridge,
she broke the silence at last.

'Long night?'

'Long week.'

Her eyes trained ahead. 'You could be happier. You and Harding blew everything wide open.' She kept her voice level and her tone stern, like she was speaking to a dog too eager to please.

David said nothing. As they passed Wapping he sensed, with a hint of trepidation, that he wasn't going home. He was being taken somewhere.

'We have a lot to talk about,' she said finally.

'Do we?'

'Don't you want to know how it all happened?'

David's composure buckled. His response caught in his throat, as if a fish hook had speared the roof of his mouth and he was trying to speak in spite of it.

Baines continued. 'Much as I'd have loved to stop you running amok — because there's no other way to put it — there are protocols, constraints. Everything that comes with the territory. I knew Bishop was on the make but I had nothing to show for it. Nothing but dozens of junkies and City traders with Nightmare in their blood. I didn't know where to look.'

She glanced at him at the next left turn.

'But you did. You're the one who led me to Larwood. He'd long been subject to a plea bargain, but we didn't know what was happening at the club. Larwood saw fit not to confess at that point. So when Lex approached the police four days ago, everything fell into its rightful place.'

David weighed that up. 'If Larwood kept quiet, how did you find out about the club?'

'Bishop,' she replied. 'Under the guise of helping my investigation. He told me narcotics had finally been traced to Larwood's nightclub.'

'How?'

'The usual channels. Undercover officers, closed-circuit cameras. He even recused himself from the case to gain my trust. But he thought Larwood had dumped the bodies the night they'd died. He thought the drugs had been disposed of. I only figured it out when I saw the tapes for myself. You'd been dredging bodies from the Thames all week. If I wanted to find out what Larwood's plan was, I had to leave you to it.'

David was lost in thought, staring unseeingly through the windscreen. Baines was citing the rule of law particular to one of the Met's directives: to 'achieve the best outcomes in the pursuit of justice and in the support of victims'. David didn't remember the rest of it. If Naomi were here, she'd have recited the whole thing.

'Naomi,' he said, the hair on his neck rising.

'Relax,' said Baines. 'She's fine. I'll see to it she's reinstated.' Though they had reached a straight in the road, she kept her eyes ahead. 'I've been throwing you bones about Lex all week. Ask yourself why you couldn't raise a missing persons case. Did that seem normal to you?'

David refused to look at her, but squirmed uncomfortably in his seat.

'Bishop was trying to hunt her down too. That "conflict on file"? That was me. I requisitioned the bodies because I needed the lab results quickly. But I knew it would trigger you — that was opportune.'

'What are you talking about?'

At the traffic lights, Baines held his gaze. 'You think your ex-wife wanted to ask for your help?'

David felt a thud in his chest. 'Audrey *knew*?'

'She had assurances in exchange for consent.'

So that was why he had not been consulted. The police hadn't sought his consent because they had got it from Audrey. She had not deliberately kept this from him, as he had believed. Rather she had neglected to mention it, as it meant Baines could keep her safe. The admission both rattled and angered him. Why hadn't *he* asked her about it?

*For the same reason we're no longer together*, he thought to himself. *You never let her in. You never talked to her about anything.*

'Why would Audrey do that?' David asked impotently.

261

'You tell me,' Baines said. 'Hell hath no fury . . . Not that I would know. I've never had much time for the trouble and strife.'

The lights changed, but as the car moved away, David's unease took root. Baines glanced over before she continued to speak. 'I've been feeding Harding case numbers. I told her to look for the bodies.'

'Why didn't she tell *me* that?'

'She didn't know it was me. Voice masking worked like a charm.'

Baines was seemingly on a roll now. 'Harding's instincts were spot on. The girls were poisoned. The drugs were spiked. It felt too easy, didn't it, when the Forensics team helped you along? The pathology results were right there — and you just took them.'

'Why . . .' David muttered. 'Why go to the effort when we could have worked together?'

'If I had done that, Bishop would have gone to ground,' Shannon said. 'Secrecy was key. If he'd known anything about Lex . . .'

She didn't need to finish that sentence. David stewed, intrigued despite himself.

'Bishop had shut himself out of the case,' Shannon continued. 'I took that as a bad sign. He suspected as much, so he played us all off against one another. You, me, Harding. Bishop promised to reinstate her if she reported back to him. He told me about the nightclub to win my trust. I take it he offered you favours in return for keeping an eye?'

David said nothing.

'You see?' Shannon said. 'Every move he made was designed to cause friction between us.'

'Why did Lex turn to you for help?' David turned on her a hard stare. 'Why didn't she come to me?'

'She *did* go to you.' She looked at him once before returning her gaze to the road. 'Remember?'

A cloying numbness swept across his brain.

*I won't get in the way.*

*You* are *in the way.*

Shame settled in his chest. All of this could have been avoided.

The car sped through Shadwell, Limehouse and Poplar, joining the Blackwall Approach heading northbound.

'You lied to us,' he rasped. 'When we came to see you, you told us you didn't know anything about it.'

A pocket of impatient air passed Baines's lips. 'I fed you what you needed to hear at the time, Cade. You didn't trust me either. You wouldn't tell me what you knew.'

David held his tongue. Shannon was right, and he knew it.

'Lex had no idea Larwood was using the Fleet. No one did. You wouldn't have figured out where and how he was dumping the girls if I'd told you where Lex was.'

'You don't know that.'

'Don't I?' She shot him a look. 'As soon as you'd ruled out the river had any connection to what was happening, you'd have walked away from the case. And I couldn't let you do that. I had a bigger fish to fry.'

David made to speak, but no sound came out. Shannon had struck upon a truth immemorial to the Marine Police. Lynch had made it so the conceit had been ingrained into his way of thinking like unbreakable code.

*Divers bring up the bodies . . .*

'You divers,' Shannon scoffed. 'You don't give a shit. You were an asset, Cade. One that turned out far better than I ever anticipated.'

David felt his confidence slip, and a curious vulnerability seeped into the space it left in its wake. 'So where is she now? Do you know where she is, or don't you?'

'You haven't asked me where we're going.'

David looked around. They were passing the Bow Locks, the Lea, and the Channelsea. City Mill River and Three Mills Lock slid by.

Baines disclosed the missing pieces of the puzzle. 'It all started with Naomi's botched raid. The dead men from the

Specialist Firearms Command were friends of mine. Bishop let the investigation and the fallout rumble on for a fortnight, before mothballing it when the time was right. I was furious. I couldn't work out why he was so apathetic about it. He'd just seemed too eager to shove it all to one side. So I began to investigate him. For ages, all I found were dangling threads, loose ends, none of which proved criminal intent.

'My back was up when Bishop told me about The Pale Horse. He'd had no reason to give me that information, and when I asked him, he gave me the usual bluster and bullshit. I had nothing to lose, so I followed the lead. I put eyes on the nightclub, and joined the dots when Lex fled the crime scene and rushed to an overnight clinic, ostensibly to get tested for an STI. She didn't want to leave, the state she was in. So the receptionist called the police. As soon as Lex mentioned The Pale Horse, I was contacted and got involved. But no matter what I said, Lex refused to say any more.

'She wanted to speak to you first,' Baines explained, 'but you sent her away. She panicked. She was terrified Larwood would come after her. She was a witness. So she called me back, and I took things from there.' Baines divulged the trap. Leave Larwood enough rope, and he'd lead them to Bishop eventually.

'But you, David. You were the wildcard . . . You were looking for Lex by then, connecting the bodies to Larwood long before I did. I needed to let out the leash, see if you could prove what I could not. And it worked. The cameras at the club and the trace DNA will do the rest.'

'Look,' David said, there's something I haven't told you about Larwood.'

Shannon kept her eyes on the road.

'We followed him to where he was dumping the bodies.'

'At the Fleet?'

David nodded.

'And?'

David shook his head this time. Shannon slowed the car. 'You have anything to do with that?'

'I saw it happen.'

'I'm asking if you killed him, Cade.'

'He was armed,' David snapped. 'I defended myself. We both did.'

'Where is he now?'

'I don't know.' It was the truth. He didn't.

'Will he turn up?'

'Maybe.'

Shannon seemed to understand what he was saying.

The car swerved off the main road, its suspension struggling as it bumped along a gravelled track. Soon they came upon a large black gate. Baines left the car, and David mulled over everything he had learnt. He was confused when his thoughts returned to his surroundings, as Baines opened the gate with a clang. What were they doing here? Did this road lead to Lex? It was so far removed from what he had imagined.

Baines returned to the car and the vehicle trundled along the track wadded by overgrown shrubland and bordered by neighbouring locks. Eventually they reached a barren forecourt.

A large building drew his eye, a relic of Victorian public works engineering. It could have been a cathedral in a past life. It had red stone dressings, round-headed windows, and a two-storey mansard roof garlanded with eaves and dormers. It had been a pumping station once upon a time.

Baines pulled up by the entrance wing and killed the engine. She nodded at the front door.

David stepped into the billowing wind. The detritus of dead leaves and dried earth skittered over the chippings at his feet, and the wind kicked up the air around him. He stared up at the timber door with its foliated ironwork, and as he stepped forwards, he heard the car's engine start. Before he had time to turn, Baines sped away to a soundtrack of shredding gravel.

David took a diver's breath and walked up to the door. Safe houses — if this was one — usually consisted of barren flats in non-descript parts of the city. The only signs they were used by the police were security cameras positioned outside and panic buttons on the walls. Noticing both as he stepped inside, David couldn't help wondering about Baines's true power. How could she command resources like this?

Inside, there was a proliferation of bolts that had been mysteriously unfastened to let him enter the building, yet there was no sign of a greeting party. The entrance hall had a gothic air, with sandstone walls and a vaulted ceiling. A sweeping iron staircase unfurled itself like a tongue. There was no furniture. All was still.

'Hello?'

The word quivered in the empty air, and hearing it made him feel stupid. A far-off sound answered him. A kind of clicking, like electricity, somewhere over his head . . .

The top-floor landing was fortified by a baluster and arched windows stretched across the expanse of the wall. He crept along, placing his steps, until he reached a passage with doors along the walls, which seemed to narrow, almost like a perspective drawing. Cabling snaked through a door at the end of the passageway.

He sensed a voice on the air. His voice. Behind the door.

David moved down the passage, walking like a clock-work soldier. His heart drummed with adrenaline. The sound he was hearing was the voicemail he'd left only an hour ago.

He listened to it. His voice was plain, but brittle.

*'I had to make you believe that you were enough. But I didn't know how to give you a life.'*

It was an unpleasant sensation, ingesting your own emotion. It was like supernatural forces had driven open an old wound, unstitching the sutures. David's heart seemed to float away from its moorings as the sound continued.

*'That's why I shunned you when you came to the dock. Because, deep down, I'm no good. Because you deserve more than a world with me in it.'*

He reached the door and opened it.

Alexis Cade was hunched on a chair facing a window. The phone was in her lap. She was so lost in the sound of his voice she didn't even hear him come in.

Time stood still.

The message drew to a close the way he knew it would.

*'I'm no match for what you are. I only wish I could tell you myself.'*

She turned and saw him, her bronze eyes welling up as she rose off the bed.

David held her in his arms, as the feelings that had been lying in wait now surfaced.

## CHAPTER FORTY-FOUR

It was late in the afternoon when Naomi returned to the house.

She'd waited several hours at the hospital but there was no lasting damage to her arm, and she had been sent packing with painkillers and strict instructions to rest. Now, as she reached the front door, she knew she wouldn't get any.

A hollow groan escaped her lips at the sight of the Porsche parked out front. Rufus emerged from the bushes and rubbed himself up her legs, causing Naomi to stumble as she entered the house. The hallway was warm and lavender-scented, thanks to a dousing of air freshener. At the sound of her arrival, a figure emerged from the kitchen, her half-moon spectacles swaying from a chord around her neck.

'Hello, Mother.' Naomi found herself being angled away from the kitchen.

'Naomi Elizabeth—'

'*Don't* full-name me, please.'

Naomi was never quite prepared to match the matriarchal glint in Judith Harding's eyes, but she noticed something else there, something unsaid. The television was on in the kitchen. Amy was sitting at the dinner table, munching on fish fingers and chips, but ignoring the peas, which were cordoned in a corner of her plate.

'Hi, Mum.'

'Hello, trouble. You OK?'

'Dad left.'

Naomi paused, and hunched down so that she was eye-level with her daughter. 'Granny pick you up from school, huh?'

Amy shrugged, then took a bite of fish finger. 'Want a chip?'

'I'm good. You enjoy it, honey. What did you learn today?'

'Naomi,' her mother cut in sharply, 'there's something you should see upstairs.'

Naomi stroked Amy's head and left the room, half trudging, half tottering up to the master bedroom. There she found a wedding band on the nightstand, along with a note that Miles had folded in half. She perched on the edge of the bed and read it.

*Don't call. I'll call you.*

The note dropped to her lap, and the wall returned her stare. She didn't know how to feel. Part of her, she knew, ought to be in pieces — yet another part knew that if she did call him, they'd hit the same impasse they'd been living with for months. Maybe years.

In any event, the decision had been made for her.

A tension buried deep inside started to waver at last. It felt inevitable. Not painful exactly, just . . . straightforward. Miles refused to be the third wheel in her affair with the Met. That was what had done for them.

She turned this thought over in her mind. She would always be a cop. It was who she was. And if it spelled the end of one thing, then so be it. It would also be the start of something.

Slowly, her weariness became readiness. Because no matter how hard and chaotic and arduous the road ahead, it was the only way to be true to herself. She supposed that's why it was going to be all right in the end.

Because she was going back.

# CHAPTER FORTY-FIVE

SATURDAY 26 JUNE
Low tide: 04.14 (1.23 m) / 16.52 (1.58 m)
High tide: 10.47 (5.92 m) / 23.18 (6.06 m)

Lex hunched on the foreshore, breathing in the aroma of silt
and algae, listening to the sound of the water drying on the
stones.

Their reunion had been a delicate renegotiation, wrought
with overly polite words and awkward conversation. David
had been feeling desperate for days on end, and because he
found it difficult to let go of that state, small spats were liable
to erupt without warning.

The first blow had struck when he'd discovered Audrey
had lied. She had emerged sheepishly from the surveillance
room at the safe house, which was brimming with staff from
Baines's squad. They'd stared at him as if he'd entered an Old
West saloon and the pianist had stopped playing.

David and Audrey had had it out there and then, while
Baines's surveillance squad had busied themselves with
packing up equipment — the missing tech from Scotland
Yard.

Even Lex hadn't managed to avoid the flack herself.

'I've been at my wit's end looking for you. I thought you'd been killed.' David's jaw muscles had jerked under his skin. 'You realize how far I had to go to—'

Lex hadn't let him finish. She'd flung herself in his arms and pressed herself to him, swearing she didn't want this, that she had done what she was told, and he needed to believe her.

Then David had taken her face in his hands and promised it would be all right. But in the moment, neither had known how it could be.

The rest of the fallout proved messier. There were statements to take and excuses to make, and questions were asked about the missing Larwood.

Audrey maintained she had done the right thing, but her sense of remorse had won over. She'd allowed Lex to stay with David to reconcile in their own way.

So now here they were on the foreshore. The afternoon was warm and bright, and the sun saturated the serene blue sky. It was a relief that the heatwave had finally managed to break.

They had struck out through the Docklands and cut down Pelican Stairs to take in the Pool of Wapping, that liminal space walled by wharves with tumbledown brickwork. It had been Lex's idea, and David watched her now, hugging her knees at the water's edge. He thought about how the tides were influenced by the earth's rotation, and wondered if they were moving towards or away from each other. He felt hot loose tears brimming in his eyes.

'So, how was it — living in a safe house for a week?'

'Cold. Sterile. You'd like it.'

Lex didn't look at him. She was trying very hard to keep her eyes on the water.

'I come here a lot, you know. When I'm by myself. I'm used to being on my own.'

That stung, but he had to admit he deserved it.

'I thought you'd grown out of it,' he said. 'Coming down here with me. I thought you hated the river.'

'You don't know me very well, Dad.'

That stung double — not because it wasn't true, but because she had called him 'Dad'.

'I don't know what to say,' he admitted.

'That's just it,' she trilled. 'Once in a while, you need to talk to me. It's always the other way round. Didn't you feel there was a problem with us?'

David bit his lip. 'I just thought it would fix itself.'

'Yeah, well. That's not how it works.'

He struggled to find her eyes. He had to hunch too. 'I'm sorry I wasn't there for you. It felt like you were slipping away, and I didn't know how to stop it from happening.'

Lex flicked the sand with a razor shell. 'Shannon, um, I mean, DCI Baines — she wouldn't let me contact you. She said it would—'

'Compromise the investigation?'

Lex nodded.

'So, are you two on first-name terms?'

'Don't be like that. She was kind to me. She came to meet me at the health clinic and . . . Well, you know the story.'

David pushed his anger aside. It could all have been avoided with one phone call — if he'd made her feel like he had time for her, that she could talk to him about her life. Baines wasn't responsible for that. He needed to find a way to atone for all that had happened.

The urge to contact Audrey returned, now that the barrier had lifted. But he quickly brushed that aside. There was no sense in reviving past wrongs. Better to leave them be.

Lex had produced a pack of cigarettes and his own lighter, and when David didn't argue, she lit one and took a drag and held it up for him to share.

'I told her everything I know,' Lex said, circling back to Baines. 'She wants me to be a prosecution witness when the time comes. Asked me to talk to you and Mum about it.'

David looked down. Her hands were shaking. Lex noticed him noticing. 'I'm OK, Dad.'

She wasn't. He could see, in her eyes, the same anxiety he'd spent his life running from. Lex had witnessed the lives of four women snuffed out, women who had been ready victims. It had been harrowing enough to view it on a computer screen, but to have been there, watching it happen in front of her eyes . . . He recognized post-traumatic stress when he saw it. He had worked for the police long enough to recognize it everywhere. He'd seen it in the Royal Marines.

Lex balled a fist, trying to control the shake. 'I'm sorry I didn't tell you.' She spoke slowly, building to something. 'I was . . . afraid of how you'd react. First boyfriend.'

He passed her the cigarette, and she aimed her gaze at the water as she took the next drag.

'How long were you together?' he asked.

'Long enough,' she said sourly. 'He wanted me to leave London with him. After that night, he wouldn't leave me alone. He kept calling. Then he just stopped.'

David watched the river, his mind somewhere he hoped she wouldn't follow.

'Shannon didn't tell me what happened to him. I guess he could still be out there.'

'He's not going to bother you again.' David savoured the hot tang of nicotine curling down his throat like liquid silver. He didn't notice Lex studying his face. The signs of his struggle were beginning to heal, but his emotions were still at the coalface.

Lex bit her lip. 'So what happens now?'

David's phone warbled in his shirt pocket. He handed her the cigarette and checked the caller ID. Lex quickly rose to her feet and skulked off, as if she'd suddenly decided that if there was news, she didn't want to hear it.

'I need you to come in.' The captain's voice down the line. 'Something you should see.'

David ended the call and loped to where Lex was standing with her back to him.

'Are you going?'

'I won't be long.'

Lex nestled her head in his shoulder. David stiffened, surprised she was willing to do it at all, and in public no less.

He reminded himself that no one knew her here. He would take what he could get.

'Don't leave me,' she murmured.

He kissed her forehead, but as he made to pull away, Lex held tight. David relaxed into it. He desperately wanted things to get better between them, but he didn't know how to get there. A relationship with Lex was like the thing you went to pick up but then found you couldn't remember what it was. He was itching to confess the truth about what had happened to the man who had taken a match and burned the very bridge that kept them out of troubled water.

'Alexis,' he whispered. 'Don't blame yourself for any of it. There was nothing you could have done.'

'You don't know that.'

'Yes. I do. I've struggled, for a long time, to protect you from all of this. You have to move on. I know that's not what you want to hear right now, but it's the truth.'

Lex stubbed the cigarette out on a stone. His cue to leave. David pressed the apartment door key in her hand, grateful that the spare could finally earn its keep. But as he made his way back to the stairs, he heard her voice again.

'Is he dead?'

There it was: the thing that would make or break them. He turned back.

'I don't know.'

'Did you ever—'

'I don't know and I don't want to know. The police are handling it. The important thing now is you're safe. That's the only thing that matters.'

'Promise me,' she said, 'that everything you've told me is true.'

David looked her in the eye, and heard himself lie. 'Promise.'

## CHAPTER FORTY-SIX

Larwood lay in the folds of the body bag wearing the blank
stare of a drunk. Every inch of exposed skin was a patchwork
of scrapes, ears fleshy where scavengers had grazed on them.
His nose was clearly broken, and he had already begun to
bloat.

David had wanted them to find the corpse. The guilt
about Larwood's death was already starting to form an ugly
crust on his conscience, to say nothing of the lie he'd told Lex
about what had happened. If she ever found out the truth, he
was certain she would never forgive him.

'Know anything about this?'

Stephen Lynch hadn't bothered to phrase the question as
anything other than rhetorical. They were standing on the dock
in the exact spot where Lynch had scolded him at the start of
the week. Early evening sunlight was drenching the harsh stone
walls, browning the dock and everything around.

The captain was standing with his hands in his pockets,
waiting for an answer.

'We find three girls over the course of a week, then this
one shows up.' Lynch looked between David and the corpse.
'Well?'

David shrugged. 'Looks familiar.'

Larwood's mugshot had been sent to every station across London as the manhunt had heated up. Finding him should have been a feather in the Marine Police's cap. When Lynch spoke again there was a noise in his throat that sounded like he was nursing a stitch. 'Don't drag it out, I know you had something to do with it.'

'Baines tell you what happened to Lex?'

'She did.'

Weathering a silence of his own making, Lynch paced to the hangar doors to watch the incoming tide. David threw a look at Larwood's body again before joining Lynch at his side.

'It's an addiction, this job. It consumes you. You don't think about anything else . . .' Lynch eyed David as he spoke. 'Or at least, that's how I'm starting to feel about it.'

If he strained to listen, David could hear exoneration behind the captain's words. The body was a Gucci now, no more or less valuable than other bets the divers had made. It would be passed along, whether he was involved or not. Larwood's demise had left its mark on David's life, but the Marine Police would not betray him for the same.

'We need you back,' Lynch said, his look of distracted anguish slowly leaving his eyes. It was replaced with a sober sort of intelligence you only find in the old guard.

'What about the suspension?'

'Never got the paperwork filed. Call it water under the bridge. As far as I'm concerned, the wheel spins on. We'll need an official ID, but if Baines says this one was a killer, that's good enough for me.'

Lynch paused, though there was nothing more to be said.

David looked over as Tunde approached, accompanied by two plain-clothes officers. Both were part of Baines's squad, the same that had taken Bishop into custody, and had come from the van parked outside the dock.

Lynch quickly pulled at the seams and zipped up the bag, concealing Larwood's face.

'What's this?' Tunde jerked his head at the bag.

'Who cares. Get rid of it.'

Tunde frowned, but Lynch kept his voice level. 'It's a Gucci. Since when do you ask questions?'

A vein beat time in the centre of David's forehead, as he realized what was happening. Lynch was saving him, and the reason for it was simple. Lynch needed the good guys to keep the river clean. He needed the ones he could trust. This was either an act of mercy or a vow of silence. Either way, the gesture would bind them together, in return for David's loyalty.

'One more for the missing persons bureau.' Lynch milked the moment just long enough to relish it, before nodding at Tunde and the officers to wheel the body out to the van.

David waited until they were out of earshot before he spoke again. 'There's another victim out there.'

'That so?'

David nodded. 'Three girls at the last count. There was another.'

'Four, you say.'

'The team didn't find her?'

'Not yet. But the day is young.'

David was in agreement. He made to walk away, but the sight of Naomi Harding stopped him in his tracks. She was waiting at one end of the dock, by the doors out to the street. The wet gear and the sling were gone. In their place was a smart jacket, culottes and heeled boots.

He met her, and she in turn took the measure of him.

'How's the arm?'

'No harm done.'

'Baines told me you'd be reinstated.'

She nodded. 'The case didn't end with Bishop. There's a mess to clean up. I guess they want my help doing that.'

'I'm happy for you.'

'Thanks.' Naomi looked away. The word felt trite somehow. 'How is she?'

'Lex?' David paused to consider his answer. 'She'll be all right.'

Naomi permitted a smile. There was a sense they were more intimate now, more involved with each other than people who were supposed to be friends. 'Walk me to my car.'

Across the street, David spotted Amy in the back of Naomi's car. She waved at him through the open window, and he returned it awkwardly.

'Taking her for pizza,' Naomi said. 'Feels like the least I could do.'

The woman in the passenger's seat was none too pleased about the arrangement.

'Who's that?'

'My mother. I'll explain another time.' She quickly changed the subject. 'Are you heading back out there?'

'Maybe. I don't know yet.'

Naomi hesitated. 'Well . . . I guess that's it.'

'Guess so.' David offered his hand. It felt so inadequate, but in that moment, standing outside on the street, he didn't know what else to do. Naomi took it in hers. It felt warm and firm. Perhaps it had all been worth it.

As she sidled back to the car, David called out. 'I never said thank you. For helping me.'

Naomi looked back as she opened the car door. 'I didn't do it for you.'

She climbed in. She'd meant what she said. Going back to the fray was a chance to be who she was, while doing something she truly believed in. The good fight was the best way she knew to make a positive change in people's lives. Her life. Because really, that's all it had ever been about.

David watched the car disappear down the street before returning to the dock. He didn't know if he would re-join the team. It had always been the one thing in his life he was certain about, but now that Lex was out of harm's way, he was worried what would happen if he returned to that life. He was scared about the future, and how, in the coming years, Lex would deal with the trauma of what she had been through.

But for now, she was safe.

David promised himself he would hold on to this feeling of relief, of finally coming home after a long journey.

He'd dredge the familiar places tonight. The tide was ebbing and would soon be at its lowest point. Zosia's body would bloat and break the water. With any luck, he'd catch her waylaid on her course to the sea.

**THE END**

## The Joffe Books Story

We began in 2014 when Jasper agreed to publish his mum's much-rejected romance novel and it became a bestseller.

Since then we've grown into the largest independent publisher in the UK. We're extremely proud to publish some of the very best writers in the world, including Joy Ellis, Faith Martin, Caro Ramsay, Helen Forrester, Simon Brett and Robert Goddard. Everyone at Joffe Books loves reading and we never forget that it all begins with the magic of an author telling a story.

We are proud to publish talented first-time authors, as well as established writers whose books we love introducing to a new generation of readers.

We have been shortlisted for Independent Publisher of the Year at the British Book Awards three times, in 2020, 2021 and 2022, and for the Diversity and Inclusivity Award at the Independent Publishing Awards in 2022.

We built this company with your help, and we love to hear from you, so please email us about absolutely anything bookish at:

feedback@joffebooks.com

If you want to receive free books every Friday and hear about all our new releases, join our mailing list: www.joffebooks.com/contact

And when you tell your friends about us, just remember: it's pronounced Joffe as in coffee or toffee!

Lightning Source UK Ltd.
Milton Keynes UK
UKHW041933170123
415517UK00006B/829

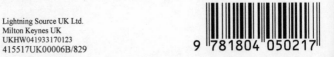